Nashville Noir

A *Murder, She Wrote* Mystery

Nashville Noir

A *Murder, She Wrote* Mystery

A NOVEL BY
JESSICA FLETCHER & DONALD BAIN

Based on the Universal television series created by
Peter S. Fischer, Richard Levinson & William Link

**Doubleday Large Print
Home Library Edition**

AN OBSIDIAN MYSTERY

This Large Print Edition, prepared especially
for Doubleday Large Print Home Library, contains
the complete, unabridged text of the original Publisher's
Edition.

OBSIDIAN
Published by New American Library, a division of
Penguin Group (USA) Inc., 375 Hudson Street,
New York, New York 10014, USA
Penguin Group (Canada), 90 Eglinton Avenue East, Suite
700, Toronto, Ontario M4P 2Y3, Canada
(a division of Pearson Penguin Canada Inc.)
Penguin Books Ltd., 80 Strand, London WC2R 0RL, En-
gland Penguin Ireland, 25 St. Stephen's Green, Dublin 2,
Ireland (a division of Penguin Books Ltd.)
Penguin Group (Australia), 250 Camberwell Road,
Camberwell, Victoria 3124, Australia
(a division of Pearson Australia Group Pty. Ltd.)
Penguin Books India Pvt. Ltd., 11 Community Centre,
Panchsheel Park, New Delhi - 110 017, India
Penguin Group (NZ), 67 Apollo Drive, Rosedale,
North Shore 0632, New Zealand
(a division of Pearson New Zealand Ltd.)
Penguin Books (South Africa) (Pty.) Ltd., 24
Sturdee Avenue, Rosebank, Johannesburg
2196, South Africa

Penguin Books Ltd., Registered Offices:
80 Strand, London WC2R 0RL, England

are used fictitiously, and any resemblance to actual persons, living or dead, business establishments, events, or locales is entirely coincidental.

The publisher does not have any control over and does not assume any responsibility for author or third-party Web sites or their content.

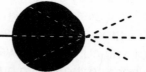

This Large Print Book carries the Seal of Approval of N.A.V.H.

For "Men with Time"—good friends and luncheon companions for whom the art of conversation is alive and well.

A tip of the hat to:

Michael Barrett

Charles Flowers

Jeff Lasdon

Phil Leshin

Ken Marsolais

Michael Millius

Tom Molito

John Shearer

And to our recently departed sage,
John Renwick.

We miss you, Johnny.

Finally to the women in our lives who keep threatening to form their own luncheon group, "Women Without Time."

ACKNOWLEDGMENTS

Nashville's Metropolitan Police Department defines "professionalism" in law enforcement. Our special thanks to its public affairs manager, Don Aaron, who so graciously and freely answered all our questions, and took the time to show us the inner workings of this exemplary police department. And thanks also to Lt. "Big Pat" Taylor and Sgt. "Little Pat" Postiglione. We hope that the real officers won't take offense that Jessica Fletcher solves the murder before our fictional officer does in the book. It seems to happen everywhere she goes.

Speaking of gracious law enforcement professionals, we're deeply indebted to Lt. Thomas A. Walker of the Davidson County Sheriff's Office. As charming as he is knowledgeable, Lt. Walker took us inside the Nashville penal system and demonstrated what an enlightened approach to incarceration can look like. And thanks also to Eric Bauder, manager of the processing unit downtown, who was so patient with our phone calls and questions.

In addition, we'd like to thank former police detective and fellow music lover Lee Lofland, author of *Police Procedure and Investigation, A Guide for Writers*, who was an invaluable source of procedural information.

Nashville is to country music songwriting what movies are to Hollywood. Debi Cochran is legislative director of the Nashville Songwriters Association International (NSAI), a dynamic organization of more than four thousand members that encourages, nurtures, teaches, and champions the creative act of writing a good song. Debi and her staff gave us a wonderful insight into how the Nashville music scene *really* works.

The collective wisdom and knowledge of those mentioned above is sprinkled liberally throughout *Nashville Noir.* We're sure they'll forgive us for having taken literary license at times with their information.

Very special thanks to our friend and award-winning songwriter David Stewart, whose song "Nashville Noir" was written especially for us and for this book. His lyrics appear at the beginning of this book. Plans for making the recording of "Nashville Noir" widely available were not finalized at the time the book was written. Information about it will be posted on my Web site at www.donaldbain.com.

D2033

Angela Landsbury A as
Jessica Fletcher

appeared in many Movies ~
a picture of Dorian
Gray.
She sang " Good - Bye Little yellow
Bird.")
"Good Bye little yellow Bird ~
O'd rather be in a barren tide
than a cage of Gold" !!

Nashville Noir

A *Murder, She Wrote* Mystery

NASHVILLE NOIR

Midnight
Waiting your turn at the
open mike
An endless procession of guitars,
cowboy hats, young unknowns
A long way from home
Take care
Somebody's watching from the
shadows out there
Is he the man that you've been
hoping to meet
Or the guy who puts the demon in
Demonbreun Street?

A little chill goes shooting down
your spine
And you're not sure if it's the good
or the bad kind
When the man says "Kid, I can
make you a star"
And you've gotten a little taste of
Nashville noir

One a.m.
Sitting and talking to your new best
friend

He's telling you that he can
open the doors
Which anyone in this town would kill for

A little chill goes shooting down
your spine
Your hand shakes as it reaches
for the dotted line
But the man says "Kid, I can make
you a star"
And you've gotten a little taste of
Nashville noir

Sometimes it's dangerous
To want something so much
You don't know what you'll do

A little chill goes shooting down
your spine
And you're not sure if it's the good
or the bad kind
When the man says "Kid, I can
make you a star"
And you've gotten a little
taste of Nashville noir

Words & Music by David A. Stewart

Chapter One

Cindy Blaskowitz held the final note of her song, allowing it to fade away to a whisper. She raised her guitar, lowered it, and bowed. There was silence in the Cabot Cove High School auditorium. Then the hundred or so people in the audience burst into applause. Some stood, prompting others to do the same.

"Bravo!" someone shouted.

"Brava!" corrected Elsie Fricket, who stood by my side.

"Thank you," Cindy said into the microphone, her face flush with emotion. "Thank you so much. Please sit down. There's something I need to say."

The clapping subsided and everyone took their seats.

Cindy cleared her throat a few times against the threat of tears. A tall, slender eighteen-year-old, she looked younger than her age, vulnerable and uncertain despite the accolades she'd received that evening. She wore a simple patterned brown-and-white dress with a high collar and a hem that reached her calves. Her cinnamon-colored hair was pulled back into a tight ponytail; the freckles on her pale face were especially prominent in the harsh glare of the spotlight.

She managed a smile and said, "You are the most wonderful people in the world. I don't even know how to begin to thank you for what you're doing for me. I do know that I'll try my very best to justify the faith you're showing in me, and that if I make it big"—she paused—"*when* I make it big"— there was a rumble of warm laughter in the audience—"I'll always remember that it was because of you."

Now the tears flowed and the applause erupted again.

Following the performance, we gathered in a large room adjacent to the auditorium for pastries, coffee or tea, and soft drinks. I was talking with Cabot Cove's mayor, Jim Shevlin, when Cindy's mother, Janet, joined us.

"I'm circling the room to make sure I don't miss anyone," she said. "How can I ever thank you for what you're doing for Cindy?"

"You must be one proud mom," Shevlin said.

"Oh, I certainly am," Mrs. Blaskowitz said, beaming. She dabbed at her eyes with a tissue. "I'm sorry," she said through her smile. "I'm such a waterworks tonight."

"Were you surprised she was chosen?"

"Not really. I don't mean to sound immodest, but I knew she'd make good from the time she was three, picking out songs on our old upright and making me play my old country tapes by Loretta Lynn and Patsy Cline over and over *and over* again. Even though I loved their albums, I thought I'd go mad if I heard them one more time. But look where it's led."

Shevlin laughed. "Just make sure we

get a copy of her first platinum CD to display in city hall."

"You can be sure of that," she said, the joyous smile seemingly permanently affixed on her face.

Janet Blaskowitz and her four daughters had lived in Cabot Cove all their lives. They'd had a tough time making ends meet after Janet's husband died. Gabe Blaskowitz had been a private pilot who ferried sport fishermen into remote areas of the backwoods between the United States and Canada. His sixty-year-old float plane had gone down when the wing tip caught on a stone outcropping as he tried a tricky landing on a lake without a name. The wealthy angler who had offered to double the fee if Blaskowitz would agree to fly out that windy day had perished as well. Cindy, oldest of the four girls, had been just eleven at the time.

With little money saved and no life insurance, Blaskowitz had left the responsibility to care for his family solely on his wife's shoulders. Janet had done an admirable job of raising the girls while holding down two full-time jobs. Her daughters were well-mannered, intelligent young women with sunny dispositions despite the hardships they'd endured. Cindy possessed those attributes, but she had also been born with musical talent—loads of it. She played piano and guitar, and had a lovely singing voice that was at once lilting and earthy. She'd won the lead in our high school musicals for the past three years, and those in attendance never failed to comment on her professionalism, the sort of poise and talent that might one day help her achieve success in show business. She also wrote country-and-western songs, some of which she'd performed this evening. Her lyrics were mature for someone so young, speaking to heartbreak and strife, as well as to soaring spirits and overcoming adversity. An impressive musical package.

"She must be thrilled about going to Nashville," I said.

"She tries not to show it," said her mother, "but I know inside she's bursting with excitement. What you and the others in the CCC have done over the years for young people like Cindy is so wonderful, Jessica."

"All we've done is to give special youngsters a chance to develop their talents,

Janet. I can't imagine a more worthwhile thing to do."

CCC stood for Cabot Cove Cares. When the organization was first established nine years ago, someone protested the name: "It sounds like the work-relief program Roosevelt put in before the war," Spencer Durkee had said. "Didn't you ever hear of the Civilian Conservation Corps?"

But he was overruled. "No one but you remembers the Civilian Conservation Corps, Durkee," another had said. And CCC began raising money for its mission: to financially back one young person each year who'd shown considerable talent in one of the arts—painting, dancing, music, writing, or acting. The recipients of the yearly grant used the money to travel to a larger venue, where they could receive more advanced professional training—which generally meant New York City or Boston. They were given enough money to live on in those cities for four to six months, and to pay for their lessons. In Cindy's case, Nashville was the logical place for her to put her songwriting and singing talents on display, and to learn more about the business of writing and performing country-and-western music.

I'd been on CCC's committee since its inception, and was active in fund-raising, donating a percentage of my book royalties each year to the organization. I took immense pride in the accomplishments of those talented young men and women who'd benefited from it. This year, we'd decided on Cindy Blaskowitz early on, and had done research into Nashville and whether that was where she should go.

I'd had no idea how popular country music was across the U.S. and Canada, nor what a dominant role Nashville played in it. I'd been there once to record one of my books, and again some years later to visit an old friend, although both visits were brief, and details about the city had been regrettably eclipsed in my memory by my involvement with a murder investigation. But that was many years ago. I knew that Nashville was called "Music City," and of course I'd heard of the Grand Ole Opry, but I was surprised to learn, as another committee member airily informed me, that Nashville was to country-and-western music what Hollywood was to the movies.

Our research showed that country music sales topped all other genres, outselling pop, urban-contemporary, rap, and jazz by a wide margin. Country radio leads all formats, with more than two thousand radio stations in the United States that program the music, with an estimated audience in excess of fifty-six million listeners. I admitted to my fellow committee members that country-and-western music wasn't my cup of tea, my musical tastes running more to Sinatra and Tony Bennett, Duke Ellington and Benny Goodman, and maybe a good Irish folk song. But once we'd chosen Cindy, I made a point of listening to her style of music on a local radio station that featured such stars as Garth Brooks, Reba McEntire, Brad Paisley, Willie Nelson, Johnny Cash, Shania Twain, and Taylor Swift, and my appreciation of the genre grew.

"I'm so pleased that Cindy has someone in Nashville who's already impressed with her talents," Janet Blaskowitz said.

"You mean that fellow Marker?" said Seth Hazlitt, who'd joined our little group.

Janet nodded. Roderick Marker was a music executive in Nashville with whom

Cindy had struck up a long-distance relationship. She'd gotten his name from a directory of Nashville song publishers—his firm was Marker & Whitson—and during her senior year in high school had sent him some of her compositions. He'd responded enthusiastically, telling her that if she ever made her way to Nashville, he would assemble a top-notch band of studio musicians to back her recorded demos, and work on her behalf to see that her songs were published, and to help advance her performing career.

Seth and I had checked him out and he seemed legitimate. Marker & Whitson was listed as having been in business for almost twenty years, and its catalogue of published songs was extensive.

"Cindy told Mr. Marker about her grant from CCC, and that she'd be coming down to Nashville after graduation," Janet said. "He sounds like a nice man, although his secretary is very rude. But he's promised to do everything he can to help Cindy along. At least she'll know one person."

There was concern, of course, about Cindy traveling alone to an unfamiliar city and being on her own there. Her mother would have liked to accompany her, but with three younger children to care for, and two jobs to maintain, she couldn't break away.

"I understand Susan Shevlin found Cindy a place to stay," I said. Susan, the mayor's wife, was also the town's leading travel agent.

"Yes. I'm so grateful to her. She was in Nashville on business and took the time to scout out possible places for Cindy to live. As far as I'm concerned, she couldn't have found a better one."

"It's a small apartment building, as I understand it," I said.

"Actually, it's a converted house with six rooms to rent. And here's the best part. The building owner, a Mrs. Granger, only wants to rent to girls like Cindy who've come to town to pursue a music career. She told Susan that she'd been a country singer in the Grand Ole Opry herself, although that must have been some time ago."

"Interesting career move," Seth said. "Being a landlady is a far cry from singing at the Opry, but it sounds like a good location for Cindy. Not too overwhelming, considerin' she's coming from a small town."

"This Mrs. Granger probably never intended to end up a landlady," Janet said. "I figure she invested in the building as a stopgap—you know, something to support her in case her career never took off. It turned out to be a lucky choice."

"Lucky for Cindy, anyway," Seth said.

"I understand that Nashville is fairly safe for a big city," I said, "but of course Cindy will still need to be careful."

"Oh, she knows that. And Susan said she heard that Mrs. Granger keeps an eye on her tenants. As a mother, that sets my mind at ease. I think it's lovely that she's looking out for these girls."

Susan had reported her discovery to CCC's committee, and with Janet's approval, a room with a shared bath had been leased for Cindy's stay, with a promise of extending it should she find work and decide to remain there.

With everything in place, Cindy was scheduled to leave in a week. Jed Richardson, a former airline pilot—and old friend of Cindy's father—who operated his own small charter air service in Cabot Cove, would fly her to Hartford, Connecticut, where she would catch a bus to Tennessee.

Jed wasn't charging for the flight, his contribution to CCC and in memory of Cindy's father.

Cindy tugged at her mother's sleeve and smiled shyly at the rest of us. "Excuse me," she said.

Janet turned to her firstborn with a warm smile. "Yes, dear?"

"A couple of the kids want to give me a going-away party. Is it okay if I go over to the Carvers' house?"

"If you take your sister. Emily is worried she'll never see you again."

"That's silly. I'll call or e-mail every day. Besides, it's not like I'm overseas or anything. She can come to the party, but please, not the little ones."

"I'll take Liz and Mia home. Just make sure you and your sister aren't back too late. We have a lot to do this week before you leave."

The prospect of her oldest chick leaving the nest in such a short time must have struck Janet at that moment. Her eyes lingered on Cindy as the young woman gathered her sister and joined her friends. Janet watched as they left for the party, their excited chatter and laughter echoing down the hall. She turned back to us.

"I keep telling myself it's such a wonderful opportunity. I know it is. It's her dream to go to Nashville. Every child should be able to follow her dream. But she's not even gone and I already miss her. She'll be okay, won't she?"

"She'll be just fine," I said.

But later, after Seth had dropped me off at home, I thought about my reassuring words and wondered if I'd said the right thing. It was natural for a mother to worry about her child leaving home for the first time, moving to a strange city, living alone. It would be a concern for any loving parent.

I took that thought to bed and awoke at two in the morning with an unfathomable nagging sense of foreboding.

You're being silly, Jessica, I muttered, and willed myself back to sleep.

The feeling was gone the next morning. But it returned three weeks later when I received a call from Cindy's mother.

in her voice on the phone mirrored by the concerned expression on her face. She passed on my offer of a sandwich and got right to the point. "Cindy has called every night since she got to Nashville," she said.

"So I hear," I said. "Good for her. Young people too often forget to stay in touch."

"She's been using the phone card I gave her."

"A wise move."

"I didn't want any of this e-mail nonsense. I wanted to hear her voice. That's how I know my children are okay. I can hear it in their voices."

"Is she okay?"

"Her calls were so upbeat the first few weeks. She sounded happy."

"I hear a very large 'but' in there, Janet."

She lowered her head and slowly shook it. When she looked up, her eyes were distressed. "But her call last night was—how should I put it?—it was anything but happy."

"What happened?"

"Well, she managed to make contact with Mr. Marker. He was difficult to get hold of. That secretary of his didn't want to put her through."

Chapter Two

"Good morning, Janet," I said. "What do you hear from Cindy?"

"That's why I'm calling, Jessica. I need to talk to you."

I knew immediately that something was wrong.

"Could I stop by later this morning?"

"Of course. Has something happened to Cindy?"

"I'll tell you all about it when I see you, Jessica. I can take an early lunch hour at eleven thirty."

"I'll be here waiting."

We sat at my kitchen table, the trouble

"That's the music publisher who's so high on her songs."

"Yes."

I had a sense of what would come next. This fellow, Roderick Marker, had brushed her off, hadn't offered the sort of support he'd promised.

It was worse.

"Cindy told me that he took one of the songs she'd sent him, her favorite, and gave it to another singer to record."

"Is that a bad thing? I thought she wanted to sell her songs."

"She does, but she knew nothing about this. He never asked her permission. She says he's publishing the song with the other singer's name on it as the cowriter. Cindy's never even met this other singer. 'Talkin' Through the Tears' was the song she was convinced would be her big hit, her best chance to become a star."

"That's outrageous," I blurted, "to say nothing of illegal. It's fraud. It's theft. It would be like taking one of my novels, putting another writer's name on it along with mine, and publishing it without my knowledge or approval."

Janet sat back and let out a sustained,

pained sigh. "She was so upset and crying on the phone, Jessica. I had to ask her a few times to repeat what she'd said because I couldn't understand her."

"She must have been devastated when she found out."

"I don't know what to do. I urged her to come back home, but she refused. She says she has another meeting set up with Mr. Marker."

"She needs a good lawyer," I said.

"There's no way we can afford a lawyer, Jessica. But maybe there's somewhere I can report this man for what he did. I suggested that to Cindy, but she begged me to not do anything until she's had a chance to talk with him again. There must be some kind of mistake, Jessica. He's been in business for a long time. You read some of his letters and e-mails to Cindy, so warm and encouraging. I can't believe he would do something so mean to a young girl."

I didn't debate it with her, although I knew from having been around the entertainment business that there are some people, who despite having impressive credentials and a pleasing manner, are sharks, out solely for themselves and without conscience no matter who they hurt. But I wasn't about to lump this Roderick Marker into that unsavory group. Maybe Janet was right, that a mistake had been made. It was best to allow Cindy to try and work it out on her own. If she failed, then it might be time for some sort of intervention by others.

"Let's see what comes from Cindy's meeting with him," I counseled. "She has a good head on her shoulders. Perhaps there was a misunderstanding between them of what he would do for her. She will be getting paid for the song—won't she?"

"Cindy said she thinks she'll get something for the song, but Mr. Marker won't be specific."

"Well," I said, "let him make his case. Then, if she's not satisfied with his explanation or with what he's offering, there's time to take other action."

Janet stood and placed a hand on my shoulder. "I'm sure you're right, Jessica. I really appreciate being able to speak with you about this."

"I'm glad you came," I said, walking her

to the front door. "Call me as soon as you hear from her again."

"It's not as unusual as you might think, Jessica. There have been a lot of composers whose songs were published under another name. It's musical ghostwriting."

I was having tea at Mara's Luncheonette with Peter Eder, the conductor of our local orchestra and another member of the CCC committee. I had called him after Janet's visit. If there was anyone in town who could give me some perspective on Cindy's situation, it was Peter.

"Of course, it's happened many times in classical music," he said, warming to the topic. "Mozart used to write pieces that his wealthy patrons would pass off as their own. It wasn't enough to be rich. They also wanted to be admired for their culture and talent."

"Did they pay him?" I asked.

"Oh, yes, if they wanted him to continue to provide works for their masquerade."

"Well, I don't think Cindy has been offered any money yet."

"In years past, putting another name on a song was the only way some black composers could get their works out to the public," Peter continued. "The early output of jazz great Duke Ellington was published by Irving Mills, who put his name as co-writer on a lot of Ellington's famous songs— 'Sophisticated Lady' for example."

"I didn't know that. Did Mills really write the songs with Ellington?"

"No, but he shared the proceeds fifty-fifty with the Duke. At the time, the word was put out that he contributed to the lyrics, but a lot of people have disputed that."

"Did Ellington?"

"Dispute it? I don't think so. It was to his advantage to have Mills promote his career, which indeed he did. Later, ironically, Ellington put his own name on some Billy Strayhorn songs. The practice was fairly common."

"Is it acceptable in country music?" I asked, trying to get the subject back to Cindy's predicament.

Peter shrugged. "There are an awful lot of songwriters working in Nashville trying to sell their work to country artists," he said. "In country, it has more to do with how the performers present themselves. If a publisher wants his artist to appear to be the complete package—singer, songwriter, guitar player—then yes, I suppose they do put their names on songs that they didn't really write. There's a lot of collaboration involved in writing country-and-western songs, at least as I understand it, lyricists teaming up with musicians. But in Cindy's case, she's the only writer. I would certainly expect her to get something out of it, credit at least."

"According to her mother, Cindy is receiving a cowriting credit, but she wasn't even consulted about it."

"That's pretty shoddy," he said. "But maybe it's a harsh lesson. Cindy has to learn who she can trust and who she can't, and how to protect herself and her songs."

"I'm not ready to throw in the towel so easily. Isn't there some way we can help, short of getting the law after him?"

"The CCC doesn't have funds for anything like that, Jessica. Frankly, I'd vote against giving Cindy any more money. It would be taking it away from other deserving youngsters we want to help."

"I didn't mean money, Peter. Is there anyone we can call, someone who could advise her on what she should do?"

"You know more people than I do," he said. "But if you take my advice, I'd let her work it out herself."

It was good advice, of course, but I didn't take it at the time. Looking back now, it might have been better if I had.

Chapter Three

"I spoke with a friend of mine in New York who knows about copyright law," I said. "There are things you can do that don't require hiring a lawyer and that don't cost very much, if anything." I was sitting in Janet Blaskowitz's house on a sunny afternoon. She had Cindy on the speakerphone.

"I don't know, Mrs. Fletcher," Cindy said, her voice hesitant. "He said this is done all the time and that I should trust him. If it becomes a big song, I can get a publishing contract and sell my other songs for a lot of money."

"That's a big 'if,'" I said. "In the meantime, he's gambling with your song, your creative work."

"And he didn't even let you sing your own song," Janet put in, leaning closer to the telephone she'd placed in the center of the kitchen table.

"Mom! He said having a good song was only the beginning, that to make it a big seller is all in the marketing, the arrangements, and the performance. And name recognition. Sally Prentice, the girl he has singing it, has already had a music video shown on Country Music Television, and—"

Janet interrupted. "I'm sure your voice would sell better than hers, whoever she is." She looked over at me. "It just burns me up, Jessica."

"Thanks, Mom. It's really great that you feel that way, but this singer is becoming a big name and I'm not—at least not yet."

I leaned toward the phone. "Did Mr. Marker give you anything in writing that spells out what he told you, that you'll be getting credit as the cowriter, and be paid?" I asked.

"No, but I didn't ask," Cindy replied. There was a distinct sigh in her voice.

"Do you think she should go back and make him put it all down in a letter?" Janet asked me, sliding a plate of cookies next to my teacup.

"Mom, I don't want to do that."

"Now listen up, young lady. Mrs. Fletcher went to a lot of trouble, and spoke to important people who know more than you do. You hear her out."

"But, Mom, Mr. Marker is a good contact. A girl who lives here, Alicia, was impressed that I even knew him. I don't want to make him angry."

"Let him be angry," Janet said. "I'm angry, too."

I put my hand on Janet's arm and shook my head. It wouldn't do to have her upset her daughter even more. Then Cindy might not listen to my advice. "Cindy," I said, "he's not a good contact if he's taking advantage of you. Why don't you let me tell you what my friend said, and then you can decide what steps you want to take, if any."

"All right. Sure. Go ahead."

I remembered what Janet had said, that she could tell how her children were doing by the sound of their voice. I envisioned Cindy with her head down, a picture of resignation as her mother and a meddling neighbor—me—told her what to do. But I wanted her at least to know her options. As a member of the CCC committee, I felt responsible for having sent her to Nashville in the first place. It was supposed to be a time for her to stretch her wings and learn more about the field she had chosen to pursue, and to improve her skills and develop as a performer and creative artist. It was supposed to be a positive experience. I didn't want it to become a negative one.

While we'd been speaking, Janet's younger daughters had edged their way though the kitchen door to eavesdrop on the conversation, taking glasses down from the cabinet next to the sink and getting a pitcher of water from the refrigerator. While Cindy had referred to them as the "little ones" on the night of the concert, Liz and Mia were thirteen and ten respectively, one on the brink of young womanhood, the other not far behind. They both had the same auburn-colored hair and freckled noses as their older sister. Only sixteen-year-old Emily, who wasn't home at the time, had inherited her father's flaming red curls.

Janet spotted the girls and got up from her seat to shoo them away.

"But, Ma, we were just getting a drink of water," came the furious whispers.

"You can drink later," she said as she escorted them from the room.

"Can we have a cookie, too?"

"Later."

I scanned the notes I'd taken from my conversation with Bart Grossman, an entertainment attorney in New York who'd been recommended to me by my publisher, Vaughan Buckley.

"First," I said, reading from my notes, "my friend said that a formal copyright is always nice, but that your copyright begins at the time you complete a song."

"How much does it cost to copyright a song, formally, I mean?" Cindy asked.

"I think he said it's thirty-five dollars if you register it online, a little more if you send in paperwork."

"Oh."

I could imagine the wheels turning in Cindy's head. At thirty-five dollars a song, with her considerable output, her small stipend could be depleted in no time. "But, as he said," I continued, "you don't need to do that to establish your copyright. Are you sure these are *your* songs? If he changed some of the music or lyrics, he could contest any copyright infringements you claim."

Janet leaned over my shoulder. "Are you writing this down, Cindy?"

"Yes, Mom."

"Mr. Grossman said that if you don't have a formal copyright you may need to present evidence that a song is yours," I said.

"I know the song is mine. Mr. Marker doesn't deny that."

"That may be true, Cindy, but it's good advice for the future. If you've written your songs on the computer, the program has a section that indicates when the song was created, and each time it was accessed or changed. If you make a demo of your songs on a disc, he told me, it's a good idea to announce your name, the name of the song, and the date you're recording it before you start to play and sing."

"Okay. I usually do that."

I paused to wonder whether Marker was being straight with her about giving her cocredit as the writer, and whether she'd ever see money from it.

"It would be a good idea, Cindy, to gather information that proves you wrote the song Mr. Marker has given to this other singer."

"But—"

"Just in case," I said. "Make copies of your original e-mails to Mr. Marker, and his e-mails to you."

"Sometimes I just talked to him on the phone."

"Did you keep any notes of your conversations?"

"I wrote about it in my diary."

"Good. Make copies of those pages. And if you spoke to friends about those calls, make a note of that, too. You'll also need a printout from the computer showing the date you started writing the song. Make copies of everything you can think of that relate to the songs, and keep them in a folder."

"What do I do with the folder?"

"Just keep it in a safe place for now," I said. "That's your paper trail. If you ever need to present evidence in court, which is highly unlikely, you have it."

"Okay. I think I can manage that. Anything else?"

"The best thing to do is to write a very polite letter notifying Mr. Marker that he's using your song without permission."

"A letter? But I already told him that."

"This is more of that paper trail I told you about," I said. "A letter, which you should send by registered mail, shows you're making a good-faith effort to resolve your differences. You state again that he doesn't have permission to give your song to this other singer, and ask him to assure you in writing that you'll receive proper credit and compensation. I'm assuming that's what you want."

"I want *Cindy* to sing it," Janet said, taking one of her own cookies. " 'Talkin' Through the Tears' was her best song."

Cindy mumbled something.

"What was that?" Janet said. "Do you have someone else there with you?"

"No, Mom. Would you please just let Mrs. Fletcher finish."

"Stop whining, Cindy. I'm sorry, Jessica. What were you going to say?"

I was beginning to think this was not a good idea. I didn't want to create a rift between Cindy and her mother. I had hoped to save Janet the expense of hiring a

lawyer, which she wouldn't have done anyway. But was I the right person to be pre-
senting this information? Legal advice is
best given in person by a lawyer rather
than over the phone by a stand-in. I wasn't
equipped to answer too many questions,
only the ones I'd happened to ask Bart. I
hurried to finish the instructions. "Cindy,
you should end the letter by telling him you'll
give him five days to respond. And then
thank him for his attention to this matter."

"I don't think he'll pay *any* attention,"
Cindy said.

"Why five days?" Janet asked.

"If you don't give him a deadline, he
might just ignore the letter and never respond. He may not respond anyway, but a
deadline indicates there will be more to
come if he doesn't."

"What more to come?" Cindy's voice
was taking on an edge of panic.

"Well, if he doesn't answer your letter,
the next step would probably be to send
Mr. Marker what's known as a C&D, a
cease-and-desist order."

"Godfrey Mighty! What's that?"

"Watch your language, Cindy," Janet
snapped.

"Sorry, Mom."

"Don't be apologizing to me, young lady. There are others here trying to help you."

"Sorry, Mrs. Fletcher."

"That's all right, dear. Let's finish this up so you can think about what you want to do." I described what a cease-and-desist order was, simply a letter threatening action if the person addressed doesn't stop what he's doing. "There are samples on the Internet you can follow if you're uncomfortable writing your own C&D."

"I'm uncomfortable with this whole thing, Mrs. Fletcher."

"Cindy—" Janet said, clearly alarmed.

"Mom, please let me talk."

There was a slight pause. I looked at Janet, whose lips were in a tight line. She was trying not to interfere, but that was difficult for her. Liz and Mia were hanging back just outside the door, out of sight from their mother, but I could see their worried expressions, eyes darting between their mother's back and the black telephone on the table.

Cindy's voice came over the line. It was reedy, and I suspected she was on the verge of tears. "Look, Mrs. Fletcher, I really,

really appreciate everything you've done for me, and what you're trying to do. And it's true that I was shocked and angry and very disappointed when I heard what he'd done." She took a deep breath.

"I understand, dear," I said. "I didn't mean to upset you."

"It's not you." We heard her sniffle, and blow her nose.

"I know that, and I know I may be putting in my two cents where it's not wanted."

"No, Jessica," Janet said.

I cocked my head and gave her a small smile, then said to the phone, "I'm going to stop now, Cindy, and let you have a nice talk with your family. The whole point of this is to remember that you don't have to feel helpless when someone takes advantage of you, that you don't have to be a victim. There are things you can do. What you *decide* to do is completely up to you, and I support whatever choice you make. By the way, have you spoken about this to anyone at that Nashville Songwriters Association we enrolled you in?"

"No, but I will."

"Good."

CCC had paid the $150 yearly dues for

Cindy to join the Nashville Songwriters Association International, NSAI, which we'd been advised was a wonderful organization in Nashville catering to songwriters, aspiring ones like Cindy and well-established veterans alike.

"Thank you, Mrs. Fletcher. Please don't think I'm ungrateful. It's just I'm such a newcomer here and don't want to do anything to jeopardize my future. If I lose a song because I was naive and trusted someone I shouldn't, well, then it's my loss and I'll know better next time. But this may turn out to be a great opportunity. I'll never know if I don't wait to see what happens."

"You're a smart girl, Cindy," I said. "I know whatever you do will be right. The most important thing is to make your time in Nashville productive. You're there to learn and, just as important, to enjoy yourself."

Janet walked me to the door. "Jessica, I'm so grateful that you're looking out for her. I feel much more confident now."

"I didn't do very much, Janet, just made a few calls."

"Oh, but you care. You can't know how much that means to me."

"Of course I care. We all do. The CCC wants this to be a positive experience for Cindy."

"But it's more. That you, a celebrity and all, would take such a personal interest in my daughter, well, I'm simply overwhelmed."

"I think you're giving me far too much credit, Janet," I said, suddenly a bit uncomfortable. "The whole community is behind Cindy. I'm only a small part of it."

But I was about to become a larger part of it, and like it or not, it was all my own doing.

Chapter Four

My deeper involvement in Cindy Blaskowitz's Nashville sojourn began on Monday
morning a week later when Emily, Cindy's
sixteen-year-old sister, showed up at my
door, dark circles beneath her eyes, her skin
so pale the umber-colored freckles stood
out in relief, making it appear as though
she'd stepped in front of a paint sprayer.

"Emily, is everything all right?" I asked,
ushering her into the kitchen and pressing
her into a chair.

"Oh, Mrs. Fletcher, my mother would kill
me if she knew I was here."

"What is it, dear?"

"It's Cindy," she moaned, drawing in a breath that ended in a hiccup.

"Has something happened to her?"

"We don't know."

"I don't understand. What don't you know?"

"We don't know where she is."

"She's missing?"

Emily nodded, and exploded into tears. I plucked tissues from the box by the phone, tucked them in her hand, sat down, pulled my chair close to hers, and waited while she gathered her emotions.

"I'm sorry," she said, blowing her nose in a tissue and wiping her cheeks and eyes with her fingers. "I'm sorry."

"Don't be sorry," I said. "Clearly you're upset. But I can't offer any help until you tell me the whole story."

"She *always* calls, the same time every night," Emily said, "but now she hasn't. We're afraid something terrible has happened."

"Let's not jump to conclusions," I said soothingly. "There could be myriad reasons why she didn't call. Perhaps she lost her cell phone or forgot to charge it. That's certainly happened to me a time or two.

Or maybe she used up all the money on the phone card your mother gave her."

Emily shook her head mutely.

"Or the cell tower might be down, or the electricity out," I said, counting the possible reasons off on my fingers. "Those kinds of things happen routinely."

Her eyes filled again.

"She might have gone away with friends for a few days," I offered.

We looked at each other in silence.

"Why do you think she's missing?" I asked.

The story came spilling out along with more tears.

Cindy had faithfully called every night at seven. Then, last Friday, she didn't, nor did she return messages her mother had left on her voice mail. Janet was worried but had come up with the same series of excuses as I had. When Cindy didn't call the next night, Janet got hold of Mrs. Granger, the landlady, who knocked on Cindy's door and reported back that she wasn't there. "Place looks normal," Mrs. Granger said. "She's pretty neat for a girl."

After Sunday night passed without hearing from Cindy, Janet called Mort Metzger, our sheriff, on this Monday morning and asked him to check with the Nashville police. While she waited impatiently for Mort to get back to her, she encouraged her daughters to question Cindy's school friends to see if any of them knew why Cindy would stop calling and not respond to messages. Had she made plans she hadn't confided to her mother? To assuage her worries, Janet called every hospital in Nashville to see if they had any unidentified patients. They didn't.

"I begged my mom to call you, but she wouldn't," Emily told me. "She said you'd done enough for our family and she didn't want to impose on you again."

"I'm sorry she felt that way," I said. "Of course I want to help, but I'm not sure what I can do. Your mother did exactly the right thing contacting Sheriff Metzger. He's probably the best person to help track Cindy down. But I'm sure it's nothing serious, Emily. In a day or two you'll probably be laughing about this."

I called Janet later that afternoon to ask whether she'd heard from Mort. According to her, our sheriff's conversation with a Nashville police contact hadn't shed any light on Cindy's whereabouts. "I'm worried sick," she said.

"Of course you are, Janet," I said, "but I think it's premature to be thinking the worst." I tried to lighten the tone of the conversation. "That's one of the problems when children promise to call on a regular schedule. The minute they forget to make a call at the appointed time, we immediately fear the worst. It used to happen to me many times with my nephew Grady. Still does, as a matter of fact, and he's all grown up with a family of his own."

"But it's been almost four days," Janet said, trying valiantly to control her emotions.

"Tell you what," I said. "Give it one more day. In the meantime, keep leaving messages for her and let her know how worried you are. Unless I miss my guess, she's probably gotten involved with friends or other performers and feels embarrassed to stop what she's doing to call her mother." I smiled, hoping the expression would come out in my voice and soothe her. "You know how young people are, Janet."

We talked a few minutes more and her mood seemed to brighten, although I was sure that her effort to seem upbeat was for my benefit.

"I'll call again," I said, "around dinner-time."

An hour later, my phone rang. It was Mort Metzger.

"Hey there, Mrs. F. Are you alone?"

"Yes, I'm alone," I said, grabbing a chair and steeling myself. From his question it was evident that what he had to say was serious.

"I'm sorry, Mrs. F., but it's about the Blaskowitz girl."

"That's what I was afraid of. What have you learned?"

"I just got off the phone with the Nash-ville police. They were all apologetic, said they didn't realize that we were looking for the same girl."

"She's not . . . ?" I couldn't bring myself to say it.

"What? No! Nothing like that, Mrs. F. She's alive. Sorry if I gave you a different impression."

"Thank goodness," I said, collapsing against the back of the chair. "Anything else will be a relief."

"Well, I'm not so sure about that."

"But they've found her?"

"Yup, they've found her."

"That's wonderful. Have you called Janet Blaskowitz yet?"

"Not yet. Tell you the truth, Mrs. F., I just don't know how to handle this. Janet Blaskowitz's one nice lady, loves those kids to death."

"What is it you need to tell her that's so difficult, Mort? An accident? She's been injured?" I hopped up from the chair and paced the room.

"I didn't know that Cindy changed her name," Mort said.

"She did? I didn't know that, either. But what does that have to do with your call? Changing her name isn't so terrible."

"Probably not, but I sure looked like a fool to the Nashville cops asking them to look for a girl whose name isn't what I told them it was."

"I'm sure they understood. Where did they find Cindy?"

"I'm not quite sure about that. They didn't give me many details."

"Mort!" I snapped. "Get to the point. *Where is she?*"

"I hate to say this, Mrs. F."

"Out with it!"

"She's in custody . . ."

I dropped back into my chair. "I never expected that. But why wouldn't she call? Why not let her mother know?"

"It's not the sort of thing you call your mother about. I mean, it's nothing to brag about. It's pretty bad, Mrs. F. She's been arrested and charged with murder. Some music producer, according to the Nashville cops."

"Roderick Marker."

"That's the one. Seems like Cindy went on the lam for a few days and had the cops searching for her. They finally found her and brought her in."

"Poor Cindy," I said, shaking my head. "I can't believe it. It doesn't sound like her at all. She's such a quiet, reserved young woman."

"You gotta watch out for the quiet ones, my old captain in New York City used to say. They're the kind who flip out when you least expect it."

"I'm sorry, but I just don't see Cindy as the flipping-out kind."

"The detective I spoke with said she was caught red-handed at the scene. He said she'd hit Marker with some kind of trophy, then ran out of the office crying, right past a security guy coming in to check on what was going on. Happened early Friday night."

"They're sure that it was Cindy Blaskowitz who ran from the scene?"

"According to the fellow I spoke with. The fact that she was seen running from the scene, and holed up somewhere for a few days after it, doesn't do much for her case, I'd say."

"No, that doesn't sound good. Still . . ."

"Thing is the victim, this fellow Marker, wasn't dead yet when she ran."

"Did he identify Cindy?"

"Nope. He wasn't in any shape to talk, says my contact in Nashville."

"How did they find her, then?"

"At first they put out an alert for her as a person of interest. Then some guy called in an anonymous tip, and the street patrol picked her up at a convenience store where she was buying a sandwich or something, brought her in for questioning, and held her for the rest of the day."

"Did she confess?"

"No, but apparently they came up with

enough evidence—the cop I spoke with wouldn't be specific—for reasonable cause to book her for felony assault. When they heard Marker passed away without regaining consciousness, they upped the charge to murder."

"If she did hit him, Mort, there had to have been a good reason. Maybe he was assaulting *her.*"

"Yeah, I thought of that, too. Only problem is the guy wasn't hit on the front of the head. He got hit from behind, walking away. At least that's what my guy in Nashville says. No court will buy that as self-defense, Mrs. F."

"Where is she now, Mort?"

"The women's prison somewhere outside of Nashville."

"This is terrible," I said.

"Doesn't sound good, Mrs. F."

"Is there anything else you can tell me, Mort, someone I can call in Nashville?"

Mort didn't have any further details, but he did give me the address and phone number of the precinct where Cindy was arrested, and the name of the detective in charge of the investigation, Perry Biddle. I dutifully wrote everything down.

"Well, Mrs. F., I suppose I'd better give Mrs. Blaskowitz a call and break the bad news."

"I don't envy you that, Mort. Will you be calling her immediately?"

"Soon as we hang up."

"Then I'll call her in fifteen or twenty minutes."

"I'm sure she'll appreciate that, Mrs. F."

My phone rang ten minutes later. It was Janet Blaskowitz.

"Jessica, I just received a call from Sheriff Metzger and . . ." She began sobbing.

"I know, Janet. I spoke with the sheriff, too."

"My God, what are we going to do? They say she murdered Mr. Marker. *Murdered him!*"

"I know, I know," I said, "but try to calm down. Above all else, Cindy needs us to think clearly. I'm sure there's been a huge mistake that can be straightened out if we put our minds to it."

"I tried to call Mr. Marker earlier today to see if he knew where Cindy might be. His secretary said he wasn't available."

An interesting way to say someone is dead.

"I'm beside myself," Janet said. "My baby! Cindy is so sweet and innocent, she'd never—"

"Why don't I come over, Janet? We can sit down and plan a course of action. Have you spoken with Cindy?"

"No. How do I reach her?"

"Wait until I get there. We'll call the police department in Nashville and see if they'll allow you to speak with her."

"To think of her in some filthy jail cell, wasting away, frightened to death. I can't stand it."

"I'll be there as soon as I can."

I called my favorite local taxi company and was soon dropped off in front of Janet's modest, well-kept house. Emily answered my knock and led me to the living room, where her mother was huddled on a couch with her two younger daughters, Mia and Liz. I'd no sooner sat when my cell phone vibrated. I opened it and saw that it was Seth Hazlitt.

"Where are you?" he asked without any preliminary words.

"I'm at Janet Blaskowitz's house."

"I figured," he said. "I just got off the

phone with Mort, heard about what happened in Nashville."

"Oh?"

"How is Mrs. Blaskowitz holding up?"

"She's distraught, as you can well imagine."

"Let me speak with her."

I handed the phone to Janet.

She could barely get out a "hello." I couldn't hear Seth's side of the conversation, but Janet nodded and said "okay" several times, before handing me back the phone.

"I'm going to drop by and give her something to help calm her down," Seth told me.

"That's a good idea," I said.

He ended the call. If there was ever a dedicated doctor, Seth Hazlitt was it. How many physicians made house calls anymore?

Janet Blaskowitz looked as though she might pass out any minute.

"Want me to make some tea?" I asked her.

"No," she said weakly. "Dr. Hazlitt said he's stopping by."

"Would you like me to stay with you until he gets here?"

"Yes, thank you. He's a little worried about my heart condition."

"Oh, Janet. I didn't know you had a heart condition. Are you in any pain?"

"What are we going to do, Jessica?"

"You're going to rest while we wait for Seth. In the meantime, why don't I go in the kitchen and do what I suggested, try to contact the Nashville police and see if you can talk with Cindy."

Her response was to close her eyes and shudder.

I called the number Mort had given me and asked whoever answered if I could speak with Detective Biddle. After a minute's wait, he came on the line. I introduced myself, said I was a close friend of Cindy Blaskowitz's mother, and asked if she could speak with Cindy.

"Sorry, ma'am, but I'm afraid that's impossible."

"Why?"

He tried to hide the pique in his voice but was only moderately successful. "Number one, Mrs.—what'd you say your name was?"

"Fletcher. Jessica Fletcher."

"Yeah. Well, number one, Mrs. Fletcher, Ms. Blaskowitz, if that's what you call her, doesn't want to talk to anybody. Number two, the chief has put a gag order on this case. Number three, she's not here at Central. She's out at CDC, the Correctional Development Center—women's jail in plain-speak. Number four, ma'am, there's a procedure everyone has to follow regarding visitation and phone calls to inmates. Does that answer your question?"

"You say Blaskowitz is what I call her. What do *you* call her?"

"I call her the name she gave us, Cyndi Gabriel. That's Cyndi with a *Y* instead of an *I*, and an *I* where a *Y*'s supposed to be. C-Y-N-D-I. Gabriel."

"I see. Does she have a lawyer?"

"She'll be assigned one. Look, like I said, you can't speak with her, and I'm done speaking about her, too."

"Can her mother speak with her?"

"No, ma'am. Thanks for the call. You have a nice evening, Mrs. Fletcher."

Seth arrived soon after I hung up.

"Were you able to reach her?" Janet asked me. Her voice sounded even weaker than before.

"Not yet," I said.

"What are we going to do?"

"What you're going to do, dear lady, is take two of these pills, help you settle down," Seth said, seating himself next to Janet and lifting her hand to take her pulse. He asked Emily to fetch a glass of water from the kitchen.

Janet looked at me. "What did they say, Jessica?"

I started to relate to Janet what Officer Biddle had said when she suddenly began turning gray and gasping for breath, her hands to her chest. Seth sprang up immediately. "Call 911," he instructed, which I did, the dispatcher assuring me that an ambulance would be there shortly. The two younger children, who'd moved from the couch to allow room for Seth, ran to their mother, but Seth shooed them away. He swung Janet's legs up on the cushions and propped pillows behind her. "Take it easy," he said as Emily delivered the water and Seth prompted Janet to take the pills.

"Will my mama be all right?" Mia, one of the young daughters, asked.

"Ayuh," Seth said, "she'll be just fine." He looked at Emily. "You have any relatives in town can stay with you and your sisters while your mother is in the hospital?"

"My mother's cousin lives nearby."

"Please call her, and tell me if she needs to speak with me."

Emily went to make the call, pulling her sisters with her. It seemed that only a minute had passed before two EMTs arrived, and under Seth's direction placed Janet on a gurney, took her to the waiting ambulance, and drove off to Cabot Cove General Hospital.

Janet's cousin agreed to keep the girls overnight, and said she'd be over to pick them up as soon as possible. I waited for her to arrive. Once I was confident that they would be properly cared for, and after issuing multiple assurances that their mother would be all right and leaving my phone number in case they wanted to speak with me, I joined Seth at the hospital, where he'd already ordered a battery of tests.

"Nothing else we can do right now," he said. "She needs to rest."

After telling Janet that he'd be by in the morning, Seth drove me home and we settled in my dining room to discuss what had transpired that night. Neither of us had had dinner, so I rustled up some leftover roast chicken, broccoli, and mashed potatoes. My appetite had flown, but Seth dug right in, pushing aside the broccoli and dipping into the potatoes. "Could use a little more butter," he decided. My dear friend and beloved Cabot Cove physician rarely follows the dietary advice he dispenses to his patients.

I ignored his call for more cholesterol and said, "You know, Seth, I had an uncomfortable feeling about Cindy's trip to Nashville from the beginning."

"The infamous 'feelings' of Jessica Fletcher," he said as he headed for the kitchen to retrieve a salt cellar from a top shelf, returning to set it down on the table with a sharp rap. "When you get a 'feeling' about the stock market, madam, I trust you'll share it with me. I can use a little more put by for my retirement." He energetically salted the chicken.

After clearing the table—I'd barely touched my dinner—we went into the living room carrying steaming mugs of coffee. "I feel as though I have to do something to help her, Seth," I said.

"Not your responsibility, Jessica. Sounds to me like it's strictly a matter for the Nashville police and its legal system."

"You're wrong, Seth. Cindy went to Nashville because the CCC raised money for her to do so, and I was an enthusiastic supporter. She's all alone there, sitting in a cell with no one to hold her hand and hear her side of the story."

"She'll have a lawyer, won't she?"

"The officer I spoke with said that one would be assigned to her, but that's a poor substitute for having a personal advocate at your side."

Seth cocked his head at me and frowned. "Why do I have this nagging feeling that you're talking yourself into going to Nashville, Jessica?"

"Is that what I'm doing?"

"I believe it is. But let me point something out to you. The way I see it—"

My ringing phone stopped him in mid-sentence. It was Evelyn Phillips, the editor of the *Cabot Cove Gazette*.

"I hope I'm not disturbing anything important, Jess," she said.

"I'm having a conversation with Seth."

"About Cindy Blaskowitz, I bet."

"You've heard."

"I just got off the phone with a reporter from the *Nashville Tennessean*. He's doing a story on her arrest and—"

"Oh my," I said. "Bad enough she's going through this without having to become a news item at home."

"You can't honestly expect me not to do a story, too, Jessica. Murder is big news. What's this business of her changing her name? The reporter told me that—"

"Evelyn, I hate to cut this short, but I really need to get back to Seth."

"Sure, only I need a statement from you about the CCC and how you were the ones who sent her to Nashville."

"I'll call you back, Evelyn, in the morning."

I hung up and started to dial another number.

"Who was that?" Seth asked.

"Evelyn Phillips."

"Who are you calling now?"

"Susan Shevlin."

"Oh?"

"I need her to book me a flight, and a hotel in Nashville."

Chapter Five

Storms in the Midwest and South the next day, Tuesday, wreaked havoc on airline schedules, and my flight, originally scheduled to land in Nashville in the afternoon, arrived at nine that night. A cab let me off in front of Cindy's "building," which turned out to be a large rambling Victorian, the original porches of which had been enclosed, making it look as though the house had been wrapped in glass-patterned paper. I knew from Susan Shevlin that it was subdivided into smaller units to accommodate the tenants, leaving the landlady, Mrs. Granger, with the largest "apartment."

Deciding to spend a night at the rooming house where Cindy had been staying was a last-minute, impetuous decision, aided by the fact that my hotel of choice couldn't accommodate me for my first night in Nashville. I'd decided to experience the flavor of Cindy's surroundings before setting off for the jail in the morning to attempt to speak with her. I'd called the landlady, Mrs. Granger, explained why I was coming to Nashville, and she graciously invited me to stay. "Terrible thing," she said, "what happened to Ms. Blaskowitz. It's got everybody in the house on edge. I'm sure she'll be glad to see a familiar face from home. Seemed like such a nice, gentle young woman, hardly capable of whackin' a music publisher in the head, not that some of them don't deserve it. I knew Marker. Heckuva way to go. Well, you get yourself here to Nashville and I'll have your room all made up for you."

Thankfully, Mrs. Granger was a night owl. When I knocked at her door at a little after ten, she waved off my apologies for the lateness of the hour. She was not only still awake but fully clothed and about to go out. "New York's not the only city with a nightlife," she told me with a grin. "If you'd come earlier, ah would've caught the show at the Bluebird. No biggie. You're here now. I can go see one of my former girls who's got a late gig at Tootsies." She glanced at her watch. "Should be able to catch the tail end of her show, but there's still time to give you a cup of coffee or something stronger—I think I got some bourbon in the kitchen—unless you want to settle in right now."

"Settling in sounds wonderful," I said. "I've spent my day in airport lounges try-ing to find a seat and keep it as the delays backed up. I've had elbows poked into my ribs, newspapers strewn across my lap, and babies thrust into my arms when their mothers took another child to the bath-room."

"Flyin's no fun anymore, so I hear," she said as she grabbed a key from a board on the wall. "Like I told you on the phone, the empty unit's not much, but the sheets are clean. It's paid up to the end of the week, so I won't charge you the full amount."

"Clean sheets are all I need at the mo-ment," I said, giving her a weary smile. "Unless—have you heard anything from Cindy?"

"No, but not that I'd expect to. Got a call from a detective who says he wants to ask me about her, why I can't imagine. All I know is that she came here to become a big star, like so many of 'em do, paid her rent, and kept pretty much to herself."

I rolled my suitcase behind her to the base of a staircase, where she paused and eyed me up and down. "It's up two flights. Can you make it?"

"I can if you can," I said.

Mrs. Granger was not what I expected. From Susan's description of the place, I'd envisioned an elderly lady in a housedress, fussing over her young charges like a mother cat with a litter of wayward kittens. But Lynee Granger was taller than I, with erect posture, and a wardrobe closer to Dolly Parton than Minnie Pearl. Her cranberry satin shirt had rhinestones along the collar and down the plackets of the sleeves. She wore her tight jeans low and tucked into red cowboy boots. Silver bangles jingled on her wrists and a rhinestone guitar hung from a silver cord around her neck. Black hair was piled high on her head, with tendrils framing her face and curling into big hoop earrings. From the back, I would thin cushion in maroon, and the chenille bedspread was dark red. The room was clean, if uninspiring.

Since most of the day had been spent waiting at airports, I'd had plenty to eat from food concessions in the terminals, so I wasn't hungry. After washing up and visiting the facilities down the hall, I tumbled into bed exhausted, only to awaken to an argument in the hall outside my room. It must have been two or three in the morning. The slit of light seeping through the bottom of my door was not enough to read my watch, but the gap was more than sufficient to allow me to hear the voices of a man and a woman, young if I had to guess.

"You promised you'd be there," the man said.

"I got held up. It's not like you were waiting around for me."

"But I was. I told them you'd be there. And everyone kept asking me where you were and I couldn't answer them."

"So what? It's not such a big deal."

"You were with someone else, weren't you?"

"I don't have to account to you for my time."

have guessed she was in her twenties
thirties. Face-to-face, and despite the a
ful hand she had with makeup, I estimat
her age at midforties, maybe a bit older.

Twenty-eight steps later—I counted
she unlocked a room labeled "Patsy Clin
and handed me the key. "There's a sink
your room, but the toilet's down the hal
she said. "Shower, too."

"Where is Cindy's room?" I asked.

"Two doors down on the left. She's
'Tammy Wynette.'"

"I'd like to ask you a few questions i
the morning, if I may."

"Sure. Anytime after ten. I sleep in when
ever I can."

I bid Mrs. Granger good night and un
packed a few things, ignoring the few wire
hangers that dangled from hooks on the
wall and behind the door, and slipping the
clothes I'd worn that day into a wooden
dresser that doubled as a nightstand. The
room was not much, as she'd said, but it
was homey, with a wide-board wooden
floor, iron bed, and battered desk in the
corner. There had been an attempt to dec-
orate; a cream-and-burgundy-striped paper covered the walls, the desk chair had a

"I can't believe you're saying that. What am I, just a guy you see when no one else is around? Are we together or not?"

"Look, I don't care to be on a leash."

"Leash! How dare you say that? I should have known better. She warned me; she said you were just a user. Leash? I can't believe you said that."

"Aw, c'mon. I didn't mean that the way it sounded."

"You use everyone you meet, you know, and where's it gotten you? You any closer to the big-time?"

"C'mon, babe, let's not argue. We can do better than that."

"I don't want to argue either, but you left me looking like a fool."

"You look pretty good to me. Do you still have that half bottle of Jack? We could share a drink. And then . . ."

"It's late. I'm going to bed."

"You're sure?"

"Yes, I'm sure."

"Just one little nip? We'll drink to better days."

The voices softened to a murmur and I heard a door close.

I'd been tempted to get out of bed and

open the door to see who they were, but two a.m. was not the time to introduce myself. Morning would come soon enough, and my hope was that Mrs. Granger's tenants would be as willing to talk to me as they were to carry on a conversation in the hall in the middle of the night.

Chapter Six

Lynee Granger poured coffee into a large brown mug shaped like a Western shirt, complete with pearl buttons down the front, and dropped in three heaping spoons of sugar. I took a sip from my yellow mug and poured in a little extra milk to counter the industrial-strength brew. It wasn't any worse than the coffee in the Cabot Cove sheriff's office, but it wasn't any better either.

I'd waited until ten to knock on her door, but I'd been up since seven, showered and dressed. I was half expecting, half hoping to encounter one of her tenants as I'd padded down the hall to the bathroom, but apparently no one had to get up early to go to work. The third floor was deathly quiet, the only sound the creaking of the worn wooden boards beneath my feet. I had paused at the Tammy Wynette room, pressed my ear to the door, and knocked softly. I'd even tried turning the knob, but the room was locked. I planned to ask Mrs. Granger to let me look around and hoped she wouldn't be offended by the request.

At eight, I'd let myself out the front door and wandered the neighborhood until coming across an open coffee shop. A pile of newspapers had been left in a recycle bin in the corner. I pulled out as many copies as I could find of the *Nashville Tennessean* and settled in a booth, where a waitress took my order of a bowl of fruit and a narrow wedge of buttermilk chess pie, a tasty but very sweet Southern specialty she'd recommended. An update on Roderick Marker's murder was on the front page of the previous day's edition. Seeing Cindy's name as the suspect in his murder sent a chill up my spine. She was described as an aspiring young songwriter and singer who'd recently come to Nashville from

Cabot Cove, Maine. The police refused to comment on the case, according to the reporter, but there was a quote from Cabot Cove's mayor, Jim Shevlin, who briefly described how CCC had chosen Cindy and provided financial support for her trip to Nashville. A photograph of Marker accompanied the article, and it ended on an inside page with a description of his career. He'd won myriad music awards, was a member of numerous city organizations, and was widely respected in the industry. His personal background included two previous marriages, and a son, Jeremy, from one of them. His widow, wife number three, was Marilyn Marker of Brentwood, Tennessee. A memorial service would take place Friday.

I made my way back to Mrs. Granger's to wait for our appointment time.

"More coffee?" she asked.

"I'm fine, thanks," I said.

Standing at the kitchen counter, Mrs. Granger took several gulps from her mug and dropped two slices of bread in the toaster. Catching sight of herself in the reflective side of the appliance, she leaned forward, licked her thumb, and swiped it under each eye to rub away a smudge of mascara that had accumulated there.

"Do you remember the last time you saw Cindy?" I asked.

"Sometime last week. Might've been on Wednesday or Thursday." She settled in a chair opposite me and pulled her pink silk kimono across her knees. "She was rushin' outta here with a bag of clothes. I figured she was going to the Laundromat—that's a big social thing with some of 'em—but maybe she had other plans. By the way, I told a few folks last night about you arriving and stayin' at my place, and somebody said you're a big-time mystery writer."

"Yes, I do write mystery novels."

"Is that why you're here, to write about Cindy and what she did?"

"Oh, no, Mrs. Granger. I came to Nashville because I was instrumental in sending her here." I explained what the CCC was and how it raised money to support Cindy's aspirations to become a successful songwriter and performer. "Her mother is in the hospital right now, and Cindy's alone here in Nashville. I wanted to show her my support."

"That's real nice of you," my landlady for one night said.

"You mentioned that you knew Mr. Marker."

"'Course I did! We lived 'round the corner from each other for years."

"Really?"

"Sure thing, sugar. Rod was a good ol' Southern boy. Smart. We didn't go to school together. His mama didn't trust her boy to the local schools. Probably right. There was a lot of gang activity then, but different gangs than they have now. He was a skinny little thing. He could take care of himself though." She sucked air through her teeth. "Too bad about him," she said, looking down. Then her eyes opened wide. "You got a mouse in your pocket?"

"I beg your pardon?"

She pointed to my hip. "Your jacket. It's moving."

"Oh!" I said, patting my pockets. "You startled me. That's my cell phone. I put it on vibrate when I don't want to be interrupted." I pulled out the phone and glanced at the screen. It was Mort Metzger. "I can return the call later," I said. "Now, where were we?"

"We were talkin' about Rod Marker."

"Right. It's my understanding from Cindy's mother that Mr. Marker had taken one of Cindy's songs and given it to another singer, and that he put this other singer's name on the song as having written it. Did Cindy ever mention that to you?"

"No, can't say that she did, but I wouldn't put much stock in that, Mrs. Fletcher. Young girls always have excuses for why they're not making it. They all dream of being the next Carrie Underwood or Taylor Swift, dolled up in heavy makeup and expensive dresses, chattin' up anyone they think can help them along. Most of 'em get disappointed and go home real fast. Good riddance, I say. You gotta make sacrifices for success. If you don't, you got nothin' to sing about. Impatient for stardom, all of 'em. Don't want to work at it like the rest of us."

"It sounds like you haven't stopped working at it," I said, smiling. "Do you still write country songs, and sing?"

"I put pencil to paper every now and then, but the only performing I do's on the demos. Got a writing partner up north, but don't tell no one about that. It's okay 'cause he's got a Southern soul. We write together whenever he comes into town. We've sold one or two, but nothin' much came from it. Nothin' big anyways. But I don't mind. I get by, and I can still go out and party."

"What about Mr. Marker? Did he have a reputation for ripping off young songwriters?"

Her smile was small but telling. "He probably cut a few corners to get ahead. Rod had a big ego for a small guy," she said, "but no more so than a few others I know. Most publishers in town are legit. The good ones don't need to rip anybody off to be successful."

"You said a detective was coming here today to interview you. That wouldn't happen to be Detective Biddle, would it?"

"I believe that's the name he gave. You know him?"

"We've spoken on the phone. I'm going to police headquarters today in the hope of seeing Cindy. Did Detective Biddle say what time he'd be here?"

She shook her head, got up, and placed her empty cup in the sink.

"I don't want to take any more of your time," I said. "If you wouldn't mind, I'd like to see the room Cindy stayed in."

"Sure. She won't be needin' it anymore. Maybe you can figure out what to do with her things. I'll be wantin' to rent that room out to somebody else." She took a key from the board and handed it to me. "You're on your own, Mrs. Fletcher. I've got some errands to run. Sure you don't want to stay more than one night? I could let you have the room for a little longer. Give you a good deal on the rent, better than any hotel."

"That's kind of you, but I've already made plans. What about the other tenants in the house? Was Cindy friendly with anyone in particular?"

Mrs. Granger stretched her arms up and cocked her head from side to side. "'Scuse me," she said around a yawn. "There's four other girls in the house, plus my nephew, Brandon, who's got a couple of rooms in the back. I guess they were friendly. They're all in the same boat, career-wise, that is. Probably tradin' tips, but not enough to give anyone an edge. Got to protect your contacts." She yawned again, more prolonged this time. "Sorry. We closed the place last night."

"Tootsies?"

"You know about Tootsies?" she said.

"Not really. You mentioned that you were going to see a former tenant sing there."

"Did I? I forgot. I'm not a fan of her writing, but she's a pretty good performer when she covers the big names."

"Covers?"

"When she sings their songs. Her own stuff is only so-so. In Nashville, it's the songs that count, the story they tell. We're a real lyric city."

My puzzled expression prompted her to explain.

"The lyric's the thing," she said. "There's just so many chords a guitar picker can use, so the song's got to tell a story, a real story that a listener can grab on to."

"I think I understand," I said.

"Good."

"May I see Cindy's room?" I asked again.

"Sure," she replied. "Go on up and look around all you want. I figure you're trustworthy."

With that vote of confidence for my character, I headed for the stairs.

Chapter Seven

The third-floor hallway was still deserted when I inserted the key in the lock of Cindy's room and opened the door. What was I hoping to find by examining this young woman's few belongings? Could I get a sense of how she'd lived her life the past weeks and what may have led her into the mess she was in? Had her experience with Roderick Marker so dashed her dreams of stardom, had it been so hurtful that it tipped her over the edge?

The Tammy Wynette room was slightly larger than the Patsy Cline but with the same sparse furnishings. Cindy's neatly made bed, with its blue spread, stood in a corner alcove. A bottle of perfume, a few magazines, and a book on songwriting sat on the combination dresser/nightstand, a match to the one in my room. Her desk and wooden chair—and mine—were identical as well. *Lynee Granger must have gotten a bargain on duplicate furniture.*

But unlike my room, Cindy's had a worn armchair upholstered in a blue plaid. Drawn up to it was a wooden stool that could serve as an ottoman, or extra seating. She also had a closet. The door was missing, but the opening was covered by a curtain that had been fashioned from a sheet. I pulled it aside. Cindy had carefully hung up her clothing, including two pairs of jeans, assorted T-shirts, and a rain slicker. The backpack that had contained the clothes she'd carried to Nashville sat on the floor next to a pair of ballet flats. A guitar case leaned against one wall. I picked it up. Judging from its weight the guitar was still inside.

The shelf above the hangers held a Grand Ole Opry ball cap and a pair of plastic bags. I held one up; it was filled with the usual toiletries, a comb and brush, deodorant, a nail file, shampoo. The other contained quite an assortment of makeup, some of it still in boxes and all purchased recently, if I had to guess.

To the right of the closet was a wall-mounted sink with a small oval mirror above it and a circular towel rack on the side. A bar of soap rested on one corner of the sink, across from a mug holding a tooth-brush and toothpaste.

I returned to the desk and sat on the wooden chair. Mort had called from his cell phone and I returned the call to that number. His voice mail picked up and I left a message.

On the desktop were a bouquet of pens and pencils in a paper cup, and an empty water bottle sporting two now-withered carnations. I reached out and touched one of the flowers. A dried petal fluttered down. Were these mementos of a happy occasion, a cheerful gift that had dried up in her absence?

A photo of Janet and her four daughters sat next to Cindy's laptop, which was closed but still plugged into a wall outlet. I was tempted to turn it on but thought better of it. How deep into Cindy's private life was I willing to go?

It was obvious that she'd intended to return to the room the last time she walked out of it. She wouldn't have left her possessions, certainly not her guitar, or the photo of her family, if she'd meant to be gone for good. The police said she'd left the scene of Marker's murder and hidden out somewhere. Where had she gone after running from Marker's office? Mrs. Granger hadn't mentioned anything about the police coming to her rooming house in search of Cindy, which meant they hadn't known where she was living. But they knew now. Detective Biddle was due to question Mrs. Granger that very day.

I slid open the desk drawers one by one, and made a mental note of their contents: a local phone directory, an envelope containing a letter from Emily, a program from a local café's talent night, several business cards, a menu from a pizzeria, two guitar picks, a box of paper clips, a lozenge-shaped gadget that I knew was a computer storage device, and three notebooks, two blank and one three-quarters full, which I pulled out to examine. I put on my glasses, opened the notebook, and paged through it.

Filling the sheets of lined paper were lyrics and chords for songs Cindy had composed. Some were clearly in the developmental stage. Erasures and cross-outs showed where she'd altered expressions, tempos, and line length. In the margins were lists of rhyming words. Some songs had a big black *X* through them, which I assumed meant that she'd abandoned their creation and gone on to something new. On several of the pages, she had drawn a musical staff and written down the notes of a melody. I tried humming one of the tunes and sighed. The CCC had chosen well in selecting Cindy as this year's grant recipient. She'd already created quite a body of work.

As I closed the notebook, I noticed writing on the back cover. It appeared that Cindy had been practicing her autograph. She had tried out "warmly" and "best wishes" and "your friend," but the name she'd written over and over with flourishes, and with a little heart over the *I,* was not Cindy Blaskowitz but "Cyndi Gabriel," the stage name she'd chosen. I had to smile. Famous and not-so-famous entertainers often changed their birth names to more mellifluous ones. In my generation, there were many Hollywood celebrities who had traded their everyday labels for fancier names, like Cary Grant, who had started life as Archibald Leach, and Rock Hudson, who was born Roy Harold Scherer Jr. I could imagine someone making the argument to an ambitious, impressionable girl that while "Cindy Blaskowitz" was perfectly respectable, it wasn't a name that trips off the tongue, nor would it be universally easy to pronounce, spell, or remember. Perhaps the late Roderick Marker had convinced her to make the change. Cyndi Gabriel. Gabriel had been her father's first name. I liked that she'd chosen to honor him by keeping his first name, if not his last. As to reversing the *I* and *Y* in Cindy, it was just what a romantic young girl might do to make herself seem more glamorous. I wondered if her mother knew she'd been considering a name change.

My vibrating cell phone interrupted my thoughts. I groped in my pocket and retrieved it.

"Good morning, Jessica. It's Seth."

"Oh, good morning, Seth."

"I'm surprised I haven't heard from you."

"I was going to call later today after I'd had a chance to gather some information. How is Janet doing?"

"She's all right, but the cardiologists still have more tests to do. Looks like she'll eventually need a pacemaker. Have you seen her daughter?"

"Not yet. I'm sitting in the room that Cindy rented, trying to make some sense out of what might have pushed her over the edge—that is, if something did. She's obviously innocent until someone proves otherwise. I haven't spoken with the police yet, but I will soon. Mort called earlier. I called back, but he must have his cell turned off."

"Haven't seen our sheriff today. How was your stay at that rooming house last night?"

"Just fine. I spoke with the landlady this morning, and hope to meet some of Cindy's friends before I head for police headquarters."

"Well, Jessica, everyone's asking for you. I suggest you get in touch regularly and keep us informed."

"I will, Seth. Thanks for calling."

The call completed, I sat back and contemplated the situation.

We now knew why Janet's daughter had disappeared. My biggest fear initially had been that she wouldn't be found, or worse, that she was dead. At least we knew where she was and that she was alive. Everything else could be addressed in time.

I was sure that Cyndi, as she now preferred to style herself, was devastated, especially if she'd been falsely accused. She was alone in a strange city, away from friends and family, from anyone who knew and cared for her, or could vouch for her. I tried to put myself in her place, to feel what she was feeling and to think the way she might be thinking as this frightening scenario unfolded.

She must have been horrified when the police took her into custody. The whole arrest process is designed to be daunting, to reinforce the impression of power the authorities hold over a suspect. She'd been sought as a person of interest, not a criminal, so hopefully she hadn't been roughly treated, although being picked up by uniformed police would be rough enough. Had they handcuffed her? Probably not. But she would have been escorted to a squad car and placed in the backseat. The door would have been shut, and she would have realized that she was in a small cage with a grill separating her from the officers in front. Had she tried to open the rear doors or windows, she would have discovered that they don't open from the inside. She wouldn't have found relief at the station house either, with steel doors slamming behind her. There, she would have faced demands to empty her pockets and purse. Everywhere her eyes rested there would be tough-looking uniformed officers carrying guns, escorting shackled prisoners, yelling phrases she didn't understand into phones or walkie-talkies. I could envision her shuddering and withdrawing into herself. She must have felt intense shame at her predicament, so much so that she hadn't even asked to call home. What could she say? What could they do? She must have been panicked about what her arrest would mean to her mother and sisters, their horrified reaction, the damage to her reputation—and theirs—in our tight-knit community, not to mention the financial burden it would impose on a family living from paycheck to paycheck. Janet had already said she couldn't afford a lawyer to advise her daughter on her rights regarding ownership of her songs. The cost of a good criminal defense lawyer would be that much more, not counting bail money to release her from jail, assuming a judge would even consider setting bail for an accused murderer.

The sound of the door opening snapped me out of my reverie.

"I thought I heard somebody up here," said a young woman, who peeked through the partially open door. All that was visible was a crown of platinum blond hair and blue eyes framed by sky blue eye shadow and thick black lashes. "Are you Cyndi's mama?" she asked in a heavy Southern accent.

"No, a friend of the family." I got up and opened the door wider so I could get a better look at my visitor. "I'm Jessica Fletcher. Who are you?"

"I'm Alicia. Alicia Piedmont. I live downstairs, right under Cyndi."

Alicia was of medium height and looked like she spent a lot of time in the gym.

She wore a powder blue sweat suit with the zippered front hanging open to reveal an orange marbleized tank top that stopped well above her navel and emphasized her full bosom. Her bright blond hair was pulled back into a curly ponytail held by a blue fabric-covered elastic. She wore silver Mary-Jane sneakers.

"I'm glad you're not her mama," she said. "I wouldn't know what to say to her."

"You know, of course, what's happened to Cyndi."

"I just found out yesterday. It was in the newspaper, on the front page. I wondered where Cyndi was. She hasn't been here, and believe me, I'd know if she was. If you think the walls are thin, you should hear what I hear through the ceiling. The girl before Cyndi used to bounce on her bed on purpose, making the springs rattle. Then she'd take off her shoes and throw them across the room at the closet, one by one. You know that phrase 'waiting for the other shoe to drop'? Well, that was me, in person. Sometimes she would only throw one shoe. Just one. I never knew if she left the other one on, or if she tiptoed across the room and put it in the closet. I think she did it just to drive me crazy. Know what I mean? Anyway, I was glad when she left. Cyndi's much quieter. I told her when she first got here that if she ever brought a boyfriend up, I'd be the first to know. Oh, but you don't have to worry. She didn't. She's a real goody-goody girl. But I'm sure you know that."

She'd walked past me while rattling on and wandered around the room, hand trailing along the front of the sink, across the curtain covering the closet opening, over the back of the chair, over the top of the dresser/night table. She picked up Cyndi's perfume, sprayed it into the air, and leaned forward to catch the droplets in her hair as they fell. She paused by the side of the bed and sat heavily on it, bouncing up and down as she'd said the previous tenant had. "I feel so bad for her," she said mournfully.

Was she about to cry? I didn't think so, although it appeared that she was attempting to summon tears.

"You and Cyndi were close friends?" I asked, taking the desk chair.

"Not really. She's only been here a couple of weeks."

"How long have you been here?" I asked.

"Too long, I guess. What I mean is, sometimes I think about heading back home, only I'm not ready just yet."

"And where is home?"

"A little town in Mississippi. You never heard of it."

"You're a singer?"

"Yup, and a good one. I write songs, too."

"Did you and Cyndi discuss your songs with each other?"

"Sometimes. She was—"

"Yes?"

"Well, she's not as good as she thinks she is. Maybe I shouldn't say that, considering the trouble she's in."

I silently agreed that she shouldn't have said that. Her comment was inappropriate given the circumstances, not to mention untrue. I thought Cyndi was very good, indeed. But I didn't express that. Instead, I asked whether Cyndi had ever confided in her about what Roderick Marker had done with some of the songs she'd sent him from Cabot Cove.

She nodded. "She told me, but I didn't believe it," she said, popping up from the bed and walking to the mirror across the room.

"Oh? Why not?"

"I figured she was just jealous, because everybody knows Mr. Marker chose Sally Prentice to be his next star, not Cyndi. Sally is just loaded with talent. She doesn't need anybody's help writing her songs. She's goin' right to the top."

"Did you also know Mr. Ma—?"

Alicia turned and interrupted me with, "Do you know if Cyndi has any coffee left? I ran out."

"I haven't seen any coffee," I said, trying to figure out this young woman who obviously wasn't what you'd call a good friend.

"I know where Cyndi keeps her coffee. She always lets me borrow some. Do you mind?"

"No."

I watched in confused wonder as Alicia skipped to the dresser and tugged on the top drawer, which opened a few inches on one side. "Darn! These things never open right." She pushed the drawer closed and tried again, easing each side forward a quarter-inch at a time until the drawer was halfway open. "Nope. Only tea. Let's see. She's got green tea and Earl Grey." Alicia puffed out her cheeks and blew out a long stream of air. "I guess I'll have to settle for Earl Grey." She pulled out a white mug and an electric coil for boiling water in a cup, and crossed to the sink to fill the mug with water. "Want one? She's got another mug here," she said, indicating the one that held Cyndi's toothbrush. "I can wash it out for you."

"I think I'll pass," I said. "When was the last time you saw Cyndi?" I asked, still amazed at how this young woman acted as though nothing of importance had happened.

"Last week sometime. She was supposed to meet me at the Douglas Corner Café Saturday night, but she never showed. I mean, it wasn't really definite or anything, but I'd told her these two guys might join us and it turned out they did, and the one guy was looking around for her all night. It was embarrassing. I told them they'd both have to settle for me." She giggled, then pouted and unplugged Cyndi's computer and plugged in the electric coil. She opened another dresser drawer, took out a roll of crackers wrapped in foil, tore at the paper, stuffed a cracker in her mouth, and held out the open package to me.

I shook my head. "If you don't rewrap that carefully," I said, "you'll attract mice."

"We already have them," she said, dropping the package on the dresser. "Brandon is talking about getting a cat. He says he had one before and his aunt never knew. He lives down the hall and around the corner. Did you meet him yet?"

"I haven't had the pleasure," I said, "but didn't I hear you talking to him in the corridor late last night? I thought I recognized your voice."

"Wasn't me. Must've been the witch."

"The witch?"

"Heather Blackwood, the 'Goth country singer.' She thinks she'll start a new trend in country music, raccoon eyes and black lipstick. I told her that her looks are fine for metal, but she'll never get by in Nashville. Those ol' country boys like to see us all-American scrubbed. Red lipstick—like mine—and flirty eyes. Glam is okay—Taylor Swift uses a lot of silver—but you shouldn't look like you just climbed out of the grave. Know what I mean?"

"I haven't met her. You're the first one to introduce yourself," I said, "apart from Mrs. Granger."

"Stranger Granger, the bitter ranger," Alicia sang. "I wrote a song about her. Well, you'll get to see them all by and by, I 'spect," she said, putting on an even deeper Southern accent. "We're all one happy family."

"How many people live here?"

She screwed up her face in exaggerated thought. "Six now, not counting the Stranger." She counted on her fingers. "Me, Cyndi, Brandon, Heather, and two more on my floor, Barrie and Sammy. They're a duo; they're on the road right now. Got a job in Branson for two weeks. They have the best luck. Oh, did you see Cyndi's new look yet?"

"What new look?"

"She's got curly hair now," she said, checking herself in the mirror again. "I gave her a permanent, and showed her how to use makeup. We had a ball at the drugstore, picking out all kinds of goodies. She looks amazing. Wait till you see."

I was sure that Cyndi looked anything but glamorous in her cell. "Your water is boiling," I said.

"Oh, right." Alicia unplugged the electric coil and dropped it in the sink. Dunking her teabag in the water, she sashayed to the door. "Gotta go now. Nice meetin' ya, as they say up here." She adopted a look of extreme anguish and caring. "You be sure to say 'lo to Cyndi when you see her. Tell her that I'm thinkin' about her. Who'd have ever thought? Oh, I'll replace the tea-bag soon as I can."

"And the mug," I reminded her.

"Yeah, and the mug."

I shut the door behind Alicia, locked it, and shook my head to clear it of the confusion Alicia had created in me. What a strange, callous young woman, I thought as I swept crumbs from the dresser into my palm and dusted my hands over the sink, washing the scraps down the drain. I returned the cooled electrical coil to where Alicia had found it, wrapped the crackers in the piece of foil, and eased the open drawer closed. I smoothed the wrinkles on the bed where she'd flopped down. On a whim, I lifted the corner of the mattress and pushed my hand between the mattress and the springs. My fingers felt a hard edge. I lifted the mattress higher and pulled out a manila envelope. The flap was open, and I sat at the desk to examine its contents.

It was the paper trail I'd advised Cyndi to

I admit to being tempted to take the envelope with me, but thought better of it. According to Mrs. Granger, the police were coming to the house that day and would want to examine Cyndi's quarters. It was bad enough that I'd already been rummaging around the room of an accused murderess; removing anything that might be considered evidence was a definite no-no. Sighing, I slid the envelope back under the mattress and left, locking the door behind me.

keep, showing the dates she'd c
her song, the one Sally Prentic
record, and when she'd sent it 1
There were notes in Cyndi's ha
from our telephone call, includir
tions on how to find a sample c
desist letter, and a copy of one
have downloaded from the Inter
was also a calendar page with la
date circled. "Mr. Marker 5:15," it

I pulled out the letter and sc
lines. Written in strong languag
paragraph and section of the
threatened damages of one hu
fifty thousand dollars. I had rec
that Cyndi send such a letter
Marker to demand that he sto
songs without permission. Ha
him this letter? Or had she d
final draft to him personall
become angry at being han
document? Had they argue
Worse, had the police found
and decided it was a motive fo

An involuntary shiver slith
back, and a fearful thought r
my mind. *Please let me no*
Cyndi the wrong advice.

Chapter Eight

I rolled my suitcase out of my room and lugged it down the two flights of stairs. Mrs. Granger met me in the foyer.

"Are you sure you don't want to stay?" Mrs. Granger asked.

"I'm afraid I can't," I replied, "but I appreciate your courtesies. And, of course, I'll stay in touch." I leaned my rolling bag against the wall and rummaged in my bag to find my notebook. I tore out a piece of paper. "Here's where I'm staying." I'd written down the name of the hotel and my cell phone number. "In case you need to reach me."

I was eager to get settled before facing the situation. I had considered calling Detective Biddle to set up an appointment but decided instead just to show up at his office later that day. It's easy to put someone off on the phone, but not so easy when you're staring them in the eye. Besides, Mrs. Granger had said he'd be stopping by sometime to interview her. I probably wouldn't have been able to reach him by phone anyway.

"What about her things?" she asked, referring to Cyndi's belongings.

I started to respond when the ringing doorbell interrupted us. Mrs. Granger opened the door. Two men stood on the porch, one in uniform, the other in plainclothes. I looked beyond them to where a marked police cruiser sat at the curb.

"Mrs. Granger?" the man in civilian clothing asked.

"Yes, sir."

"I'm Detective Biddle. Called yesterday."

"Sure," she said. "Come on in."

As they stepped into the foyer, Biddle eyed me.

"I'm Jessica Fletcher," I said. "We spoke on the phone."

"Yes, ma'am, I remember," he said.

"I was going to stop in later this afternoon to see if I could speak with Ms. Blaskowitz, or rather Ms. Gabriel."

"Had a hunch you'd be showing up," he said, not sounding pleased. "That sheriff of yours is a persistent sort."

I smiled. "He is when he wants something."

"Called twice this morning about you. Says you're a good friend of the kid's family and that you'd be the only friend she has here in Nashville. Mother's in the hospital and all that."

"Yes, it's a sad situation," I said. "I hope you'll let me speak with Cyndi."

"You're pretty persistent, too, Mrs. Fletcher." He shrugged. "But in any case, it's not up to me. It's up to her, and the sheriff's department that runs the women's prison out in Antioch. They've got their rules. Besides, heard she refused to put any names on her visitor list. She's got a lawyer now. I'll get you the name. Why don't you take it up with him?"

"Thank you. I'll do that."

He turned to Mrs. Granger. "In the meantime, I have some questions for you."

"Do you mind if I sit in?" I asked.

Detective Biddle rolled his eyes and looked at me as though I'd uttered a crude four-letter word.

"I'd like her with me," Mrs. Granger said. "She's a famous mystery writer."

"So I hear," he said.

"I've already been through Cyndi's room," I said, "and—"

Now his expression said I'd come out with a string of expletives.

"I stayed here overnight and—"

"Touch anything in her room?" he asked.

"A few things. It's not taped off as a crime scene. I didn't see anything wrong with looking around and trying to understand what led up to what—well, what she's accused of doing."

His long sigh said many things, none of them favorable. "Stay out of her room, okay?" he said. "Leastways till we get finished with it."

"Certainly, if you wish."

Although he'd not responded to my request to join them, I followed anyway into the kitchen, where he and Mrs. Granger sat at the table. The uniformed officer stood near the door; I chose an inconspicuous spot on the opposite side of the room. If Biddle realized I was there, he didn't say anything. He asked Mrs. Granger a series of questions that didn't elicit any useful information as far as I was concerned. When the questioning was concluded, Mrs. Granger led Biddle and the uniformed officer up to the third floor, where they spent a half hour in Cyndi's room. I stayed in the kitchen until they returned carrying Cyndi's laptop computer, guitar case, backpack, and an evidence bag holding whatever else they'd taken from the room.

"Doubt if we need to tape off the room," Biddle announced. "We did a thorough search, got everything there was to find."

"Did you look under the mattress?" I asked.

He chuckled. "You read too many mysteries, Mrs. Fletcher. Nobody hides things under their mattress these days."

I raised my brows but didn't say anything. There was a moment of uncomfortable silence.

A look of consternation crossed Biddle's face. He turned to the uniformed officer. "Go on up again and look under the mattress," he said.

The officer returned a few minutes later, waving the manila envelope.

Biddle scowled at me, and I feared that I'd made an enemy.

I'd hated to have to tell them about the envelope. But if Cyndi was guilty, the police were entitled to see it, and if she was innocent, well, the same still held true. The fact of the matter was, I couldn't live with myself if I'd been responsible for knowingly withholding evidence.

"Have a car here in Nashville, Mrs. Fletcher?" Biddle asked, interrupting my thoughts. He seemed to have gotten over his pique at me.

"No. I'm afraid I don't drive."

A prolonged sigh. "Come on, then, I'll give you a lift down to headquarters. Get you her lawyer's name. Maybe he'll agree to let you see the accused, but he'll have to convince her that it's okay."

"I understand perfectly, Detective Biddle, and I very much appreciate what you're doing."

When we arrived at the Nashville Metropolitan Police Department's central precinct, a fairly new redbrick building on what's called James Robertson Parkway in downtown Nashville, he led me to an office on the top floor of the building. "You can park your bag over there," he said, pointing to an empty space next to a bookcase. "Have a seat. I'll be back."

I followed his instruction and swiveled in my chair to take in my surroundings. Mort Metzger's office is fairly organized, although on occasion it looks as though a whirlwind has hit it. No one would ever accuse him of being naturally neat. Biddle's environment, on the other hand, reflected someone who might be obsessive-compulsive. Every piece of paper was squared on the desk, and pens and pencils were lined up evenly. No photograph or citation hanging on the walls was even slightly crooked. Books on a series of shelves behind the desk stood neatly in rows, not one protruding farther out than any other.

I was perusing the books on Biddle's shelf when he returned. He took a candy bar from his pocket and put it on the desk, then removed his suit jacket and carefully draped it over the back of his chair. He was a short, stocky man with a thick neck, large chest, and muscular arms that were evident beneath his shirtsleeves. He wore a starched pale yellow shirt with a purple tie and suspenders to match. He was a fussy dresser, if not one I would describe as particularly stylish.

"This isn't my office," he declared. "I work out of the west precinct. We cover Music Row, where the murder took place, but we're undergoing renovations of the building so I hang out here." He grimaced for a moment against an unspecified pain and said, "Okay, Mrs. Fletcher, here's the deal. Just talked to the DA's office. As it happens, Ms. Gabriel's court-appointed attorney is in the records room now, going over some reports. When he comes out, you can ask him about putting you on the young lady's visitor list. Judging from the way she's been acting since we picked her up, she might not want to see you. Don't be insulted if she stiffs you."

"I hope she doesn't," I said, "but that's her decision. I won't be offended if she declines to talk with me."

"I'll say this for her," he said, "she aced the alcohol and drug screenings. Clean as a whistle. Hasn't seen the shrink yet, though. We put in for it, but the guy's so busy he can't do her until tomorrow. That's what happens when you have all these whackos on the streets. We arrest one hundred and forty people a day in this city. Hard to keep up." He ran a hand over his bald spot, a circle of pink scalp peeking out from beneath brindle-colored wavy hair.

"And the charge against Cyndi is murder?" I asked.

"The prosecutor will probably go for murder-two, unless her lawyer can negotiate it down to manslaughter."

"Has she admitted to the assault?"

"No, ma'am. Says she saw him there, got scared, and ran out to call the cops. Of course, she never made that call. She just disappeared."

"Did she give a reason for why she was there in the first place?"

"Says she had an appointment, but he kept her twiddlin' her thumbs. Said she went in to tell him she couldn't wait around anymore and found him on the floor. That's her story, but we don't believe it's how it went down."

"So far it sounds pretty circumstantial to me. Have you looked into any other possible suspects?"

Biddle picked up the candy bar he'd left

on the desk and tore open the wrapper. "Want one?" he asked. "Got another in my jacket pocket."

"No thanks," I replied.

"It's a Goo Goo Cluster," he said, eyeing me.

"Should I know what that is?"

"Made right here in Nashville. Can't call yourself a Southerner if you've never had a Goo Goo."

I smiled. "I'll have to try one some other time."

He shrugged and leaned back, his leather chair squeaking under his weight. He munched on the candy bar, his face thoughtful. Finally he sighed and said, "We're professionals, Mrs. Fletcher. Fact remains, your girl was at the scene, and her prints are on the trophy she used to kill him."

"A trophy?"

"Award, then. Same as."

"Like a Grammy or an Oscar?"

"A CMA, Country Music Award. Big and heavy. And before you ask again, yes, I had my guys check out the staff and whoever else was in the building."

"And?"

"His secretary, a Ms. Anderson—Edwina's her first name—said he was alive when she left for home at five and passed your girl in the hall coming in."

"Is she the only one who saw Cyndi?"

"No, ma'am. The security fellow—" Biddle leaned forward, winced at the chair's creaky objection, and ran his index finger down the front page of the report on his desk. "Clevon Morgan of Smoky Mountain Security Services said that when he tried the door to Marker's suite at five forty-five, she came flying out of there like a bat out of you-know-where, crying and hysterical."

"It's not surprising that she'd be hysterical at discovering a man fatally injured. She might not even have known that he was still alive."

Biddle sucked a bit of chocolate off his thumb and nodded. "If she hadn't taken off, her story might carry more weight. But she hid out until we found her. Juries tend to see that as an indication of guilt."

"She was obviously frightened and not thinking clearly at that moment," I offered.

"Had a lot of time to think in the days after. Never came forward."

"She's very young, Detective Biddle."

"The jails are full of young people, Mrs. Fletcher."

"Unfortunately true, but—"

Biddle raised his hand to stop me. He eased back in the chair, again to the accompanying creaks. "Tell you this. Don't know if she went in meaning to kill him or not. The shrink will give us a better idea. But these things happen. From what I hear, this type of situation is not unfamiliar to someone like you who writes about crime, so you know how people can snap if they're under pressure. Found a letter on his desk signed by Cyndi Gabriel, accusing the deceased of having stolen songs from her and demanding payment. Mentioned that to your Sheriff Metzger and he confirmed it, said he'd heard that from people in— What's the name of that town you're from?"

"Cabot Cove."

"Right. Cabot Cove. Anyway, that letter, and your sheriff's confirmation, ties a neat bow on it for me."

"Did you respond to the call from the scene yourself?" I asked.

"Yes, ma'am. Call that came in said the victim was dead, so we got involved. Was me along with our west precinct commander, our ranking officer, and a crime scene investigator to collect evidence. Because the vic was still breathing, the fire department sent EMTs, who took him to the Vanderbilt University Medical Center. They've got the Level One trauma center for this area."

"Did he ever regain consciousness?"

"No, ma'am, and we had a twenty-four-hour guard on him, but no opportunity to question him about the attack. Once Marker gave it up, the case moved from aggravated assault to murder."

"And you arrested Cyndi."

"Yes, ma'am. Once we finished questioning her here, she was run past our night court commissioner. He advised her she was being held for a capital offense and denied her bond. We turned her over to the sheriff's office, the ones who run the jail."

"How is she?" I asked.

"What I hear, she's doing okay. I called out there to check on her. She's sort of a fragile type, so I asked them to handle her with kid gloves, keep her away from the hardened criminals. They're very sharp out there. Already had her in isolation for her own safety. Don't worry, she hasn't been abused or browbeaten. But they can watch her more carefully, make sure she doesn't become a suicide risk."

"Good heavens! Is that a possibility?"

"You never know, especially with first-timers."

"How long do you think the lawyer will be?" I asked, anxious to see Cyndi and gauge her frame of mind for myself.

He shrugged. "Could be some time." He heaved himself out of the chair, which continued rocking as if his body were still sitting in it. "I'll go check," he said, leaving me alone in his office.

The detective had been remarkably cordial and forthcoming, considering we'd never met, and looking back at the rocky start we'd had over the phone. I had to credit our Cabot Cove sheriff for that. Mort had paved the way, giving me not only Biddle's name, but calling the detective in advance and alerting him to my interest in the case. What was distressing me at that moment was a suspicion that the Nashville police were convinced that they had already solved the crime, convinced that Cyndi

n-striped suit that draped nicely on his
me, white button-down shirt, and muted
aroon tie.

"This is Jamal Washburn, Mrs. Fletcher,
ndi's court-appointed attorney."

Mr. Washburn extended his hand and
e shook.

"I understand from the detective that
u'd like to go see my client," he said,
eing my rolling suitcase.

"That's right," I said, "with your permis-
on."

"You know you're not allowed to bring
r anything."

"Of course," I said. "This is mine. I just
ven't had a chance to check into my ho-
yet."

We stood talking while Detective Biddle
oved away to speak with an officer at the
ception desk.

"Your visiting her is fine with me, Mrs.
etcher," he said. "I'm glad that you're
re. At first she didn't want to see anyone
m home. Now she's changed her mind.
nce you're a pretty famous person
ere she lives, I imagine she trusts you."

"I certainly hope so," I said. "But before I
e her, could we have a moment to talk?"

was Marker's killer and disintereste
suing other leads, other suspects.
that wasn't the case. A rush to j
wasn't unusual in other cases in
unfortunately ended up involved,
my dismay and to Seth Hazlitt's ch

The police feel under pressure
a crime, especially murder, with
eight hours. After that, the thinki
witnesses begin to forget what the
don't remember it as clearly as th
closer to the commission of the c
even the accused may lose tra
details. Television and news acco
also influence memory, as well
borhood gossip and the opinions
and friends.

I pulled out a small notepad
shoulder bag and wrote down th
of Marker's secretary, Edwina
and the security man, Clevon N
Smoky Mountain Security Servic
finished when Biddle returned to
and invited me to accompany h
stairs. In the lobby of the buildi
troduced me to a tall, young
African-American man wearin

"We can have more than a moment," he said. "We can sit there if you like"—he indicated a row of chairs against the wall—"but frankly, I'd like to grab some lunch first, if you don't mind."

"Not at all," I replied. "I could use something to eat, myself."

"Great. Then we'll drive out to Antioch to the women's facility. There'll be plenty of time to talk."

Before we left, I shook hands with Detective Biddle. "Thank you so much," I said.

"Not at all, Mrs. Fletcher," he said. "Glad to oblige a fellow officer. You say hi to Sheriff Metzger for me. It was nice to meet you."

"It's nice to meet you, too, Detective, but don't think you can get rid of me so easily. If Cyndi is innocent, as I suspect she is, I'll be back."

"Is that a threat or a promise, Mrs. Fletcher?"

I smiled to soften my answer. "Maybe a little bit of both."

Chapter Nine

Jamal Washburn turned his Saturn onto Interstate 24 and headed east, my suitcase safely stowed in the trunk. We'd stopped for sandwiches at a noisy luncheonette not too far from police headquarters. The tables were all occupied, so we sat at the counter hemmed in by construction workers in hard hats working on a building across the street. I'd refrained from asking the attorney any questions out of a reluctance to shout over the conversations of others and be overheard. However, now that I was alone with him in the car, I gathered my thoughts. I didn't want to waste this opportunity to learn as much as possible about the case against Cyndi.

"Detective Biddle has been extremely gracious about sharing information with me," I said. "I'm hoping you can add to what I now know."

"Biddle's a good guy," Washburn said. "He's been the lead on a number of cases I've been assigned to. I like him. He's a straight shooter, at least most of the time. He's got his job to do, and I've got mine."

"Of course. From the little I've learned, the case against Cyndi sounds almost totally circumstantial."

Washburn nodded, but quickly said, "Sometimes circumstantial cases are the toughest to defend."

"I can understand why." I paused. "Mr. Washburn, Detective Biddle said that Cyndi absolutely denies having had anything to do with Mr. Marker's death."

"That's right."

"Do you believe her?"

His laugh was sardonic. "It really doesn't matter," he said. "It's my job to give every one of my clients the best possible defense, whether they're guilty or not. But in Cyndi's case, yes, I do believe her. I don't know who killed Roderick Marker, but it wasn't Cyndi."

I sighed with relief. "I needed to hear that," I said.

"I not only believe it, Mrs. Fletcher," he added, "I'll do everything I can to absolve her in court, but I need her help. Right now she isn't being as cooperative as she could be."

"Perhaps I can convince her to do better."

"That's what I'm hoping. I'm sure you've noticed that I'm not a veteran attorney. I graduated from Vanderbilt University Law School right here in Nashville three years ago, and passed the bar two years ago. I'm on a list of attorneys the court appoints to cases where the accused don't have lawyers of their own. Relatively speaking, I'm fairly new at this game, but I don't want you to think just because I'm young that I'm green. Court-appointed lawyers get to work on a lot of cases."

"Age and experience aren't necessarily a plus," I said. "The real question is, are you good?"

He broke out into a laugh. "If I didn't think I was, I'd give up law practice and write country-and-western songs." He turned on the radio, and a woman's voice floated out over the speakers singing, *"Guilty, baby, I'm guilty. And I'll be guilty the rest of my life."* Washburn gave a soft snort, flipped off the radio, and pressed down the car's directional signal. "I'm glad you're coming to see Cyndi," he said. "She needs a familiar face."

Fifteen minutes later, we pulled into a large parking lot. Ahead of us were a series of imposing buildings. Washburn pointed to the one directly before us, a one-story tan building with a stone front. He then indicated a pair of two-story white stucco buildings up a hill to our left, surrounded by a chain-link fence topped with coiled razor wire. "That's where the female prisoners are housed," he said as we walked in the direction of the one-story facility. "Here's where we check in," he said, holding the door open for me.

He announced us to a woman at a desk to our right, and led me to a row of blue plastic chairs with black armrests. "This is the way it works," he said in a low voice. "A prisoner's lawyer can visit anytime, and for any length of time, between eight in the morning and ten at night. I can also bring along an assistant, a paralegal, anyone involved with me on the case. That'll be you."

"I'm your assistant?"

"If you want to go in with me to see her."

"I do," I said.

We sat back and waited for someone to bring us to where I'd have my first chance to be face-to-face with Cindy, or Cyndi as she now called herself. I took the opportunity to observe my surroundings. I'd been in a number of prisons before—never my favorite places to visit—but this particular one didn't seem as depressing as most of the others I'd seen. It was brightly lit, and clean. There was a touch-screen unit in the corner where visitors could use their credit cards to deposit funds into prisoners' prison bank accounts. Farther down the wall were blue lockers, where visitors could secure those possessions that they were forbidden to bring inside with them. And there was music softly playing, definitely a country-and-western song performed by a musical group unknown to me. Of course, knowing that women were caged in cells nearby was depressing enough to mitigate these attempts at civility. I thought of those who'd been wrongly incarcerated. How utterly frustrating and frightening that must be for them, as I was sure it was for Cyndi Gabriel.

A few minutes later, a stocky African-American man in uniform came through a door and approached us. "I'm Lieutenant Atkinson," he said pleasantly. "I understand you want to visit with Ms. Gabriel."

"That's right, Lieutenant," Washburn said, standing and shaking the officer's hand. "I'm listed as her attorney, and this is Mrs. Fletcher, Jessica Fletcher, who'll be assisting me. She's from the prisoner's hometown in Maine and has come to Nashville to work on the case."

"You're not an attorney," Atkinson said.

"No, I'm not," I confirmed.

"You're a famous mystery writer."

My heart sank. Did this mean I'd be precluded from accompanying Washburn to see Cyndi?

The lieutenant flashed an engaging smile. "It's a pleasure meeting you, Mrs. Fletcher," he said. "Detective Biddle told me about your involvement."

"That was good of him."

"If Mr. Washburn wants you on his team, that's fine with me. Come on. I've already called for the prisoner to be brought down to this building. Let's go through Security and get you settled before she arrives."

We stepped through a metal detector, and I handed my purse to a female officer. She gave it a thorough examination before handing it back, and returned Washburn's briefcase to him. Lieutenant Atkinson escorted us into a spacious room that at first glance reminded me of a school cafeteria. Gray plastic tables were arranged in a large square. The chairs were a vibrant blue, and the floor was a blue-and-white checkered pattern. Large windows along one wall allowed plenty of sunlight to pour into the room, adding to its already sunny atmosphere. I turned to take in a brightly lit alcove where the walls were decorated with a hand-painted series of Disney characters—Cinderella in a pink gown, the fairy godmother, and the mice in their pointy caps and little shirts. I laughed in appreciation.

"An inmate painted that in honor of a little girl who died of leukemia," Atkinson said. "She was the daughter of one of our officers."

"What a loving gesture," I said.

"She's a good artist," Atkinson said. "Last I heard, she's doing well on the outside. We like to keep things as light and bright as possible. Lifts the spirits. I'll leave now. The officer will bring her in shortly."

"I'd prefer you not to touch her when she comes in," Washburn cautioned me after the lieutenant had left. "This is not a family visit, and we don't want to alarm the guard with behavior they're not used to seeing in a lawyer. They might suspect you were passing something to her."

"I'll remember," I said.

Several minutes later, the door opened and Cyndi and her guard entered. Janet's eldest daughter wore navy blue pants and shirt, and matching tennis shoes. Her hands were manacled, her eyes without expression. An angry pimple on her forehead, and red blotches on her chin, testified to the stress she was under. Her formerly straight hair was a stringy mass of curls, thanks to the ministrations of Alicia, her downstairs neighbor at Mrs. Granger's, and looked as if it needed washing. She carried with her a file folder that she dropped on the table.

"Does she need to sign anything?" the guard asked.

"Yes," Washburn said.

The officer who'd escorted her unlocked the handcuffs and waited until Washburn and I took chairs at the table; Cyndi was directed to sit on the inside of the square, across from us. "Standard procedure," Washburn told me. The officer moved to a seat on the other side of the room to give us some privacy, but she never took her gaze off Cyndi.

"Officers can't be within hearing distance during attorney-client visits," Washburn said softly, "but she'll keep an eye on us."

Cyndi perched awkwardly on her chair. She didn't look up, but sat glumly with her arms tightly folded across her chest, eyes fixed on the tabletop.

"Hey, champ," Washburn said, "you've got a visitor."

"Hello, Cyndi," I said.

Slowly she raised her eyes, blinked back tears, and wrapped her arms even tighter around herself as though that would squeeze away the pain.

I resisted gently patting her arm. "It'll be

all right," I said. "Everything will work out." It seemed the right thing to say under the circumstances, although I had no idea whether things would, in fact, work out.

"I'm so sorry," she whispered.

I pulled a tissue from a packet and placed it on the table. She picked it up and dabbed at her eyes, then dropped her head, staring at her fists tightly clenched around the tissue. "Thanks for coming, Mrs. Fletcher," she managed in a soft voice.

"You're welcome. How are you feeling?"

"I'm okay. How's my mother?" she asked, looking up again. "They told me that she's in the hospital." She hesitated. "Is that because of me?"

"You didn't cause your mother's heart condition, if that's what you're asking," I said. "That's something that takes a long time to develop. But stress of any kind isn't good for someone with health problems."

"That's why I didn't call her. I was afraid she'd have a heart attack right on the phone and I couldn't do anything to help."

"There was no way your news wouldn't be stressful for her," I said, "but I think she'd much rather hear from you than not. She's more worried about you than she is about herself."

"Is Mama gonna be all right? I mean, is she very sick?"

"Dr. Hazlitt says she'll be fine. He's the best. He's taking care of her, brought in specialists to run some tests. She should be going home soon. Don't you think you ought to call her at some point?"

"I can't," she said, a hiccup in her voice. "I'm so ashamed."

"If you killed Mr. Marker, you should be ashamed."

Cyndi gasped. Her eyes flew to mine, their expression panicked. "I never. I swear. I never touched him. I didn't kill him. I saw him on the floor. I thought he was dead. There was blood all over his head. I didn't know what to do, so I just ran. But I swear, Mrs. Fletcher, I didn't kill him. I could never do anything like that. Never! Please believe me. Please."

"I believe you."

"You do?"

"You're telling me the truth, aren't you?"

"Absolutely." She raised her hands, palms facing me. "I didn't kill him. I swear it. Please get them to give me a lie detector test. I told them I would take it. I'm telling the truth."

"That's something for you to discuss with Mr. Washburn," I said, looking over at him. He nodded, and seemed to be content to have the conversation involve only Cyndi and me.

"Why were your fingerprints on the trophy that was used to kill him?" I asked.

Cyndi took a deep breath. Her gaze roamed the ceiling, picturing the scene. "I was waiting in his secretary's office. He'd told me to wait there."

"Wait! You saw him that night?"

"No, not actually," she said, her eyes meeting mine. "Not until—" She stopped, then started again. "He'd told me that over the phone."

"Okay," I said. "Start from the beginning. Who called who to arrange this meeting?"

"He called me, but it was because I'd dropped off the C&D letter with his secretary, you know, the one you advised me to give him. I wasn't sure if I should do it, but he wasn't returning my calls. And I was getting desperate."

"Did you see him right away?"

"No. I saw the award lying on the floor, and I said, 'Oh, Mr. Marker, your CMA award fell down.' I picked it up—it's really heavy—and put it back on the corner of the desk. That's when I saw blood on my hand, and I wiped it on my jeans. And when I looked up I saw him lying on the floor on the other side of his chair."

"Did you know he was still alive?"

"No! I didn't. I was sure he was dead. He wasn't moving. And his blood was on my hand and on my pants. I got so scared, I started to scream and ran out the door, but the guard was there. He yelled at me, grabbed my arms, and pushed me into a seat in the waiting area. He told me to stay there until he came back." She had been speaking quickly, then stopped. She took a shaky breath, and a sob escaped. "But I didn't."

"You didn't what?" I said, providing another tissue.

"I didn't wait," she said in a long moan. Her shoulders heaved up and down and she put her head in her hands, sobbing, curled over, her whole body convulsed in grief. It was as if the misery she'd been

"So you got his attention once h
your letter in hand."

"Yes. He called and said we had
He said to come at five fifteen and w
side his office. He was very busy th
but he would get to me when he was

"And he never did?"

"No. I waited as long as I could
supposed to try out for a gig dov
and I was afraid if I was late they
let me audition."

"So what happened while yo
waiting?"

"Nothing. I just sat there, lookir
watch. After about forty minutes I
I couldn't wait any longer, so I kn
his door."

"How did you know he was ev
office?"

"I didn't at first, but then I heard
Not real well. I couldn't hear wh
saying, but I could tell it was him.
like he was arguing with someb
phone. I waited, and when I didn
again for a long time, I knocked

"And then?"

"He didn't answer, but I thou
he didn't hear me so I turned th

holding in so long finally had a chance to escape and she could no longer stop it.

I watched her cry, sad that I couldn't hug or comfort her in any way. Her attorney had warned me not to touch her, and I needed to follow his directions if I hoped to be of any help in the future.

Her sobs slowly subsided, and her breath came out in hiccups. She used the wadded tissues in her fist to dab at her red eyes and nose. After several deep breaths, she was able to contain herself.

"Why, Cyndi?" I asked softly. "Why didn't you do what the guard told you to?"

"I was . . . I was sure he thought I'd killed Mr. Marker. He'd said to me, 'What did you do? What did you do?' And I had blood on me. I didn't even think about the award when I saw it lying there. I just picked it up. I didn't see it had blood on it until it was too late. I thought they'd never believe me. Who am I? A nothing from a little town in Maine. And he's an important publisher, with a Country Music Award, lots of them. So I ran."

I sighed. "You know that in doing that you've made it more difficult for yourself."

"Yes." She swallowed visibly. "I realize that now."

"Where did you go?"

"I don't even know. I just wandered around the city. I was upset. I was too afraid to go back home, I mean to Mrs. Granger's. I thought that would be the first place the police would look, so I stayed away and just wandered around."

"You were gone for three nights? Where did you sleep?"

She bit her bottom lip and shrugged, eyes falling to her hands again.

"Cyndi?"

Washburn interjected, "I've been asking that same question."

"I don't remember. Really. It's all a blur until the police found me."

"You don't remember?" I said, incredulous.

"No," she said, picking at a cuticle on her thumb.

There was something she was holding back, a lot she was holding back. I didn't want to tell myself she was lying—I believed her when she said she hadn't killed Marker—but there was definitely a hole in this story big enough for a steamship to sail through, and a prosecutor would have a field day cross-examining her. I decided to change the topic.

"I stayed at Mrs. Granger's house last night, and spent some time in your room," I said.

That got her eyes up again. "You did? Why?"

"I wanted to get a sense of your surroundings since coming to Nashville."

"Pretty tacky, huh?"

"I didn't think it was so bad."

"Oh! I didn't mean to be ungrateful, Mrs. Fletcher. I know Mrs. Shevlin did the best she could. And, of course, it isn't a lot of money, the rent at Mrs. Granger's, that is, and that's important. It'll let me stay in the city longer and use my funds for lessons or whatever else I need. And I'm learning how to live on my own with a budget."

I could hear her mother's words coming from Cyndi's mouth. Obviously, she hadn't been pleased with her Nashville quarters, and Janet had chided her to be grateful for what she had received.

I interrupted her little speech. "I saw the

copy of the cease-and-desist letter you wrote to Mr. Marker," I said. "When you gave it to him, did he—?"

"I never gave it to him in person," she said, sitting up straight.

"Did you mail it? The detective says they found it on his desk."

"I was too nervous to give it to him directly, but I was afraid if I mailed it and he didn't respond, I'd never know if he got it or not. So I dropped it off with his secretary. She gave it to him."

"It was signed by Cyndi Gabriel. When did you change your name?"

A faint smile crossed her thin lips. "Sounds stupid, huh?"

"Not at all. Did Mr. Marker suggest it?"

"No."

"Who did?"

"Oh." She looked up at the ceiling. "A lot of people told me that Blaskowitz wasn't, um, well, it's not really a pretty name, and it's hard to remember or spell, so I changed it."

"Look," Washburn said, pulling papers from his briefcase, "we have to get some work done here. I need you to sign these papers acknowledging that I've been retained to act as your attorney." He slid the papers across the table to her, along with a pen.

"What name should I use?"

"For now, I think you'd better go with your legal name."

After Washburn thoroughly reviewed the legal papers he'd brought for his new client, and Cyndi signed "Cindy Blaskowitz" where he indicated, I asked what was in the file folder she'd brought into the room.

"Just some songs I wrote."

"Since you've been here?" I asked, incredulous.

"Just a couple."

"Like Johnny Cash with 'Folsom Prison Blues,'" Washburn said with a chuckle. "Some say a jail experience is good for a country composer."

Cyndi looked self-conscious. "Not really," she said. "It's just there's not that much to do. They have me all by myself."

"May I see them?" I asked.

She opened the folder and flipped through a few papers.

"Do you want me to save them for you?" I asked.

"Yes, please," she said. "They won't do me any good here."

"I'll give them back after you're re-leased."

"Right," she said, but the word was laced with irony.

Before I could take the folder, Cyndi slid out two songs, folded them neatly into halves, and then into quarters. "These are junk," she said. "Those other two are maybe okay."

"Let me take them anyway," I said, tucking them back into the folder. "You may change your mind."

"We should be leaving," Washburn said. "I have a downtown meeting with another client in an hour."

"Cyndi, before we go," I said urgently, "I really wish you'd tell us where you spent those two days after you ran from Mr. Marker's office. Mr. Washburn can't help you unless you're completely open and honest with him."

Cyndi swallowed audibly. "I don't want to get anybody in trouble," she said.

"You're in the most trouble," I said. "You can't afford to shield someone if it will make things worse for you. Would this person really want you to do that, to make yourself more vulnerable? What kind of friend would ask that?"

"But I promised I wouldn't say anything."

Washburn snapped his briefcase shut. "If the DA finds out who it is," he said, "and you didn't come clean on this, it'll make my job defending you a lot harder."

"Please, Cyndi," I said. "Trust us. We're here to help you."

"Remember, Cyndi," Washburn added, "anything you tell me is confidential, and I'm sure Mrs. Fletcher will respect that, too."

"Of course I will."

Cyndi slowly shook her head before drawing a deep, pained breath. "Wally," she said so softly that I barely heard her.

"Who's Wally?" Washburn asked.

"Wally Brolin."

"Is he a friend?" I asked.

She started crying again as she said, "The only real friend I have here in Nashville. He's a musician. He let me stay with him after I went to Marker's office."

"And he lives where?" Washburn asked.

Cyndi gave him an address in East Nashville.

Washburn jotted down the information

on a legal pad, returned it to his briefcase, and made a show of looking at his watch. "Time to go," he said, standing.

"Will I see you again?" Cyndi asked as the officer stood and walked toward her holding the handcuffs.

"You bet you will," Washburn said. "We're a team now."

"You, Mrs. Fletcher?" Cyndi asked as she extended her slender wrists to the officer.

"I'll be here every chance I get," I assured, "and I'll be working on your behalf when I'm not here."

Once back in Washburn's car, I asked, "I will be allowed to see her again, won't I?"

He nodded. "As long as we're together. Sorry, but you're stuck with me."

"Frankly," I said, "I'd prefer it that way."

"Welcome to the Washburn defense team," he said lightly.

"Thank you," I said, "for everything. You know, I think I know the key to defending Cyndi."

"Oh? Tell me."

"The key," I said, "is to discover who really killed Roderick Marker, and to find out fast."

Chapter Ten

"Would you like me to drop you off at your hotel?" Washburn asked as we headed back to the city.

"That would be wonderful," I said. "I'm staying at the Renaissance Hotel downtown."

"I know it well. It's my mother's favorite place when she visits from L.A."

"So you're not from here. How did you end up practicing law in Nashville?" I asked.

"Well, it's really just a short story. I came here for Vanderbilt's law school, ended up clerking with a local judge, liked the city, decided to stay, passed the Tennessee bar, and here I am."

"A nice concise tale. What appealed to you about Nashville?"

"It's a little like Los Angeles in a way, in the sense that it's mostly a one-industry town. That's not to say that there aren't lots of other corporations and businesses here, but country music is at the heart of Nashville, and everything revolves around it in the same way Los Angeles is all about the film business. The local media cover the industry. Many of the people here come from somewhere else. Yet everyone I've met, from my local dry cleaner, to the lady in the bank, to the guy who picks up the trash is a country-and-western fan, and some are remarkably knowledgeable about country music. The fellow who set up my computer can tell you the difference between the original Jimmie Rodgers and the one who had a TV show, that Loretta Lynn was the first female country singer to have a gold album, and even who Vernon Dalhart was."

"Who *was* Vernon Dalhart?"

"Vernon Dalhart was one of over one hundred names used by a Texas singer named Marion Try Slaughter, back when country was known as hillbilly music. He's in the Hall of Fame."

"Does that mean you're a lover of country music, too?"

He laughed. "I wasn't when I first came here, but I'm a convert now."

He dropped me at the front of the hotel, where a bellman relieved me of my rolling suitcase. "Thanks so much, Mr. Washburn," I said through the open window of his car.

"It's Jamal. You up for dinner, Mrs. Fletcher?"

"Why yes, I am. And it's Jessica."

"I thought we should get to know each other a little better and see how we can work together to help Cyndi."

"I like that idea."

"My treat," he said. "I have a favorite place I think you'll enjoy." He consulted his watch. "It's almost four thirty. Shall I pick you up at six? Will that give you enough time?"

"Make it six thirty," I said.

"I'll be back at six thirty."

"I'll be waiting."

My room at the hotel was a far cry from

the one I'd slept in at Mrs. Granger's rooming house. I pulled back the drapes to uncover an expanse of glass and a lovely view of downtown Nashville. I quickly unpacked, put everything away, and checked out the bathroom. It was spacious and nicely appointed; a terry-cloth robe hung on the back of the door. I was tempted to slip out of my clothes and bundle up in the robe, but I had things to do. Before I got to them, however, I called Seth to see how Janet Blaskowitz was faring.

"Doing all right," Seth said, "but there has been a complication. The cardiologists are working on it now."

"Seth, is this complication life-threatening?"

"Doesn't appear to be. Why do you ask?"

"First, because I'm concerned about Janet, and second, because I haven't been able to convince her daughter to call yet. I think it would be healing for both of them to speak with each other."

"I take it that means you've gotten in touch with Janet's daughter. How is she?"

"I just left the jail where she's being held. I'm having dinner tonight with her court-appointed attorney. He's a nice young

man who I believe has Cyndi's best interests at heart."

"And how does it look to you?"

"How does *what* look to me?"

"Her predicament. Do you think she'll
be found guilty of murdering that man?"

"I certainly hope not. I don't think she
killed him, but I'll have a better grip on her
chances for acquittal after dinner. Everything all right at home?"

"Fine, just fine, busy as ever. Mayor Shevlin was askin' after you. He's concerned
about the girl. Told him we'd be speaking
soon. Think he wants to talk to you about
fund-raising for the legal defense."

"That's very generous of him, but I can't
call him right now. Would you mind giving
him an update for me, Seth? I've got to run
out."

"Will do. Soon's I get off with you."

After hanging up, I jotted down notes
from my visit with Cyndi, my conversations
with Detective Biddle, and everything I
could remember of what Cyndi had said.
The notes didn't amount to much. I'd had
abbreviated time with her, and she'd basi-
cally told me what I'd already learned from
Biddle. The only revelation was the name

of the person with whom she'd holed up after running from Roderick Marker's office, a Nashville musician named Wally Brolin, and his address. I'd follow up with him at the first possible opportunity. But what was on my agenda at that moment was to go to the scene of the crime, Roderick Marker's office.

The cabdriver dropped me off in front of Marker & Whitson Music Publishers. A large banner fluttered from the top floor of the modern tan stone building, congratulating SALLY PRENTICE, NASHVILLE'S RISING STAR.

I waited while a flow of people exited the building, and entered when a gentleman held open the large glass door for me. No guard was on duty in the lobby. I could have asked someone for the location of Marker's office, but the few people crossing the marble floor looked to be in a hurry. A wall directory told me the firm I sought was on the third floor. When the elevator opened, I stepped into a carpeted hallway, which extended in both directions. Ahead of me was a huge circular glass partition—to suggest a record or CD,

"It's no trouble at all," I said, picking up
e box. "Where were you going with all
is?"

"Just around the corner at the end of the
ll. Typical of him, waiting until after busi-
ss hours to make the move. I could have
ne this anytime today and gotten some
lp, but no, God forbid we disturb the
ff people during work time—except, of
urse, for this staff person. I'm Buddy,
the way, chief cook and bottle washer
all things no one else wants to do at
rker & Whitson."

He walked past the glass entrance to
other end of the hall and turned left. I
owed him. "Here we are," he said, stop-
g in front of a door next to the fire exit.
leaned back, the boxes in his arms
ing into his cheek as he groped for the
rknob with one barely free hand.

Here, let me get that," I said, putting
box I held on the floor and opening the
r for him.

e turned his body and sidestepped
ugh the opening before squatting down
depositing his burden on a glass cock-
able in front of a long gray sofa.

oked around the large office. Windows

perhaps—with a glass door in i
The name of the firm was spell
gold letters in an arc over the ent
M&W logo, also in gold letters, w
door. I could see the reception
waiting area, but no one was ther
door was locked. I looked at m
was after five. I wandered down
my left, looking for another doc
on in case someone was work
man came around the corner f
end, a pile of cardboard file bo:
in his arms, obscuring his vision
knocked me over, sending one
from the pile, hitting the floor,
some of its contents.

He slammed himself agai
and peered at me over one sh
sorry, ma'am," he said. "Are \
I didn't see you."

"I'm not surprised," I said
pick up the papers. "I'm fir
quite a load you're carrying."

"You don't have to pick tho
he said, juggling his cargo
losing another box. "I'll just
my way back. Don't trouble
carrying more than I should

overlooked the street, which must have given the room a lot of light when the blinds were open. Several boxes sat atop the desk and matching credenza, and it appeared as though the original occupant of the office had moved out and someone new was moving in.

Buddy returned to the hall to kick the box I'd carried for him through the doorway, giving it a good shove with a green-sneakered foot.

"Is that table strong enough to hold all that weight?" I asked.

"Oh sure. It looks like glass, but it's real thick, probably strong as iron. I've seen people climb up on it when one of our clients topped the *Billboard* chart for hot country songs."

"Really? Who would take that chance?"

"The president. The president that was. You heard about what happened here, I suppose."

"Um . . ." I started.

"'Course you did. It was all over the TV, the radio, the papers."

"You're talking about Mr. Marker."

"The very same, killed right here in his office, this room, over there by the credenza.

Well. Almost. Didn't die right away, lasted a coupla days." He pointed to an area behind a large mahogany desk. "Girl whacked him with one of his CMA awards. We haven't gotten it back from the police yet, but we've got others on the shelf. See 'em? They're the same thing."

Buddy didn't seem particularly sorry that the firm had lost its president, and I found that curious. I walked to a bookcase where two of the awards he'd pointed out were displayed. "May I?" I asked.

"Sure. Knock yourself out." He winced. "I didn't mean that literally."

I picked up one of the awards. It was a very heavy piece of crystal in the shape of a flame, pointed at the top and mounted on a square base. It wouldn't be easy to hold on to and swing, but it was certainly weighty enough to do some damage. I replaced it on the shelf.

"Did you know the young woman who was arrested?"

"Nope. Never met her, but it's not surprising. There are people in and out of here all the time."

"Were you here when he was found?" I

asked, walking nonchalantly toward the desk.

"No, thank goodness. The security guard caught her. Careful now, don't trip on that rug. Eddy put it there to hide the stain. Suppose they'll have to replace it soon. Shame. This carpet cost a fortune."

I stepped back from the small area rug.

"Didn't mean to gross you out," he said.

"That's quite all right. Who's Eddy?"

"Edwina Anderson, Mr. Marker's secretary. She's been here since the vinyl age." He opened the top box and transferred its files into a tall cabinet near another door.

"I know the name," I said.

"A real battle-ax. Rumor has it she was a wild teen—can't quite envision it—and got into legal trouble."

"What did she do?"

He shrugged. "I hear she ran over some guy in a parking lot. Went straight after that. Went rigid is more like it. Anyway, Eddy's the only one knows this place inside and out, so they can't fire her. He tried once or twice, and brought in a pretty young thing to sit at Eddy's desk and smile at everybody coming in, but he had to hire Eddy back after his wife found out. He didn't want an old bat out front, but Marilyn had a fit when she saw the new girl. A blond bombshell, to coin a phrase. Not that he was henpecked or anything, but their marriage wasn't made in heaven, if you catch my drift. Can you pass me the next box?"

I lifted it off the pile on the table and handed it to Buddy. "Marilyn was his wife, I take it."

"The queen of green, I call her. She spent it as fast as he could make it." He held up one pinkie, miming someone drinking tea. "Rules were not made for the queen," he said in a fake English accent, before lapsing into his Southern drawl. "She fritters away more on parking tickets than I make in a month."

"Where does Eddy sit?" I asked.

"Out there in the reception room." Buddy pointed to the door next to the file cabinet he was filling.

I looked behind me. "But we came in—"

"The other door," Buddy supplied. "Mr. Marker liked to be able to come and go without anyone, meaning you-know-who, the wiser." He pointed at the door through which he'd said Marker's secretary sat.

"And he had the occasional lady friend that he wasn't eager for anyone else to see." He gave me a wink. "So he had the second door installed. Mr. Whitson likes that, too."

"Is Mr. Whitson moving into Mr. Marker's office?"

Buddy did a double take. "Why, o'course! Why else would I be hauling all these files up and down the hall and putting them in this cabinet?"

"I don't know," I said. "I just arrived."

"Oh, 'scuse me," he said. "Where are you from?"

"Cabot Cove, Maine."

"A Yankee! Well, we all have burdens to bear. Who were you looking for before I banged into you?"

"Actually, I think I was looking for Eddy."

"Well, you're too late for her. She's out of here like a shot on the dot of five. I might be able to find someone else for you, but it's probably better to come back tomorrow. Are you a writer?"

He must've seen the surprise on my face because he chuckled.

"How did you know?" I asked.

He flapped a hand at me. "I can always spot a writer, but I gotta tell you, you can't just waltz up to a publisher and expect anyone to help you."

"I can't?"

"Nope. You need a plugger."

"A what?"

"You *are* from out of town. A song plugger. The publishers don't listen to just anyone who shows up. It's the pluggers who have access. They bring them all the good CDs from the songwriters they represent, and the bigwigs here and sometimes the performers—names you would surely know—sit 'round the table in the conference room and play, maybe ten seconds from each cut before they turn them down."

"Ten seconds. That's not very long."

"Maybe it's a little longer, but not much. You gotta be good right from the first word and first note. Anyway, get a plugger if you want Mr. Whitson to hear your song, but make sure you get a good one. Some of them are unscrupulous." His rolled his eyes and cocked his head in the direction of the desk. "Speaking of—" He shook his head. "Forget what I said. My mama taught me not to speak ill of the dead."

A man's voice boomed from down the hall. "Buddy, where the hell are you?"

"My master's voice," Buddy said, picking up two boxes he had already emptied.

"Do you mind if I follow you and meet Mr. Whitson?" I asked.

"Honey, he won't talk to you, believe me. But you can try. It never hurts to try."

I trailed down the hall in Buddy's wake. He held an empty box in each hand, and cursed each time he banged them into the walls, which was often. Rounding the corner, I nearly collided with him again when he stopped before an open door.

A tall, handsome man with dark hair slicked back on the sides and pulled forward a bit over his forehead—reminiscent of Elvis—stood behind a desk littered with piles of files and a jumble of office materials: a tape dispenser, rubber bands, a stapler, boxes of paper clips, pens and pencils, sticky note pads, paperweights, a calculator, CDs, and who knows what else. It looked as if he'd taken out a desk drawer and simply upended it over his desk.

"I can't find the key to the other file cabinet," he complained. "Did Eddy go home?"

"Gone at the stroke of five," Buddy told him, flinging the empty boxes to one side of the room.

"She knew we were moving the office tonight. Where could she have put it? I don't want to start again in the morning. I want everything in place, and it *will* be in place if it takes all night. Understand?"

"Yes, sir," Buddy said with a mock salute. "I'll check her desk." He turned and saw me. "Oh, by the way, this lovely lady came to see you. This is Mr. Whitson."

"I'm Jessica Fletcher," I said, moving around Buddy and extending my hand to his boss, who took the tips of my fingers as if afraid I might contaminate him. "It's a pleasure. I can see I'm getting you at a difficult moment, but I was hoping you might give me a few minutes of your time."

"She's a songwriter," Buddy said as he left the room.

"Well, that isn't quite accurate," I began.

Mr. Whitson came from behind his desk and took my elbow. "Ms. Fletcher, as you can see, I really don't have any time to spare." He steered me toward the door.

"But it's terribly important. A young woman's life is at stake, and—"

"I've heard that before. If you'd like to make an appointment tomorrow, I'm sure we can work something out."

"But, Mr. Whitson, I don't want to talk to you about songwriting. Actually, I wanted to ask you some questions about your partner."

"Of course you do. Call Ms. Anderson. She handles the press. She'll be very helpful, I'm sure."

"Mr. Whitson, it's not what you think."

"It never is. Goodbye, Ms. Fletcher." He pushed me into the hall and closed the door. I heard the snick of a lock.

Well, I thought, *that was quite the bum's rush. I haven't been thrown out of an office in some time now.* I was tempted to pound on Whitson's door and tell him I'd be back, but of course I didn't. Instead, I tugged at the hem of my jacket, smoothed down my hair, straightened the strap of my bag on my shoulder, and retraced my steps to the elevator. At least I had a dinner date with someone who *did* want to talk to me.

Chapter Eleven

I was tempted to take a nap when I got back to my room at the hotel. I was feeling jet-lagged although there's only a one-hour time difference between Nashville and Cabot Cove. Maybe "travel-tired" is a better way to describe it. But I knew that if I fell asleep, I'd be groggy when it was time to meet Washburn. Instead, I took a quick shower, relying on it to wake me up, dressed in an outfit that I felt would be appropriate for any restaurant setting, and was waiting for him in the lobby when he arrived.

The restaurant was only a short ride

from the hotel, in an old, three-story brick building on Broadway. A sign announced that it was called Merchants.

We passed through an attractive grill downstairs and were escorted to a second-floor dining room, where a pianist played show tunes on a small, white grand piano. Our table was nicely set on a sparkling white tablecloth. Jamal ordered a perfect Manhattan; I opted for a glass of house white wine.

Our waiter left us menus and a sheet recounting the history of the building before it was a restaurant and during the time when lower Broadway was not the flourishing neighborhood it is now.

Built around 1870, it originally housed various businesses, including a drug company that advertised "blood medicine," a concoction of alcohol and opium. A pharmacy on the first floor dispensed ice cream sodas, which contained, among other things, cocaine.

When a hotel was added in 1892, Nashville was booming. Steamboat trade on the Cumberland River opened up the town to a post–Civil War prosperity, providing plenty of customers for Merchants Hotel, who paid twenty-five cents for a night's lodging, and twenty-five cents for a meal. With the launch of the Grand Ole Opry at the Ryman Auditorium across the street, all the greats of country-and-western music stayed at the Merchants Hotel—Roy Acuff, Patsy Cline, Loretta Lynn, Dolly Parton, and Hank Williams, to name a few. Will Rogers often stayed there; so did Wild Bill Hickok and the James boys (one of them shot someone dead outside).

The hotel deteriorated. During the Roaring Twenties, it became a speakeasy, one of Al Capone's places. It became a brothel in the 1940s and a "dive bar" in the seventies. The building was about to be demolished in the 1980s, but the owner of the current restaurant, Ed Stolman, and the Nashville Arts Commission saved it by arranging for it to be listed in the National Register of Historic Places. Stolman opened the restaurant in 1988, a time when lower Broadway wasn't an especially nice, peaceful neighborhood. All that has changed now, and it's become the core of Nashville's vibrant nightlife scene.

"I latched on to this place while I was a student at Vanderbilt," Jamal said with a chuckle. "Of course, I couldn't afford to come here very often, but I always liked it. I'm not a big fan of down-home Southern cooking. This place is more straight ahead."

"I'm sure I'll like it," I said.

After our drinks were delivered and we'd had some idle conversation about Nashville and his favorite places in the city, I raised the subject of Cyndi Gabriel. "I didn't have much time with her, and I have so many questions."

"I'll be happy to answer the ones that I can, only you'll have to respect the attorney-client privilege."

"Of course. But if Cyndi were to waive that privilege—"

"That would change things."

"The police were looking for her for three nights and two days following the assault. I'm wondering if she was with this musician, Wally Brolin, the whole time. I assume you'll be getting in touch with him."

"Soon as I can. "

"I'd like to be with you when you visit him."

"Absolutely, partner."

I smiled. "From the looks of Cyndi's room at Mrs. Granger's house, it's unlikely she returned there during the time she was missing. Somehow, I think that if she really meant to run, she would have found a way to take her guitar, if nothing else."

"What do you know about her claim that Marker had ripped off some of her songs?"

"Just that," I said. "Marker had arranged for this up-and-comer, Sally Prentice, to record a song that Cyndi was counting on performing herself. I don't really know much beyond that."

"He took away her opportunity for stardom, huh? Makes for a strong motive, unfortunately. Explaining her running away is tricky, but the big problem may be the cease-and-desist letter with her signature on it that was found on Marker's desk."

"Yes. Detective Biddle told me about that. Why is that a big problem?"

"Tends to confirm that motive. Proves she was angry with the deceased, maybe angry enough to kill him."

"Oh."

"Something wrong?"

"I have something to admit. I'm afraid I may have complicated things."

"How's that?"

I recounted for him Cyndi's tearful call to

her mother, my consultation with an entertainment lawyer, and the advice I'd tried to give. "I saw a draft of that letter in an envelope in her room," I said. "The police have it, too. Even though we have to assume she was upset when she delivered the letter, she agreed to meet with him later to discuss it. That's a good sign. You can make the case that she hoped that she and Marker would be able to come to some sort of agreement without her resorting to legal means."

"Or violent ones."

"I just don't believe it's in Cyndi's nature to be a violent person."

"I happen to agree. I think that's a fair assumption, Mrs. Fletcher."

"Jessica. After all, we are partners."

"Right, Jessica," he said through a gentle laugh.

"There's something that's puzzling me," I said. "Maybe you can explain it."

"What's that?"

"They say the fingerprints on the murder weapon match hers," I said. "How could they have determined that *before* they arrested her? As far as I know, she'd never been fingerprinted before. What were they comparing the prints on the murder weapon to?"

Jamal gave me a wry smile, and cocked his head. "Yeah, well, the police can be pretty cagey at times. From what I understand, during their initial questioning— before I was assigned to the case, I might add—they offered her a can of Coke. She was obviously nervous and dry-mouthed. So, of course, she accepted. Also, she's pretty naive and wouldn't have suspected anything. They took her prints off the can so they would have a set to compare to those on the murder weapon. When it came back positive, they made it official and arrested her."

"Sneaky," I said, "but clever."

"Very. And perfectly legal."

"What happens now? Has she been arraigned?"

"Tomorrow. Technically it's called a jail docket," Jamal said, "part of the General Sessions Court. I'll ask for a reconsideration of her bail, but it's unlikely the judge will grant it, not in a murder case. But nothing ventured, nothing gained."

"I'd like to be there, too."

A nod from the young attorney. "I'm sure

she'd appreciate that." He took a sip of his drink and set the glass down. "I have something to ask you, Mrs. Fl . . . I mean, Jessica."

"Go ahead."

"How long do you intend to stay around Nashville?"

"I want to stay as long as it takes to see Cyndi walk free. I feel responsible for her being here in the first place." I told him about CCC and how we'd raised the money for her to come to Nashville to pursue her dream.

"That's an admirable project, Jessica. It's a shame it's ended up like this."

"But that's my whole point for being here, Jamal. I'm determined that it won't end up this way. I can't stay here months and months. I realize that's unrealistic. But if we can learn enough to raise reasonable doubt in a potential jury, or better still, find out who really did kill Marker, we'll have served Cyndi well."

"That's for sure," he said, opening his menu. "I hope you're right for all concerned. Shall we order?"

He steered me toward the Southern chicken cordon bleu, which the waiter indicated was breaded with pecans and stuffed with ham, Swiss cheese, and sage, sprinkled with a Dijon cream sauce, and served with sausage grit cakes and spinach. "I won't be able to eat anything else for days," I said, "but lunch was a long time ago and I'm hungry enough to eat a moose."

"I figure you'll be busy enough to work it off," he said, ordering Merchants' meat loaf. "Comfort food," he said with a laugh. "Got me through some tough law exams."

He offered to drive me to the court the following morning, but I declined. "I'm sure you have plenty to do," I told him. "I'll find my way there just fine."

His parting words as I got out of his car in front of the hotel were, "I'm glad you're here, Jessica. You know the defendant well. You got her to answer a question that she wouldn't answer for me. That was a positive development."

"Well, thank you. I'm hoping I can be of service."

"You already have. And believe me, in this case I can use all the help I can get."

Somehow, that didn't sound terribly positive.

Chapter Twelve

I was forty-five minutes early for the General Sessions Court the next morning, but Jamal Washburn had beaten me there. He saw me walk through the door, got up from where he'd been sitting on a wooden bench outside the courtroom, and escorted me back outside.

"I was hoping we'd have time before court convenes," he said. "I have a suggestion to run past you."

"I'm listening."

"Getting a judge, especially Judge Grimes, to release someone charged with murder without bail is a stretch, a definite long shot. Usually, it's the trial judge who hears pleas for reduced bail, but that will mean a long delay. I'm hoping we can present this judge with a creative reason for allowing Cyndi to go free without bond until her trial comes up."

"A *creative* reason?" I said.

He smiled. "The law is pretty cut-and-dried," he said, "but there's always room for a little creative thinking. I asked around about Judge Grimes and was told that she's a dedicated fan of murder mystery novels."

"That's always good to hear."

"I'm sure she's well aware of your stature as a writer."

"What are you getting at?" I asked.

"There was a case a year or so ago where a young man charged with second-degree murder was released into the custody of his uncle, a well-known Tennessee businessman, no bail. The accused had to live at his uncle's house, wear a monitor on his ankle, and wasn't allowed to leave the house except for medical and court visits."

"Are you suggesting that—?"

He nodded. "If you'd be willing to take responsibility for Cyndi here in Nashville, I might be able to persuade Judge Grimes to release her into your custody, with the usual restrictions, of course."

"But I don't have a home in Nashville."

"Home is a relative term. You are staying in a hotel. If you could arrange to keep her with you, it might fly."

"Oh, Jamal," I said. "I just don't see that working. Cyndi's trial won't be for months. I couldn't possibly stay here that long. Certainly not in one room."

"I understand. But you *did* say that the key to saving Cyndi was to identify the real murderer. If we work on that together, it could only be days or weeks at the most. I did a little checking on you, too, Jessica. Your reputation precedes you, not only as a successful writer, but as someone who's solved more than her fair share of *real* murders. I'm betting on you to do what you've done many times before, find out who killed Marker."

"It's hardly a reputation I covet, Jamal. But what happens if we don't find Mr. Marker's murderer in days, or weeks?"

"That's a bridge we can cross when we get to it. The important thing is to get Cyndi out of prison. She's a vulnerable kid. Prison can't be good for her. If you have to leave, maybe the judge will allow her to stay at Mrs. Granger's again. As I say, we'll deal with that when we have to. Game?"

I nodded, without conviction. Chances were that the judge wouldn't go for this scheme anyway.

"How about checking with the hotel to see if they have a two-bedroom suite available? It might help if the judge knows arrangements have already been nailed down."

I called the Renaissance Hotel, was told there were a few such suites available, and reported that to Washburn. As much as I wanted Cyndi released from jail, I wasn't sure I was up to babysitting an emotional teenager, not to mention the time it would take away from any investigation.

"If Judge Grimes even considers my plea, she'll want to hear from you. Up for that?"

"No, but let's not let that stand in the way. I'll do my best."

"Can't ask for more than that."

Judge Candice Grimes was a no-nonsense woman with little patience for sob stories and less patience for bumbling attorneys. As we waited for Cyndi's case to be called, the judge dispensed with several others, bringing her gavel down with a sharp crack as she set stiff amounts of

bail and remanded prisoners back to jail.
Not one to trust promises to show up in
court without a monetary guarantee, Judge
Grimes let no one out on their own recognizance, and chastised defense lawyers who
tried to argue for a lower bond.

Jamal and I sat in the back of the court
until Cyndi and several other defendants
were brought in by the marshals, and we
moved up to the front row. As each case
was called, the defendant rose, then sat
as the judge and lawyers argued the mer-
its of bail. Decision made, the gavel came
down and the defendant shuffled out, escorted by a marshal.

"The State of Tennessee versus Cindy
Blaskowitz, aka Cyndi Gabriel. Accused is
charged with murder in the second degree.
How does your client plead, Mr. Washburn?"

"My client pleads not guilty, Your Honor."

"I see you're asking for her to be released
on her own recognizance, Mr. Washburn."
The smirk on her face said volumes. "Does
the prosecution have a comment on this?"

"This is news to me, Your Honor," the prosecutor, a rotund, red-faced, older gentleman
said, the expression on his round face mir-
roring the judge's. "Of course, considerin'

the charge, Judge, I don't imagine this court would be comfortable havin' a murderer runnin' around loose in our fair city."

Judge Grimes picked up her gavel and was prepared to bring it down when Washburn spoke. "Your Honor," he said, "I realize that asking for no bail for the defendant is unusual in such a case, but I also know that Your Honor has an open mind."

"Do I, Mr. Washburn?"

"Yes, ma'am. I've been joined in my defense of the defendant by none other than Jessica Fletcher, an esteemed writer of bestselling murder mysteries *and*, I might add, a respected and upstanding member of the community from which the defendant has come. Mrs. Fletcher is here at her own expense because she believes, as I do, in the defendant's innocence, believes in it to such an extent that she has offered to share a two-bedroom suite at the Renaissance Hotel with Ms. Gabriel, and to take full responsibility for her."

The judge lowered her chin and looked at me. "You are Jessica Fletcher?" she said.

Washburn nudged me, and I stood. "Yes, Your Honor," I said.

"I love your books, Mrs. Fletcher," Grimes

said, "especially some of the more recent ones."

"Thank you, Your Honor. That's kind of you to say."

"Which is *your* favorite?"

"That's like asking a mother to pick out her favorite child," I replied, smiling.

The judge let out a belly laugh, drawing all eyes around us, and there was a discernible easing of tension in the court.

Judge Grimes asked the prosecutor whether the defendant had any prior criminal history.

"No, Your Honor, she does not, but that doesn't mean that—"

"I see that she's eighteen years old," the judge said.

"That's correct," Washburn confirmed.

"And you're willing to take responsibility for the defendant, Mrs. Fletcher?"

The words caught in my throat: "Yes, I am, Your Honor."

"Any final objections, Mr. Laidlow?" she asked the prosecutor.

"I've plenty of 'em, Judge, but ah've got this feeling that you don't want to hear 'em."

She smiled sweetly at him before saying, "The defendant will be released in the care of Jessica Fletcher, and will be sequestered in accommodations provided by Mrs. Fletcher at the Renaissance Hotel in Nashville. Defendant will be fitted with an ankle monitoring device and shall wear it at all times, except for showering. She shall not leave her quarters at the hotel except for medical emergencies, or for matters relating to her case. Any meetings with her court-appointed attorney shall take place at the hotel. Anything else?"

Laidlow, the prosecutor, glared at Washburn, who returned a wide, victorious smile.

Judge Grimes instructed Cyndi, Washburn, and me to meet with her in chambers. We were there almost an hour. During that time, she gave Cyndi a harsh reminder of what would happen to her if she violated any of her instructions. As we were leaving, she said to me, "I've always enjoyed your books, Mrs. Fletcher, and I'm also aware that you've ended up solving real crimes during your long and illustrious career. I hope you don't mind me saying that you've taken on a huge responsibility with serious legal consequences should things go awry. I hope you know what you're doing!"

Chapter Thirteen

Jamal Washburn and I drove from the courthouse to the jail, where Cyndi was processed out. Her personal belongings and clothing, which had been secured in a locked blue hang-up bag, were returned to her, and she handed over her two-piece prison uniform to the female officer in charge.

"You get to keep the underwear and the shoes," the officer told her, as Cyndi opened the door to the changing room.

"I don't think I'll wear them again," Cyndi said.

"Suit yourself, but those are quality goods."

It was almost one that afternoon before we left the facility and drove to the hotel, where an assistant manager showed us to the suite they'd set aside for me. If he noticed Cyndi's electronic ankle bracelet, which had been attached at the jail, his expression didn't reveal it. My belongings had already been transferred to the new quarters and my clothing neatly tucked away in the dresser drawers of the room with a king-sized bed. Across the living room, what the assistant manager called "the parlor," was the second bedroom, which Cyndi would occupy, a room with two queen beds. We each had our own bathroom.

Cyndi had said little during our drive from the jail to the hotel, but once in the suite she perked up. "This is beautiful," she said, taking in the airy living room, and walking to the huge windows that flooded the space with filtered sunlight through gossamer drapes. She parted the curtain and looked at the view of downtown Nashville. "But it's too bad I won't be able to go outside." She leaned her forehead against the glass.

"You heard the judge's rules," Washburn said. "Violate any one of them and you'll be back in prison. I'm sure you don't want that to happen, or for Mrs. Fletcher to end up in trouble with the law. She's really sticking her neck out for you."

"I won't break the rules. I promise," she said, turning away from the view. "I know how lucky I am to have people like you supporting me, Mrs. Fletcher, and you, too, Mr. Washburn. How can I ever repay either of you?"

"You can start by telling us about this friend of yours, Brolin," I said.

"Wally?" She brightened for a moment before a cloud descended over her features. "He won't end up in trouble, will he?"

"Is there a reason he should?" I asked.

She shook her head. "I guess not, except that he helped me. He's such a good friend, a sweet guy."

"I'm sure he is," I said, "but we have to talk. How do we reach him?"

"I know his cell number."

I wrote down the number she recited.

"He's a musician," she said, "and keeps really late hours. He's a good guitar player, better than some of the others who get the gigs because they play up to the producers and studios."

My assumption was that Cyndi was parroting what this Wally Brolin had told her.

"We were going to cut some demos together."

"I'm sure you will once we get your legal situation cleared up."

I picked up the phone and dialed the number she'd given me.

"I hope he won't be angry that I told you about him," Cyndi said. "Could he be arrested for harboring a felon?"

"I doubt it," I said, listening to a series of rings on the other end of the line. I was about to hang up, but a sleepy male voice stopped me. "Yeah?"

"Mr. Brolin?"

A loud yawn preceded, "Uh-huh. Who's this?"

I introduced myself and said I was calling on Cyndi Gabriel's behalf, which injected a semblance of life into him. "Is Cyndi okay?" he asked.

"Yes, she is. She's right here, in fact. It's important that her attorney, Mr. Washburn, and I speak with you."

"She's out of jail? Can I talk to her?"

"Another time. First, I'd like to arrange to meet today. Will you be available, say in an hour?"

"An hour? No, I don't think I can. I've got a recording session in an hour."

I wondered whether he'd have awakened for his recording date if I hadn't called.

"How about after your recording?" I asked. "I can meet you there."

"I suppose that'd be okay." He gave me the address of the studio, and we ended the call.

"I should have asked you before I made the appointment," I said to Jamal. "Will you be able to come with me?"

"I can't," he said. "I'm already running late for a meeting, but that's all right. You keep the appointment, Jessica, and fill me in later."

I admit I was worried about leaving Cyndi alone, and was sure that Jamal, too, shared my concern. "You'll be okay while we're gone?" I asked her.

She evidently read our minds. "You don't have to worry about me, Mrs. Fletcher. I'm not going anywhere. I don't want to get sent back to jail." She gave an involuntary shudder, then sighed. "But I wish I could get my things from Mrs. Granger's, especially my guitar. It would help me pass the time if I could do some playing and writing."

"I understand," I said, "but the police took several things from your room, including the guitar."

"I'll stop in after my meeting and see if they'll release it to me," Washburn said.

"And I'll call Lieutenant Biddle and ask when I can collect the rest of your things from Mrs. Granger's."

We rode down together in the elevator.

"You're a real trouper to do this for her," he said.

"I'm just surprised that it worked, that the judge went along with it. Do you think we can count on Cyndi—?" I was afraid to finish the sentence.

"To stay put? She's a smart girl. Let's hope she doesn't decide to do anything stupid, like running the way she did last time."

Yes, please don't let that happen, I silently thought.

The recording studio where I was to meet Wally Brolin was on a block of small houses, most of them craftsman-style bungalows. It was a two-story, yellow stucco home with a front porch atop a gray stone wall. Four stone pillars held up the roof of the porch, two at either end, and a pair flanking the steps up to the front door. An old green metal chair and a dead potted plant were the only outside furnishings on the wood planks. A sign next to the door said WHIZ STUDIOS. Standing next to it was a five-foot-tall plastic purple-and-white guitar sculpture. I knocked. There was no answer. A shade had been drawn partway down the glass panel of the door. I bent down and peered beneath the shade. The room appeared to be a reception area, so I walked in. As I stood there alone, I heard the faint strains of music emanating from somewhere to the rear of the house. I doubted if it was being played by Wally Brolin. I'd gotten to the studio in less than an hour.

The source of the music was evident ten minutes later when a door opened and three people joined me in the anteroom: a pretty young woman with very long brunette hair carrying a guitar, an older man wearing a large black Stetson hat and also with a guitar in his arms, and a painfully thin middle-aged man with thick glasses and a large pair of earphones draped around his neck. His salt-and-pepper hair was tied back into a ponytail that reached halfway down his back. The two musicians ignored me and left.

"Can I help you?" the skinny fellow asked in a nasal voice.

"I'm here to see Wally Brolin," I said.

"Here he is now."

The front door opened and a bearded, roly-poly bear of a man entered carrying a coffee container and a guitar. He, too, wore a black Stetson hat. A scuffed pair of tan cowboy boots protruded from the bottom of his faded jeans. His shirt was a lighter shade of blue denim with a garland of tiny red-and-white horses embroidered on the chest.

"Mr. Brolin?" I said.

"This woman says she's waiting for you," the thin fellow said.

He crossed the room and extended a beefy hand, which I took. "Name's Wally Brolin."

"And mine is Jessica Fletcher," I said. "I know I got here early, and I don't want to get in the way of your recording. I'll just wait, if you don't mind."

The door opened again and a middle-aged woman entered wearing jeans, boots, and a denim jacket with her name stitched on the back. "Hey, Wally B., mah main man," she said in a heavy Southern accent.

"'Lo, Millie," Brolin said. He turned to me. "Millie and I are recording a demo of a coupla tunes she's written. No problem if you want to come on in and listen."

He introduced me to the thin man with glasses. "This here's Jack. He's the engineer."

I followed them into a small but cozy studio in what would have been a living room if the house were set up as a home. Two microphones were on stands in front of chairs that faced each other. I was given a seat in the "control room," which must have formerly been a bedroom, where Jack-the-engineer fiddled with his equipment until he said into his own microphone, "All right, let's rock 'n' roll. Take one. Wally B. and Millie Travis."

I spent the next forty-five minutes listening to them do multiple takes of three songs.

Millie had an appealing husky voice that spoke of having lived a hard life that included plenty of cigarettes. The guitar looked ridiculously small against Brolin's large chest. He hunched over the instrument, his body moving as though trying to wring a more mournful sound from it. To my untrained ear, Millie's melodies sounded similar to me, and her lyrics weren't very different, either, all lamenting the loss of a lover, how she yearned for him to go, and now wished he'd return.

When they were finished, Brolin and Millie came into the control room and heard the recordings played back. "I like that third take on number one the best," Millie said, and Brolin agreed. She gave Brolin a hug as she left. After saying goodbye to Jack, Brolin and I walked out to the street.

"Can we sit down somewhere and talk?" I asked. "Coffee? Something stronger?"

"I wouldn't mind a beer," he said. "Dan McGuinness's over on Demonbreun is close."

"Wherever you say."

We drove to the Irish pub in Brolin's pickup truck, a well-worn Chevy with plenty of discarded food wrappers and other debris on the floor, and a gun rack behind our heads. Once there, we took a tall table with stools in a far corner near a window. He ordered a draft beer; I had lemonade.

"I don't know where to start," I said. Cigarette smoke wafted in our direction, and, surprised, I turned to see that it came from another table.

"Places that don't allow customers in younger than eighteen can have smoking," he said. "Sorry."

"It's okay," I said.

"You Cyndi's lawyer?" he asked.

"No. I'm working with her attorney, however," I said, purposely leaving my "official" capacity vague. "Did you visit Cyndi in prison, Mr. Brolin?"

"No. She didn't want me to get involved."

"But you *were* involved. It's my understanding that she was with you for those days after the murder of Mr. Marker, before the police caught up with her."

He nodded ruefully and sipped his beer. "So she told you that, huh?"

"After a lot of convincing. Tell me, how did that come about?"

He took another swig before replying. "Cyndi showed up at my door that Friday night. She was in a panic, crying, hysterical. I got her to calm down and tell me what happened. She was a mess, a real mess."

"For good reason," I said, "finding a man she thought had been murdered."

"Yeah, sure, of course. I tried to convince her to go see the cops—I said I'd go with her—but she kept saying they'd think she killed him."

"And she stayed with you on those nights?"

"Uh-huh."

"Where?"

"At my house over in East Nashville."

"Were you and Cyndi, well, boyfriend and girlfriend?" I asked, realizing as I did that my phraseology might be old-fashioned.

"No. Just good friends. We met the first night she was in Nashville, at a club. A gal I know introduced us. We got to talking and started hanging out together, writing a few songs, you know, just making the Nashville scene. I'll tell you this. She was some talent."

"She still is."

"Right. How'd she get out of the slam-mer?"

I explained what had happened at court that morning, and how we'd moved in together at the hotel.

"That beats all! She's lucky to have a friend like you, ma'am."

"And you, too, Wally."

"You say she can't leave the hotel," he said.

"That's right, except for very special needs."

"That's a bummer."

"Better than a jail cell."

"I mean 'cause of the Bluebird gig."

"The nightclub," I said, remembering that Mrs. Granger had mentioned it the night I arrived.

"I got her into one of the auditions there and they loved her. They called yesterday. I guess they don't read the papers. Anyway, it's *the* place to get your name known, really tough to get a gig there."

"Do you mind if I tell her that she passed the audition?"

"No, except it'll break her heart." He smiled for the first time since we'd met. "She'll probably write a song about it."

He asked if he could visit her at the hotel, but I said the judge didn't want her to have any visitors before her next court appearance. He ordered a second beer

"Did she tell you about her belief that Mr. Marker had taken one of her songs and given it to another singer?" I asked.

"Yeah, she did. He gave it to Sally Prentice."

"You know her?"

"Sure. I played on some of her early demos. I'm hoping to get called to play on her CD. She's movin' up fast."

"From what Cyndi told me, this Sally Prentice will be credited as cowriter of the song."

"That's the way it usually works," he said. "Sally's headed for the big time. She's got it all—looks, a great voice, terrific stage presence. I told Cyndi to let it go, take the cowriter credit and use it to help build her career."

"But Cyndi didn't see it that way."

"She's young, Jessica. I probably would've felt the same way when I first came to Nashville fifteen years ago. But you mellow out after a while, roll with the punches, take the bitter with the sweet, if you know what I mean."

"Not an easy thing for a young girl like Cyndi to do," I said.

"I suppose not. You hungry?"

"No, but you go ahead and eat. My treat."

He ordered a corned beef sandwich on rye, with a side of fries.

I asked him what Cyndi had told him about discovering Marker's body, and his response matched what she'd told me, the police, and Jamal Washburn. His sandwich arrived and he ate with enthusiasm after slathering on a lot of mustard. The conversation drifted to him, his background, musical experiences, and aspirations. He was originally from New Jersey, although he'd moved frequently; his father was in the military. He started playing the guitar while living in Texas, and decided to make it his career. A friend suggested they travel to Nashville together, and at the age of eighteen he headed for Music City with his eye on a successful career in country music.

"Have you found it?" I asked. "A successful career?"

"I've managed to make a living as a

studio musician, and helping lyricists develop their songs. I'm a good musician, Jessica, but the town is crawling with good musicians, four-thousand of 'em registered with the Nashville union. You grab what jobs you can get, mostly demos, and hope that some producer will hear you and decide to put you on his A-team. Those are the guys who've been around a long time and are always called for major recordings." He grinned. "You keep waiting for one of them to burn out and decide to pack it in so you can take his place. Hasn't happened to me yet. Meanwhile I keep at it, recording where I can, picking up an occasional gig at some of the smaller clubs, and practicing."

"You said you thought that Cyndi has talent. Enough to make it big?"

He took the last bite of his sandwich, wiped the remnants of mustard from his mouth, and said, "With the right people to get her name around, and maybe a stylist to glam her up, she could've made it big, maybe really big."

"And are you one of the 'right people to get her name around,' Wally?"

"I coulda been."

"Why past tense?"

"Her name's known in town now, but only because of this murder mess she's in."

"It's a mess I'm determined to get her out of."

"And how're you gonna do that?"

"By finding out who really killed Roderick Marker."

"Yeah? I didn't take you for a cop or a PI."

"I'm not a policeman, just a concerned citizen. By the way, did you know Marker?"

He winced before answering. "I met him a few times, did a bunch of demos with songwriters he had under contract. Not my favorite guy, that's for sure. He's a sleaze. Took advantage of the young girls, the vulnerable types, if you know what I mean. Plus, he was slow to pay. I know some musicians who've been stiffed by him."

"Which means he had lots of enemies?"

"I don't know about *lots* of enemies, but you probably could start with his business partner, Whitson, or his wife, Marilyn."

"I have their names from the newspaper article about the murder. Tell me more about them."

"I only know what I've heard. Mostly, that is. I've met Whitson, too slick by half, struts around like he's the second coming of Elvis, but underneath he was just Marker's lackey."

"And Mrs. Marker?"

"I never saw Marker's wife, except for in the papers. She's his third. Apparently he liked 'em blond and . . . uh . . . with big—" He made a gesture with his hands.

"I get the picture," I said.

"She's in the gossip columns a lot. She's big with the charities, but a classic gold digger, if you ask me. And I heard she's a swinger. Lookin' for her next mark, I bet." He chuckled. "Hey, that's funny. Marilyn Marker lookin' for her next mark."

"Not a very flattering view of either of them."

"Just the way I see them. Look, I really should go. I'm meeting a lyricist in a half hour. Not much talent, but she's got plenty of money from her daddy to cut demos until the cows come home. Thanks for the beer and sandwich."

"It was my pleasure, Wally."

I asked him to drop me at the hotel, which he did. As I climbed down from his truck, he called out, "Hey, tell Cyndi I'm thinkin' of her, and hope everything works out. You let me know if there's anything I can do."

"If there is, Wally, you'll certainly hear from me."

As I watched him drive away, I realized that I was quickly getting to know a lot about this place called Music City—for better or for worse. What was more important, however, was for me to get to know those things, and those people, who could lead me to Marker's killer.

I knew one thing for certain: With the cost of a two-bedroom suite, and commitments back home that would start piling up, I'd better do it soon.

Chapter Fourteen

I couldn't help but smile as I approached the door to the suite at the Renaissance Hotel and heard the faint strains of a guitar, and a sweet voice emanating from inside. Jamal Washburn had obviously been successful in getting Cyndi's guitar back from the police.

I opened the door and stepped inside. Cyndi, wearing one of the hotel's fluffy robes, was seated in a large, overstuffed chair by the window. She'd propped up pieces of paper on a desk chair and leaned forward to read what was on them while playing the guitar. She was so engrossed in her task that she failed to hear me come in.

"Hello," I announced in a loud voice.

She stopped strumming and turned to me. "Oh, hi," she said.

"Nice to see you enjoying your music again," I said, taking a chair close to her. "I just came from a meeting with your friend Wally Brolin."

"Is he mad at me for telling you about him?" she asked.

"He didn't sound angry. In fact, he sends his best. He wanted to visit you here, but I don't think Judge Grimes would go along with that, not at this juncture."

Her face sagged. "I wish I could see him," she said sadly.

"You will soon enough," I said. "Has anyone called while I was gone?"

She shrugged. "The telephone rang a few times, but I didn't answer because I couldn't tell who was calling."

"That's fine. I'll check the voice mail for messages."

"Mrs. Fletcher," she said, "do you really think there's a chance they'll know I'm innocent and let me go?"

"I can't promise you anything, Cyndi,

but that's what Mr. Washburn and I are determined to see happen."

She took a shaky breath and nodded. "Okay."

"Now, what I thought we should do tonight is enjoy the evening together," I said, injecting some enthusiasm in my voice. "In a little while, we can order up some dinner, and use the time to get to know each other better. Would you like that?"

"I guess," she said. "I'm not going anywhere anyway."

Hardly a stirring endorsement of my suggestion, but I understood her mood.

I spent an hour in my bedroom adding to my notes from the previous day, including a recap of my conversation with Brolin, and checking phone messages, both those on the hotel's voice mail and those I'd let my cell phone pick up while I was busy. Seth Hazlitt had called. So had Susan Shevlin and Mort Metzger. Jamal Washburn had left a message saying that he'd been successful in retrieving Cyndi's guitar from the police and would drop it at the hotel, which he had. The only message that caused me concern was from a columnist from the *Nashville Tennessean*, Brian Krupp, who said it was urgent that I return his call. He left both his office and cell numbers.

I changed into a favorite soft, comfortable, pale blue two-piece pantsuit and rejoined Cyndi. She'd stopped playing and had turned on the large, flat-screen TV on which a country music singer was performing.

"Country music certainly is popular," I commented, joining her on the couch.

"I wonder if I'll ever end up on TV singing my songs," she said to no one.

"Let's assume that you will, Cyndi. You have to think positive at a time like this."

We consulted the room service menu and I called in our selections. Cyndi picked at her food, leaving half of it uneaten. We kept the country-and-western music channel on during dinner, which covered frequent lulls in our conversation.

"I'm going to Roderick Marker's memorial service tomorrow morning," I said when we'd retreated again to the couch. "And I'll stop by Mrs. Granger's to see if I can pick up what things of yours are still there."

"I feel bad for Mr. Marker and his family," she said, "even though he broke his promises."

"Your friend Wally told me that he encouraged you to go to the police. Why didn't you listen to him?"

"He said that?"

I nodded.

"He never said that to me."

I covered my surprise. Had I misinterpreted what Wally said? I thought over our conversation. No, he was very clear. His words to me were "I tried to convince her to go see the cops."

"What else did he say?" Cyndi asked.

"Well—he said that your audition at the Bluebird Café went well. They want to book you."

It was as though I'd punched her. She squeezed her eyes shut and doubled over.

"I'm sure they'll still want you when this whole legal mess has been straightened out," I said.

"The Bluebird," she moaned, sitting up, her eyes moist. "Do you know what a gig at the Bluebird means, Mrs. Fletcher? It's like . . . it's where . . ." She groped for words. "It's such an honor, and great things can happen to a singer who gets to perform at the Bluebird. People have gotten record deals after playing at the Bluebird."

"So I've heard. But as I said, they'll still be there when you're free to take that job. Or I should say gig." I quickly changed the subject. "Tell me about friends you've made here other than Wally Brolin."

"I haven't been here that long," she replied. "I met some great people at NSAI."

"The Nashville Songwriters Association."

"Yes. Everybody there really wants to help young songwriters."

"What about the other boarders at Mrs. Granger's? Alicia?"

"Oh, her," she said in a dismissive voice.

"You don't sound very positive about her."

"Alicia is okay, I guess, but she's not really a friend. She likes to play at knowing a lot more than you do. Look what she did to my hair." She pushed her hand into the pile of curls and made a face. "Plus, she has what my mother would call an 'active imagination.'"

"You mean she lies?"

Cyndi shrugged. "I didn't want to say that."

"Hard to be friends with someone who lies," I said. "Did you go out together, double-date, things like that?"

"I haven't had any dates since I've been

here," she said through a small laugh. "That's been the last thing on my mind."

"I just thought that you and Wally might have been dating."

"No, nothing like that. He's just a good friend who has my best interests at heart. Besides, he has girlfriends."

"Plural?"

She nodded.

"Did he warn you at all about Roderick Marker? He said he had a bad reputation with young girls, and also told me he knew musicians who hadn't been paid, at least in a timely fashion."

She got up, went to the window, and stared through it. I joined her and placed an arm over her shoulder. She turned to face me and said, "He kind of did. And Alicia did, too. She told me not to be in a room alone with Marker if I could help it, that he was a notorious womanizer. I thought she was jealous that I knew him and she didn't. I thought she was just trying to scare me off."

Alicia's advice to Cyndi made me wonder if indeed the young woman was simply parroting what she'd heard about Marker's reputation. Or had she learned

about his inclinations from firsthand experience?

"In any case, I didn't pay any attention
to what either of them said. If I had, I'd
never have been at his office after hours,
and I'd never have walked in on . . . on . . .
What a mess I've made of things."

"I agree that you're *in* a mess, Cyndi,
but it wasn't your doing. Have you called
your mother or sisters?"

She lowered her head and slowly
shook it.

"Let's remedy that right now," I said, leading her to the phone, where I dialed Seth's
number. When he answered, I put Cyndi
on. She asked about her mother, was reas-
sured that she would be all right and would
be coming home from the hospital in a few
days, and was given the number of a direct
line to Janet's room. I went back into my
bedroom to afford her privacy, but could
hear what sounded from Cyndi's end like a
tearful, then cheerful conversation. Her
sisters were at the hospital, too, and the
girls chatted for almost a half hour. When I
heard silence from the living room, I returned. Cyndi's mood had brightened con-
siderably.

"Feel better?" I said.

"Much. I've been so stupid avoiding calling. Thanks for getting me to do it."

A few minutes later, I picked up the ringing phone.

"Jessica Fletcher? This is Brian Krupp of the *Tennessean*."

"Oh, yes, Mr. Krupp. What can I do for you?"

"I understand that you've joined Cyndi Gabriel's legal defense team."

"I wouldn't say I've joined it, Mr. Krupp. It's more a matter of—"

"It's unusual having a murder mystery writer helping defend an accused murderer in court, isn't it?"

I glanced over at Cyndi, who'd picked up her guitar and softly strummed it.

"Mr. Krupp, I appreciate that you have your job to do as a reporter, but I don't think that it's appropriate for me to comment on an ongoing case."

"Suit yourself, Mrs. Fletcher, but I really would appreciate being able to ask you a few questions about your connection with the accused. I've already spoken to people in Cabot Cove so I know all about that association you have there that sent her to

Nashville, and how you've come here to help her out."

I was tempted to ask to whom he'd spoken back home but didn't want to prolong the conversation.

"Do you believe she's innocent?" he asked.

"Of course I do."

"Rod Marker was an important part of the music scene here, Mrs. Fletcher. This story won't go away anytime soon."

"I'm sure you're right, Mr. Krupp, but I really must go. Someone is—someone is waiting for me."

"If you play ball with me, maybe I can help you. Can we get together? Buy you dinner, lunch, whatever?"

"I really don't think that would be a good idea," I said. "Thank you for calling."

"Okay," he said, "but I hope you enjoy my piece in tomorrow's paper. Have a good night."

His call ensured that the night would be anything but "good."

Much of the night had been spent listening to Cyndi play and sing some of her compositions. That she was a talented young lady was beyond debate, but then I already knew that from hearing her perform back in Cabot Cove. She shared with me her turmoil over not being able to pursue her career in Nashville aggressively because of this unfortunate, tragic event that had intruded into her life. I had the feeling she didn't have a firm grasp on how precarious her future actually was. I kept reminding myself that I was there to prevent an innocent woman from being convicted and sent to jail for a crime she hadn't committed, and therefore it was imperative that I remain optimistic.

The following morning, I walked from our hotel to where the memorial service was being held for Roderick Marker at the national historical landmark and Mother Church of Country Music—the Ryman Auditorium. Perhaps the most famous home of the Grand Ole Opry until it moved to its custom-built quarters on the outskirts of Nashville at Opryland USA, the Ryman first opened its doors in 1892. A beautiful redbrick and white stone building, it had been constructed by a riverboat captain, Thomas Ryman, as a tabernacle for one of the early revivalists, Sam Jones. As a consequence, the elegant auditorium includes pew seating and stained-glass windows, an appropriate backdrop for those mourning the passing of Roderick Marker, who'd spent his life developing country stars with ambitions to perform at the Ryman.

An usher handed me a program as I entered the hall, and I walked down the aisle. There were too many attending Marker's service to hold the ceremony on the stage, but far too few to fill the seats of the main floor, much less the balcony. The four sections in the front had been left open, but the eight sections in the rear had been roped off to ensure the seats closest to the stage were filled before any additional rows were released.

I took a seat on the aisle in the last row and studied the program, which included a history of the auditorium. Marker's was hardly the first memorial service the Ryman had hosted. A full house, more than two thousand people, had turned out for the funeral of Bill Monroe, hailed as the father of bluegrass. And Waylon Jennings, Johnny Cash, and Tammy Wynette had been memorialized there, among many others. With acoustics second only to the home of the Mormon Tabernacle Choir in Salt Lake City, Utah, Nashville's Ryman had been voted among the top five places to hear live music in America in a national poll conducted by Citysearch.com. There wasn't any live music at the moment, but a recording of a female country music singer wafted over the hushed conversational buzz in the room.

I stood when someone asked to sit in my row and was surprised to find Detective Biddle taking the seat next to mine.

"You're quite the celebrity," he said.

"Oh?"

"This morning's paper. Nice picture of you."

"I haven't seen it."

"Looks like it might have been taken a few years back."

I laughed softly. "You certainly know how to compliment a woman, Detective."

"Just an observation. The article says you're here in Nashville snooping around to find Marker's real killer."

"That's quite an assumption on the part of the reporter who wrote the piece. But I would like to find out who murdered Mr.

Marker, as I'm sure you would. I don't believe for a moment it was Cyndi Gabriel."

Biddle didn't rise to my bait and I directed my attention to the area in front of the stage, where a small, somber group had gathered.

"Is that Mr. Marker's wife?" I asked, referring to a striking woman dressed in a snug black sheath, with a large gold and diamond broach on her shoulder. Her platinum-blond hair was pulled back in an elegant chignon, exposing earrings to match her pin, and she wore a pillbox hat with a dotted veil that covered half her face. Even through the veil, I could see that she was carefully made up including pale pink lipstick, which gave her a delicate and serious appearance. She carried a black snakeskin clutch and an embroidered handkerchief, edged in lace.

"Yup, that's her," Biddle said. "The grieving widow."

I turned to him. "Are you suggesting that she *isn't* grieving?" I asked.

He shrugged.

"She's beautiful," I said.

"I hadn't noticed," he said.

But of course he had.

"Are you here because *you're* grieving?" I asked.

My question brought a smile to his lips. "Nope. Just figured I'd like to see the rest of the players in Marker's life close up."

His response gave me a momentary glimmer of hope that he was, in fact, continuing to investigate the murder without having prematurely settled on Cyndi to the exclusion of others.

He excused himself and walked to another part of the auditorium. I looked to my right and saw Buddy, Marker & Whitson's jack-of-all-trades, standing alone in the aisle.

I got up and greeted him. "Hello," I said. "Remember me?"

"Oh, yeah, sure. How'd your meeting with Whitson go?"

"About as you predicted."

"How come you're here?" he asked.

"Just paying my respects," I said.

"That's funny, seeing as you never even met him." He looked around as the seats began to fill. "But I guess there's a lot of people here never met the guy."

"I imagine you're right," I said.

He narrowed his eyes and looked intently at me. "Hey, I saw your picture in the paper."

"Yes, I heard it was in this morning's edition."

"I didn't read the piece, but it was a nice picture."

"It was taken a while back."

After further scrutiny of me, he said, "Yeah, I guess it was."

"Who are the people up there at the front of the auditorium?" I asked. "I know that the blond woman is his wife."

"Madame Marker," Buddy said, his brows rising and falling in an expression of disgust.

I let it go and asked about a tall young man whom I judged to be in his early twenties.

"Him? Jeremy, the wayward son, Marker's kid from his first marriage. There was no love lost between him and his old man, or with Madame."

"How unfortunate," I said.

"Money never did buy happiness for anybody, that's for sure."

"Which one is Eddy Anderson? Can you point her out to me?"

"Eddy? Oh for goodness' sake, there's too many people down there for me to find one. She must be somewhere up front, and I'd better make myself seen. You didn't come here just to make a contact, did you? I thought you were classier than that."

"No. Of course I didn't," I said, but he had already moved away, walking down the aisle toward the seats nearer the stage.

Fifteen minutes later, the distinctly non-religious service started. Whitson, whom I recognized from our brief encounter the other day, spoke about losing a treasured business partner—and dear friend. He introduced a young woman with a guitar, Sally Prentice, as "Rod's brilliant pick as our next big country star."

Sally was a pretty blonde, but apparently unsure how to dress for a memorial service. She wore a full-length beaded gown in a teal green with a slit down the front revealing a blue lining, something more suitable for a concert, I thought, but perhaps in Nashville these things were done differently than in Cabot Cove. Of course, we

didn't have a theater or auditorium anywhere near the size of the Ryman. Maybe
Sally's choice in dress was acknowledging
the historical importance of the venue
rather than the purpose of the observance
taking place. Whitson had set a standing
microphone in front of her, and she played
and sang "Amazing Grace," with many in
the audience humming along.

I listened carefully, trying to gauge
why Marker thought it was better for Sally
to present Cyndi's song rather than the
singer/songwriter herself. In my admittedly
biased view, Sally's voice was pleasant,
but not as distinctive as Cyndi's, and I also
thought that Cyndi's looks were at least
as appealing as Sally's, who resembled
every pretty face in the department store
flyers that accompanied my Sunday newspaper.

After Sally sang, a few people I didn't
know also weighed in with platitudes for
the deceased. Marker's wife, Marilyn,
spoke for only a minute, citing the years of
bliss they'd enjoyed together. The final
speaker was the son, Jeremy. Without
mentioning their relationship, he focused
on his father's devotion to business, his

canny musical ear, and the hours he spent promoting his country music favorites. The implication was that the father had found little time for his son, whose talents, if any, lay elsewhere. Jeremy's tone was matter-of-fact, at times bordering on belligerent. He finished reading off cards he'd carried to the lectern and walked away from the others, his stride purposeful and with anger in each step.

Outside, the crowd lingered as the principals climbed into waiting limousines. I was walking up the block toward Commerce Street when I heard someone call my name. It was Detective Biddle.

"Hello again," I said, tipping my head to the side.

"Won't hold you up. Figured we, you and me, could sit down sometime today and, I don't know, maybe compare notes."

I thought for a moment before saying, "I'd like that very much, Detective. Yes, I would like to do that very much."

"I'll be in the office from three on, Mrs. Fletcher. Swing by if you have a minute."

"You can count on my being there, Detective."

Chapter Fifteen

Lynee Granger's stereo was pumping out Reba McEntire's "I'm Gonna Take That Mountain" at an ear-splitting level when I knocked on her door.

"Just go on in. She'll never hear you," said a young woman wearing a backpack, who rushed past me in the hall and bounded up the stairs, two at a time, before I had a chance to see what she looked like.

I turned the knob, poked my head in, and called out, "Hello!"

Mrs. Granger was vacuuming and singing along with the CD. Her dark hair was up in rollers, covered with a scarf tied behind her neck, and she had on the same pink kimono she'd worn the morning we'd first sat down to talk. I waited until she turned the vacuum cleaner in my direction, then waved to capture her attention. She motioned me in, clicked off the machine, and lowered the volume on Reba. "Sorry," she said. "I get carried away when I'm listening to music."

"I understand," I said. "I tried knocking. Sorry to disturb you, but I need the key to Cyndi's room."

"Did you come to get her things?" she asked, crossing to the board on the wall that held keys to all the rooms. She lifted the one from the hook labeled "Tammy Wynette" and handed it to me.

"Yes," I said, "whatever's left there."

"How's she doin'?"

"Considering all she's been through, not too bad."

"Had some guy from the *Tennessean* stop by yesterday, askin' me all sorts a questions about her. Told me she got out of jail. That was a pretty piece of work you and the lawyer pulled off. Read about it in the paper this morning."

"The judge is letting her stay with me at

the hotel, pending the grand jury proceedings. Once that's over, the court will reconsider whether she can remain out of jail. But she's not allowed to leave the hotel other than for special circumstances. Since we don't know where she'll end up, I thought it best to collect her belongings. We discussed it and agreed that we didn't want to delay you in case you found another tenant for her room."

"Appreciate that. Not that I have anyone in mind right now," she said, tucking a wayward strand of hair under her scarf, "but this old house is my income as well as my home. I like to keep it filled up."

"Naturally."

"Are the police sure she's the actual killer? She's such a skinny thing, you wouldn't think she'd have the strength to lift that big award, much less bash someone's head in with it."

I winced at the image. "They're going forward with the case," I said, "so I have to assume they believe she's guilty. But I'm hoping to prove them wrong." I put my hand on the doorknob. "I won't keep you any longer. Would you like me just to put the key back on the board when I'm finished?"

"That'll be fine. You say hi to her for me, now."

"I'll do just that."

I climbed the stairs to the third floor, pausing at the first landing to peer down the hall on the chance Alicia was about. She wasn't, and I continued up. I wasn't exactly eager to see her, but I thought if we happened to meet, I'd ask her whether she knew any of Cyndi's friends, including Wally Brolin.

I reached the third floor, unlocked Cyndi's room, and began to gather whatever the police had left behind. Her computer and guitar were gone, of course, as was her backpack, but her clothing was still hanging in the closet and folded in the dresser drawers. I opened a plastic laundry bag I'd taken from the hotel and placed her clothing in it along with toiletries. After a struggle to open them, I emptied the dresser drawers and noticed that the roll of crackers and boxes of tea were gone.

The police had taken Cyndi's small storage device from the desk—I believe it's called a flash drive—as well as her song notebook, but had left the two unused spiral-bound books. I took those, the picture from home, and Emily's letter.

The packing didn't take me more than ten minutes. I looked around the empty room to see if I'd missed anything. Something was nagging at me, but I couldn't quite put my finger on what it was. I rechecked the desk, pulling out the drawers to see if any papers had fallen behind them, and did the same with the dresser. I got down on my knees and peered under the bed. Not even a dust bunny.

I hoisted the full laundry bag, took another fast look around Cyndi's space, and retreated to the hall to lock the door.

"Hi! Are you related to Cyndi?" said a voice behind me.

I turned to see a pale young woman holding a canvas laundry bag. Several inches shorter than I, she had straight black hair reaching to her shoulders, black bangs on her forehead, and eyes outlined in black pencil, making her appear not unlike the depictions of ancient Egyptians I've seen in museums. From Alicia's description, I assumed this was Heather Blackwood, the "Goth country singer."

"Hello," I said. "I'm an old family friend

of Cyndi and her mother. Do you live here, too?"

She introduced herself and confirmed my guess as to her identity.

"I stopped by to pick up Cyndi's things for her," I said.

"Oh, is she moving out?"

I hesitated. "Yes, at least for now," I said. "You didn't know?"

"Nobody tells me anything. I just got back from Jacksonville, visiting the folks, so I haven't seen anyone yet."

"How long were you in Florida?" I asked.

"Just a week. Enough time to remind me why I left home." She tilted her head and gave me a wry smile. "I'm on my way to the Laundromat. Do you want me to throw in some of Cyndi's stuff with mine? I don't mind."

"That's very generous of you," I said. "Perhaps another time."

"Where is she, by the way?"

"She's staying at my hotel with me while I'm in town," I said, wanting to avoid a long conversation.

"Wow! Lucky her. It's nice to get time in more posh surroundings, huh?"

"Not precisely, but it's a long story, and

I'm afraid I have to get back." I lifted the bag and headed for the stairs.

"Sure. Didn't mean to keep you."

"You haven't," I said, feeling regretful that I was brushing her off. I turned at the last minute. "I'm sorry to be in such a rush. Alicia will fill you in, I'm sure," I said. "Ask her."

Heather gave a half laugh, half snort. "She who leaves no truth unmauled? You can never get anything reliable from her, but okay, I'll ask Alicia. Say hi to Cyndi for me."

As I walked down the stairs, it occurred to me that if she'd been absent from the rooming house for the past week, she couldn't have been the one I'd heard in the hall in the middle of the night, despite Alicia's claim. Who was it, then? I'd thought it had been Alicia. Now I was convinced of it.

When I reached the downstairs hall, Lynee Granger was coming out of her apartment. She'd changed into a blue denim skirt with a wide flare, a multicolored patchwork shirt, and cowboy boots.

"On your way out?" I asked.

"My cowriter is in from Rhode Island. We've booked a writing room at the Music

Mill. He's got some song ideas, bless his Yankee heart."

"I hope you end up with a gold record," I said. "Do you happen to know a musician named Wally Brolin?"

Her laugh was gentle. "Sure I know Wally," she said. "Wally the bear. He's a good man and a damn good guitar picker. Got a temper, too, that sometimes keeps him from gettin' the gigs he deserves. Why do you ask?"

"Oh, just that he and Cyndi were friends."

A sly smile crossed Granger's face. "Ol' Wally may not look like some leading man movie star, but the girls sure go for him. I suppose they like that macho spirit; he don't take no guff from nobody. Hard to find a man like that these days."

"Interesting. He didn't strike me that way," I said. "He seemed very laid-back."

"Maybe he's a whatchamacallit, a multiple-personality," she said. "Anyway, glad to have met a famous writer like you. You tell your friend to keep her chin up and hope things work out. And if she wants to move back, just give me a ring."

She called a taxi for me, and I directed the driver to stop at the hotel, where I gave a bellman the bag of Cyndi's clothes to deliver to the suite. Then we continued on to Music Row to the offices of Marker & Whitson Music Publishers.

Since my last visit to the scene of the murder, something had been circulating around in my brain that I couldn't pin down. But it came to me as I was packing up Cyndi's things. Marker's office had two doors, which as Buddy had told me was to allow him to come and go unnoticed. Buddy had also subtly indicated with a wink and a nod that the second door was used on those occasions when Marker was entertaining a female other than his wife, and Brolin, too, knew about this aspect of Marker's personal life. Not that I cared whether he was a man who arranged for trysts in his office. But that second door was likely the one through which his killer had fled. Cyndi had said she'd heard Marker arguing with someone on the phone, but perhaps he'd been talking to that someone in person. Of course, conjuring this scenario didn't help identify who'd been in the office while Cyndi waited outside in the reception area, but it was a place to start.

I was taking a chance that the office

would be open, since the service for
Marker had been only that morning. But
sure enough, when I stepped out of the
elevator, ahead of me was a woman seated
behind a desk in the reception area of
Marker & Whitson. She was in her midfif-
ties with short wispy hair, a sallow com-
plexion, and thin lips set in a hard line.
Narrow reading glasses were balanced on
the tip of her pug nose. I wasn't certain if
this was Marker's secretary, Edwina Anderson, whom Buddy had referred to as "a
battle-ax," but I could see how a man his
age might describe this woman that way.
Marker had wanted someone more attractive in her position, and while I objected to
the idea of discarding an efficient and
loyal worker because time, and perhaps
genetics, had not been kind to her, this
lady certainly made no effort to be wel-
coming. A smile would have gone a long
way to overcoming her deficiencies.

"May I help you?" she said, barely looking up from some papers on her desk.

"Yes, I hope you will. My name is Jessica Fletcher."

A ray of recognition crossed her face.
"Oh, yes, the writer. I read about you in the

paper this morning." She removed her glasses and folded her hands on the desk.

"And you're Edwina Anderson, I presume."

She didn't reply, simply stared at me.

"Well, I'm—as you probably learned by reading the article, I'm working with the defense team for Ms. Gabriel."

"Yes, I did read that. Frankly, Mrs. Fletcher, I'm not of a mind to cooperate with anyone looking to get that young woman off the hook."

"Even if she's innocent?"

"But she's not. I've read the accounts of Mr. Marker's death. She's obviously as guilty as sin, if you'll pardon my use of a cliché."

"Pardon granted," I said, "but I strongly believe that Cyndi has been wrongly accused."

"Just because you believe it doesn't make it so," she sniffed.

"That's true," I said, "but it would be a travesty of justice if a thorough investigation were not conducted, taking into account a history of the victim and all the people he knew who may have had issues with him. Everything is not always as clear-cut as it appears initially."

"Are you questioning the authorities? Nashville has an excellent police department."

"I absolutely agree," I said, "but that doesn't mean they can't use a little extra help from time to time. I'm simply hoping to point out possibilities they may not have considered."

"Well, what do you want from me?"

"I understand on the night Mr. Marker was attacked, you saw Cyndi coming into the building when you were leaving for the day."

"That's what I told the police."

"So I heard. Had Cyndi made her appointment to see Mr. Marker through you?"

"She did not have an appointment."

"Was anyone with Mr. Marker when you left the office?"

"No."

"At least not that you knew about," I said. "But Mr. Marker didn't always tell you about everyone he saw in his office, did he?"

"I don't know where you're getting your information," she said.

"I stopped in the other day and had a brief conversation with Mr. Whitson, and with Buddy."

She rolled her eyes at the mention of Buddy. "Really?" she said in a stern, haughty voice. "I don't have time to deal in innuendo and rumor. Is there something specific you want?"

"As a matter of fact, there is. I wanted to take another look at Mr. Marker's office."

"May I ask why?"

"I'd like to examine the other door in the office and where it leads."

"And if I say 'no'?" she said with a smirk.

I decided I could be just as obstinate. I straightened up and said in my best school-teacher voice, "You should know I'm not only working with Ms. Gabriel's defense attorney, I'm discussing the case with the lead detective, Detective Biddle. You'll only delay me for a short time. I'm sure I can arrange for a warrant to allow me to take another look at the crime scene."

I had no idea whether I could do as threatened, but it seemed an officious thing to say. It obviously had some effect, because her expression changed from abject defiance to something closer to reflection.

"But Mr. Whitson isn't in right now," she said, a blatant attempt to shift the direction of the conversation.

"That's perfect," I said. "I won't take up a lot of your time. I need to spend only a few minutes in his office. There's an emergency exit outside that door, isn't that right?"

"That's correct."

"Where does it lead?"

"To the parking lot in the back."

"And do people use that entrance to come into the building from the parking lot?"

"No. The door is locked. Everyone comes in the front entrance."

"If the door is locked, then that implies a key. Can people with a key use that door?"

Her sigh was dismissive. "I suppose so," she said, "if they have one."

"Do you have one?" I asked.

"Yes, but I don't use it. I come in and out the front entrance like everyone else."

"But if you have the key, I assume that others may also have a key. Perhaps Mr. Marker gave a key to someone who could then have access to his second door from the parking lot."

"I wouldn't know about that."

"Just an assumption," I said pleasantly. "Now, may I see the office again?"

Another sigh, more prolonged this time. "Mr. Whitson won't be pleased."

I said conspiratorially, "He never even has to know."

She got up from her chair with exaggerated effort and came around the desk. She was a tall, solidly built woman whose floral dress reached to her calves and came high up around her neck. She led the way into Marker's office, which now belonged to his business partner, Lewis Whitson. *Was gaining a larger, more elaborately furnished office—and one with a second door—motive enough to kill?* The question crossed my mind. Marker's partner had not wasted any time taking over the larger office, and I wondered if there were others who would have a claim on the partnership, if Whitson was marking his territory, so to speak. Then too, Whitson may have had a lot more to gain by Marker's death than simply a more impressive office. Or could Edwina Anderson have secured her position by ridding herself of a boss who clearly wanted to fire her? I'd slipped into my "what if?" frame of mind, which opened the door to any and all possibilities without self-censoring.

The office looked markedly different than the last time I'd seen it, which was only two days ago. The rose-colored plush carpet was new. Marker's desk was gone, replaced by a large glass one. Whitson's high-back chair was red, as opposed to the black tufted seat I'd seen in the office before. An overstuffed green leather couch substituted for the long gray sofa, and where the glass coffee table had stood, there was now a series of three small tables—not one of them strong enough to support an exuberant dancer when the latest M&W talent topped the charts. I glanced at the walls. Many of the same photographs of their more famous clients were still there, augmented by a grouping of color shots that appeared to be family photos. Marilyn Marker wasn't in those pictures; they must have been Whitson's family.

"I see that you've changed the decor," I said.

"Mr. Whitson wanted the office to reflect himself."

"And not reminders of his partner's demise," I added.

"Satisfied?" she asked.

"Almost," I said, going to the second

door and opening it. It was unlocked. I stepped into the hallway and looked at the fire door.

"And these stairs lead to the parking lot," I said to myself.

"I already told you that," she said, making a point of looking at her watch.

Back inside, I stood in the center of the room and tried to envision the murder scene. I saw someone—I wasn't sure whether it was a man or woman—arguing with Marker over something. A business deal gone sour? Money promised and unpaid. A vow broken? A jealous competitor. A betrayal of a lover—or a wife? All possible motivations were on the table at this point.

I turned and looked at the first door to the office, the one through which we'd just passed. I could see Cyndi, frustrated and impatient, waiting in the reception area to see the man she felt had taken away her best chance for stardom, hoping to change his mind. She comes through that door and looks for him, doesn't see anyone. She spots the music award on the floor, picks it up to place it on the corner of his desk, puts it there, realizes there's blood on it, wipes her hand on her jeans, and sees him lying facedown on the floor behind the desk, not moving.

She panics, turns, and runs from the office into the arms of the building's security guard, who pushes her down into a chair in the reception area. While he goes into the office to see what has happened, she panics even more and races down the main stairs, out into the street, and tries to think of a safe haven where she can stay until she decides what to do next.

I wiped that vision from my mind and looked at the second door again. Cyndi had heard Marker arguing with someone while she waited to see him. No, that wasn't entirely accurate. She thought he was on the phone, which meant she hadn't heard a second voice. Was he on the phone? Possibly not. Maybe he was talking in person with the man or woman who would murder him. I made a mental note to encourage Cyndi to try and remember whether she ever heard a second voice through the closed office door.

"You've had enough time to do whatever it is you're doing," Ms. Anderson, better known as Eddy, said sharply.

"Yes, and thank you for your courtesy," I said. "I think I'll leave by the fire door, if that's all right with you. Is it alarmed?"

"Should be. I've told Buddy it should be, but he functions in his own little world. They all do."

"They?"

"His type. Suit yourself. Goodbye."

She waited until I left by the second door and locked it behind me. I opened the fire door and peered down the stairs, seeing in my mind someone rushing down the steps, realizing what he or she had just done, desperate to flee the premises.

I slowly descended, reached the steel fire door, which opened from the inside with a bar release. I pressed it, and the door swung open easily. I stepped outside and looked around. The parking lot was half full. The door slammed closed behind me. I turned and tried to reopen it, but there was no latch on the outside, only a pull and a keyhole. Clearly, anyone who would enter the building through this door needed a key. Marker & Whitson might require their staff who parked in the lot to walk around the building and come in the front entrance, but there could be a select few who were given the key and used this door, even people who didn't work in the building.

I peered up into a pewter sky that promised rain, and followed a sidewalk around to the front of the building, where I entered again. A guard, who hadn't been there earlier, was standing at the counter. A burly man with a paunch hanging over his black leather belt, he wore a gray uniform with a shoulder patch on which the letters SMSS were superimposed over an embroidered image of a mountaintop. Detective Biddle had said the guard who caught Cyndi was from the Smoky Mountain Security Services.

"By any chance, are you Clevon Morgan?" I asked.

He straightened. "Yes, ma'am. How can I help you?"

I didn't want to confess that I was looking to find evidence to exonerate Cyndi, especially to the man who'd been hailed for catching a killer. Instead I put on my best impression of a gossipy biddy and batted my lashes at him.

"I read about you in the *Tennessean*," I said, slapping the counter. "Terrible shame about Mr. Marker. I heard *you* were the one who found him—and the girl."

He smiled. "Yes, ma'am. Got her red-handed. In fact, really red-handed; the blood was still on her fingers. Told the police that. Gave them a good description. That's how they found her. Took a coupla days, though. I should've locked her up good, so's she couldn't run. Still riled about that."

"No need at all. My goodness, you're a hero! Your family must be so proud."

"Yes, ma'am. They are."

"It's got to be so difficult trying to guard this place, what with people coming and going all the time and using the back door to the parking lot."

"You got that right. That back door is a pain in my butt, if you'll excuse my French."

"Of course," I said, injecting my voice with sympathy. "When she escaped, did the killer run out that back door?"

"No, ma'am. She sneaked out the front when I was callin' the cops."

"How can you be so sure she went out the front?"

"Easy. Mr. Marker, he had a second door in his office, right outside them stairs leadin' to the parking lot. If she'd gone out that way, I'd know."

"And you can see right through his door. Is it glass?"

"No, ma'am. It's wood, but it was open."

"Of course. How silly of me."

"If I'da seen her, I woulda caught her again. She wouldn'ta got away from me then."

I left the building and paused on the sidewalk, peering down the street in hopes of spotting a taxi. As I stood there, someone in a shiny silver Jaguar with tinted windows pulled up next to a fire hydrant and turned off the engine. Lewis Whitson emerged from the passenger door and walked around the car to the driver's side. He held out his hand to the driver. A long black-stockinged leg appeared, and then the rest of the woman in black. It was Marilyn Marker. Whitson's back was to me, but Marilyn scanned my face, and there was a fleeting hint of recognition in her eyes. However, she said nothing. Whitson took her elbow and they hurried into the building.

I looked at my watch. It was almost three. *How interesting,* I thought, *that the widow of the victim and his business partner arrived together. And what business could they need to address at the office on the day of Marker's memorial service?*

An empty cab turned the corner. I hailed it and asked the driver to take me to central police headquarters. If Detective Biddle was serious about meeting to, as he put it, compare notes, I didn't want to waste any time taking him up on it.

Chapter Sixteen

Biddle was in a meeting when I arrived at the central precinct, but sent out word that he'd be free in fifteen minutes. I sat in a hallway outside the honeycomb of offices until he emerged. "Come on in," he said. "Sorry to keep you waiting."

"This is the cold case office," Biddle said, as we passed a half-dozen cubicles in which other detectives were on the phone or working with their computers. We reached the office he'd said was his temporarily while the department finished renovating the west precinct, and he closed the door behind us.

"Cold cases," I said. "How successful are you in solving old cases?"

"Do okay. Have a seat."

We looked at each other for a few seconds without saying anything. He broke the ice by opening the desk drawer and holding out a Goo Goo Cluster to me. This time I accepted his offer. He took one, too. "Don't want to give you the wrong impression, Mrs. Fletcher, by asking you to come by," he said, tearing the wrapper off the candy. "I'm not looking for a partner. But—well, it's just that there's something gnawing at me about the Marker case, and I hate it when something gnaws at me." He took a bite of the candy and chewed thoughtfully.

"Like a circumstantial case?" I said, nibbling at the marshmallow, chocolate, peanut, and caramel confection.

He smiled. "Something like that," he said. "I got a call from Marker's office a few minutes ago."

"Oh? And?"

"It was the deceased's partner, Whitson, complaining that you'd been there using my name to get inside Marker's office."

"I did go there," I replied, "and I'm afraid

I did use your name to gain access. But it's not what you think. All I said was—"

He waved his hand in the air. "It's okay, it's okay. I don't care about Whitson. Guy's a loudmouth. I bring it up because you're obviously somebody who won't take no for an answer."

I nodded cautiously. I certainly couldn't deny the truth, but I wondered where he was taking this.

Biddle continued. "You've gotten yourself on Gabriel's defense team—nice work, by the way, getting her out of jail without bail—and you're letting it be known around town that you're playing detective." He waved a copy of the morning newspaper at me. "Not good for my reputation. The duty officer passed a comment."

"I don't consider it playing detective. But I do believe in Cyndi's innocence and feel a responsibility to do everything I can to help her."

"Like showing up at Marker's memorial this morning."

"Is there something wrong with my being there? You were there, too."

"No, no, nothing wrong at all."

"I was hoping that *your* presence meant you're interested in developing other leads," I said.

Biddle hesitated a long time, contemplating the candy wrapper as if it held a secret he was trying to divine.

"Are you?" I asked. "Developing other leads?"

"Matter of fact, Mrs. Fletcher, I've come into some information that might—and I stress *might*—have a bearing on the case."

The news buoyed me, but I was careful not to react too strongly. "I'd love to hear about it," I said, breaking off a piece of candy and popping it in my mouth.

"Between us?"

This time I was the one who hesitated, then said, "If it helps Cyndi, I'd naturally want to share it with her attorney, Mr. Washburn."

"But nobody beyond him."

"Fair enough."

He leaned back and finished off his Goo Goo, chewing while he decided what to say, and how to put it. "Okay," he finally said. "We put out some feelers around town, people who know the music scene and what's going down."

"Informants?"

"Yeah, one of them, too. Learned that Marker had been having a fling with a young country singer. I'm thinking it might have been Sally Prentice, the one who sang at the memorial service today."

"Sounds like something for the tabloids," I said.

"You didn't hear it from me."

"Of course not," I said, wrapping up what was left of my candy and tucking it in my bag. "This was delicious, by the way. I'm going to save the other half for later."

"We'll make a Southerner of you yet."

"I'm afraid you have a long way to go with this dyed-in-the-wool Maine Yankee."

Biddle shrugged. "You know, this sort of philandering isn't exactly a shock," he continued, relaxing into his subject. "In any glamour field, guys in top places, guys with influence, have been known to take advantage of the vulnerable ones. In Hollywood you'd expect it. It's no surprise it's here in Nashville, too."

"There are disreputable people in every business, Detective. I don't have to tell you that."

"Sources tell me Marker's gone through

quite a few women, most of 'em young and looking for a break, or a mentor, or a king-maker, maybe I should say 'queen-maker.' Easy pickin's."

"You're not suggesting that Cyndi Gabriel was one of them, are you?"

"No, ma'am. I wouldn't have ruled her out, but fact of the matter is she doesn't fit Marker's MO, method of operation. For one thing, she's not blond—his preferred . . . well, let's say game. And she's not an es-pecially provocative dresser. Plus, even though I don't know her well, your girl doesn't strike me as the kind of young woman to sacrifice her scruples on the al-tar of fame."

"I agree, which is why I don't believe she'd kill anyone just because he didn't live up to his promises. This is a young woman who's had a lot of disappointments in life. Nothing's been given to her. Any-time she's been faced with obstacles, she's simply worked harder to achieve her goals. She was disillusioned with Marker—I know she was. She was upset and angry—with justification. But vengeful or violent? No. I just don't believe that's true."

"Maybe," he said.

But I had a feeling he was coming around to thinking Cyndi wasn't the best candidate for prosecution in this case.

"To fuel you with a bit more gossip, Mrs. Fletcher, the talk says Marker's wife, the grieving widow, has been known to show up in somebody else's bed as well."

"Whitson's?"

"Don't have a name yet."

"Or one you're willing to reveal," I said. "Well, if Whitson and Marilyn are having an affair, that could give both of them motives to get Marker out of the way."

"Could."

"Where is all this leading, Detective Biddle?"

He'd been leaning back in his squeaky chair and now let the seat propel him forward. "Don't really know," he said, sighing. "Yeah, there are others might've had a motive to kill him. Problem is, I keep coming back to the fact that your girl is the one who sent the threatening letter."

"I know you think that's strong evidence against Cyndi," I said. "In fact, if my memory serves me, you said it tied up the case in a neat bow for you. But if Marker was in the habit of stealing songs from young, unrepresented songwriters—and if that's a valid motive to kill—then there's a good chance there are others who've suffered that same fate. You could even take it further and say that if *anyone* knew about Cyndi's letter, he or she could use it to set her up as the killer."

"You think she's been framed?"

"It's not out of the realm of possibility," I said.

He chuckled. "In crime, nothing is out of the realm of possibility." He leaned back in his chair again. "So," he said, "tell me about your visit to Marker's office."

"I wanted to check out the second door in Marker's office," I said, telling him what the guard said about it being open, and laying out for him my theory of how the murderer used that door and the fire stairs to access the office, and to flee the scene.

"We dusted all of them, including the one leading to the parking lot, for prints. There were so many prints we couldn't come up with a specific one."

"I'm not surprised," I said.

"There's always at least one surprise in a murder investigation," he said through a chortle.

"And I hope that's the case with this one," I said. "If we knew the names of everyone who had a key to that outside door at the foot of the fire stairs, and to that second door to his office, we'd have a pretty good list of suspects."

"Nice theory," he said, "but I doubt we'd ever be able to get all the names."

"The office probably has a list. Did you ask for keys to those doors as part of your investigation, Detective?"

"No. What would that accomplish?"

"If we know what those keys look like, we could check other suspects' keys to find a match."

"What's to keep the murderer from throwing away the keys?"

"Nothing, of course. But it would still help to know who was issued a key. And if the killer didn't think to throw away the keys, finding them in someone's possession, someone without an alibi, perhaps, could point us in a different direction."

Biddle opened the desk drawer and stared down at a small pile of silver-wrapped Goo Goo Clusters, as if debating whether he should have another. Apparently deciding against it, he closed the drawer and said, "I'll send an officer to get a copy of the keys from the building manager and a list of who had them. Anything else you can think of? Any other suspects you have in mind?"

"I heard Marker tried to fire Edwina Anderson, but his wife intervened."

"Firing's not a killing offense."

"It has been many times in the past. Have you done a background check on her?"

He grunted, then shook his head. "We'll look into it. Anyone else?"

"Mr. Marker's son was at the service this morning," I said. "I'm told that their relationship was not particularly close."

"I interviewed him at the hospital while Marker was lingering on the edge. The son arrived in Nashville the day before his father was assaulted. He was pretty up-front about his feelings. He and his father didn't get along, and had as little to do with each other as possible. But you could see he was worried that his father was dying. Of course, he was living off his old man, receiving regular checks. Maybe the father truly wanted to help, or maybe he was paying him to stay away. There was no love lost between him and his stepmother, either, the current Mrs. Marker. They barely said two words to each other in the waiting room."

"Not a Norman Rockwell family," I commented.

"Meaning?"

"Not the sort of loving family the artist depicted in his paintings," I explained.

"Not at all."

"So where does this leave us?"

"Until we have another viable suspect, it leaves us exactly where we are." He picked up the newspaper again and tapped it on his desk. "I don't object to you poking around, but I gotta ask you to be discreet. Not a good reflection on the department to have stories in the paper hinting we're not doing our job."

"I certainly never said any such thing. May I see that?" I asked, pointing to the *Tennessean*. "It seems that everyone in Nashville has read about me *except* me."

"Go ahead and take it. I'm done with it. Brian Krupp is a pit bull when it comes to getting a story. He's gravel in our craw here at MPD, but I have to admit he's good."

I mentioned the call I'd received from him at the hotel.

"Just watch what you say to him," Biddle counseled. "He picks up on everything."

"Thanks for the warning, Detective. I really appreciate having this chance to sit down with you. I'm sure we'll be running into each other again."

"I don't doubt that for a minute."

He walked me from the office, stayed with me on the elevator, and escorted me to the street, where we shook hands.

"Mind another warning, Mrs. Fletcher?" he said.

I cocked my head as an invitation for him to continue.

"Whoever killed Rod Marker, assuming for the moment it wasn't Cyndi Gabriel, knows that you're here in Nashville to find out who that person is. I'd watch my back if I were you. Once someone has taken a life, it's not as hard to do it again."

"I—"

"Stay in touch," he said, and walked back into the building.

Chapter Seventeen

When I got back to the hotel, Cyndi was lying on her bed, watching a movie on TV. I went to my own room and used the time while she was distracted to read the Brian Krupp article in the *Tennessean* that I'd taken from Biddle's office. While the details of Marker's assault and subsequent death were rehashed in the piece, and Cyndi's alleged involvement in it highlighted, much of the article focused on me and my trip to Nashville. It made me sound like a caped crusader who'd flown in to rescue a damsel in distress, an overly dramatic portrayal of my trip and its purpose.

My inclusion on Cyndi's defense team was duly noted, and the prosecutor was quoted as being shocked, as well as dismayed at the judge's decision to release her into my custody without any bail to bind her to Nashville. And there was my photo, larger than either Cyndi's or Marker's.

I wasn't certain if I should show the article about Marker to Cyndi. She hadn't shown any interest in watching the news or reading a paper since Jamal and I had picked her up in the jail and brought her to the hotel. Perhaps it was her way of avoiding the ugly reality facing her: She very well could be brought to trial for a murder she hadn't committed. If she asked to see a newspaper, I would show it to her. But until then, I would take my cues from her behavior and let her decide when she was ready to see how the news was portraying the case against her.

I'd finished reading the feature and was skimming the rest of the paper when one item caught my eye in the entertainment section. Sally Prentice, the up-and-coming country-and-western star who'd been given Cyndi's song, would begin recording her new CD that night at a Nashville studio. It was a short mention accompanied by a head shot of the singer.

I folded the paper and tucked it into a drawer in the nightstand next to my bed. When I returned to the living room, Cyndi was engrossed in playing and singing a new song.

"Sounds nice," I said.

"I got up in the middle of the night to write it down," she said proudly. "I think it's as good as 'Talkin' Through the Tears.'"

"That's wonderful, Cyndi. I'm impressed with how you can continue to create under these circumstances."

"I think I'd go crazy if I didn't have my music," she said, hugging her guitar to her chest. "Don't take this the wrong way, Mrs. Fletcher, but there's nothing else for me to do here. In the jail, they had classes from morning to night. At least it passed the time." She looked around the room. "How many hours can you spend sleeping or showering or watching TV?" She gave a soft snort. "I've never been so clean."

I started to say something but she rushed to add, "Gosh, I hope you don't think—I absolutely do *not* wish I was back in jail. I will be eternally grateful that you rescued me from that. All I'm trying to say is: I need to occupy my mind, to keep being creative. If I allow myself to think about the trouble I'm in—" Her voice broke and she struggled to regain control of her emotions. "Anyway, not to sound too big-headed about it, my music is my escape. I think what I'm writing is good—at least I hope what I'm writing is good. But good or bad, I need to keep doing it."

I understood what she meant, and was grateful that she had her music as a creative outlet to occupy her mind. "I'm sorry to have to leave you alone so much," I said. "I know it must be difficult for you, but you understand it's all for your benefit. I'm talking to people, trying to find out the truth."

"I know that. Besides I don't mind being alone. I mean it. I don't. When you have three younger sisters at home, you're always looking for a place to be alone." She smiled thinking of them. "Anyway, this hotel's really nice. I feel a lot safer here than I did at the correctional facility even though they were watching me every minute of the day." She gave a little shiver. "I don't think I'll want to wear navy blue for a long time."

"The color of the jail uniform?"

She nodded. "If you didn't make any trouble. The troublemakers had to wear yellow. I don't like that color either. You could pick them out a mile away. And white, the women who were pregnant wore white. And the ones who worked in the kitchen wore gray." She made a face.

I laughed. "You're kind of limiting the choices in your wardrobe if you avoid all those colors," I said.

Cyndi laughed, too. "If I get out of this, I'm sticking with pink. That's the one color I never saw in jail."

"*When* you get out of this," I said.

"*When* I get out of this."

I hated to break her lighter mood, but I had some questions that had been rattling around in my brain, and we needed to address them. "Let's talk about the case for a few minutes," I said, taking a seat on the red sofa across from her. "The best way to defend you is to find out who was in Mr. Marker's office before you opened the door, because in all likelihood, that's who the killer is."

Cyndi nodded and set her guitar down on the floor. "I didn't see anyone go in there."

"But someone may have already been inside when you arrived."

"I didn't think of that."

"You said you heard him arguing with someone on the phone."

"I just assumed it was on the phone."

"That's what I thought. Now think real hard. Could you possibly have heard another voice, the voice of the person he was arguing with?"

"I don't think so. But he had music playing, so it was hard to hear anything."

"You never said he had music playing. Did you tell that to the police?"

"I didn't remember it until now."

"And the voice you heard. Are you sure it was Marker's?"

"It was a man's voice; that's for sure. I thought it was his voice, but I guess it could have been someone else." She was grinning at me now.

"Don't get excited yet," I said. "There's still a long way to go."

"I know, but at least now it's beginning to make sense to me. It didn't before. Could that person have been hiding in the office when I came in?"

"Probably not. There's a second door from that office that goes into the hall."

"There is? I don't remember it at all. I'd just been in his office once before, and the only thing I noticed were the awards in his bookcase and on his desk. He'd won so many awards."

"Well, there *is* a second door," I said, "and there are two ways to reach that door, either by walking down the hall from the elevator or by coming up the fire stairs from the parking lot at the rear of the building. Now, you wouldn't know if anyone came in from the parking lot, but you could have seen someone get off the elevator and walk down the hall. Do you remember anyone in the hall?"

"Let me think." She looked uncomfortable. "You know I've been trying so hard to forget that night that I think I blanked on whatever I saw, if I saw anything at all."

"Take your time," I said. "See if you can picture the elevator door opening. Does anyone get out?"

She shook her head. "I didn't see anyone. I kept going over in my head what I would say to Mr. Marker when I saw him.

When I couldn't concentrate on that, I flipped through *Country Weekly* magazine. I was tapping my feet to the music being played, checking my watch. I wasn't paying any attention to anything outside in the hall."

"That's all right," I said, giving her a small smile, "it's not critical, but all the same, if something occurs to you, or if you remember any detail you haven't told me, please make certain you let me know." I stood up. "Now, you'll have to excuse me; I need to make a few phone calls."

"Sure," she said, her mind elsewhere. "I can't believe I forgot there was music playing till now."

I was halfway to my room, when she called out, "Oh, I almost forgot. Mr. Washburn was here this afternoon."

"Good," I said, turning. "I'm hoping to catch up with him later. What did he have to say?"

"A lot of legal mumbo jumbo, something about motions he has to file with the court, and dispositions he has to do."

"You mean depositions."

"I guess so. He said he expected the

case would go to the grand jury next week."
She looked down at her hands and sighed,
then picked up the guitar and strummed
softly.

I watched her for a moment, then went
into my bedroom to make the calls. It was
good to have discussed that night again.
I had been dancing around the subject
a bit, trying not to add to the pressure
she was under, but if we were to make
progress, Cyndi would have to help us,
too. It was time to face the facts, no matter how painful.

My first call was to Lynee Granger.
"Hello, Mrs. Granger," I said. "It's Jessica
Fletcher."

"How're ya doin'?"

"I'm calling for some advice. I see in the
newspaper that Sally Prentice is recording
a new CD tonight at a studio called BIG-
Sound, on Division Street."

"I know all about that," Granger said.
"BIGSound's owner is an old pal of mine.
So's the keyboard player on that session."

"Really?"

"Yup. A real fine musician, on the A-list
for studio sessions."

"Well," I said, "I was wondering whether it would be possible for me to attend the recording session."

She laughed. "I figured that's what you'd be asking. As a matter of fact, I was planning on goin' there myself tonight. They don't let many spectators in for sessions like this one, but my pal invited me this afternoon. I should warn you that it won't be a finished recording, more like a rehearsal, a run-through for the musicians before they get down to business. Still, if you'd be interested I can bring you along with me."

"I would love that, Mrs. Granger."

"Seems like we should maybe be callin' each other by our given names by now. Whaddya think, Jessica?"

"I agree, Lynee."

"You don't have a car, do you?"

"Unfortunately, I don't."

"Well, then, suppose I pick you up about seven thirty. That all right?"

"That's fine, Lynee. Thank you so much."

I made a series of calls to Cabot Cove, speaking first with Seth Hazlitt, who took my call despite having a patient with him. Janet Blaskowitz, he reported, had a pacemaker implanted, was doing fine, and would be going home the following day.

Buoyed by that good news, I called city hall and spoke with Major Shevlin.

"Great hearing from you, Jessica," he said. "How are things going?"

I filled him in the best I could, and he talked for a few minutes about the legal defense fund he'd spearheaded for Cyndi. "We've already got over a thousand dollars in it, Jessica."

"Splendid. I know Cyndi will feel terrific knowing that people back home are supporting her."

I caught Mort Metzger just as he'd arrived at police headquarters after having participated in the arrest of a parole violator from another county who'd decided to hide out in Cabot Cove.

"Guy's a moron," Mort told me. "Thought by moving a county away he'd be safe. Took us just two days to find him living over at Pete Rollins's motel."

"Glad you nabbed him," I said, and gave our sheriff the same report about Cyndi that I'd passed on to Seth, adding that Detective Biddle had been especially cooperative thanks to Mort's intervention.

"Glad I could be of some help, Mrs. F. You take care now, and stay in touch."

I had a message on my cell phone from Evelyn Phillips, the editor of the *Cabot Cove Gazette,* and reluctantly returned the call, although I would have preferred not to. I love Evelyn as a person, but her aggressiveness as editor of the town's only newspaper can occasionally rub some people, including me, the wrong way. She answered on the first ring and sounded out of breath.

"Jessica," she said upon hearing my voice, "what perfect timing. I've wanted to talk with you. You got my message?"

"That's why I'm calling, Evelyn."

"I've had a brilliant idea. There you are in Nashville, Tennessee, trying to help our own little country music star, Cindy Blaskowitz, who's been accused of murdering in cold blood one of Nashville's top music executives. Could I convince you to write a daily report for the *Gazette* about how the case is going, your involvement in it? It would be wonderful to get some insight into Cindy's frame of mind, human interest pieces that my readers would absolutely love. Then, too, it might give a big boost to the mayor's fund-raising campaign for Cindy. That's what I call a win-win. What do you say?"

"I'm afraid not, Evelyn. I'm going to have to say no."

"No? Just like that?"

"I know you mean well and you want the *Gazette* to appeal to everyone in town. And I'm sure you have Cindy's best interests at heart," I said, not entirely certain that last part was true. "But I just don't have time for writing articles. There's too much to do. I'm sorry to be so blunt, but it's out of the question."

There was silence on her end.

"Evelyn?"

"It was just a suggestion," she said glumly.

"And a good one," I said, "just not one I can take up right now. I have to run. We'll talk another time."

I hated to end the call so rudely but didn't want to discuss her "suggestion" for even a moment longer. I returned to the living room, or parlor as it was called by the hotel, and relayed the information about the mayor's campaign and about Janet Blaskowitz from my talk with Seth.

"I know," Cyndi said. "I talked to Mama earlier and she told me she was doing a lot better. She thinks the world of Dr. Hazlitt, says he hung the moon."

"I tend to agree," I said.

"She said everyone in town has been so supportive. Her boss told her she should just take her time getting better and not worry about rushing back to work."

"Good advice."

I told Cyndi of my plans for the evening. Initially I'd considered not confiding in her, but decided that she was entitled to know everything and anything that had a possible bearing upon her predicament.

"You're going to see Sally Prentice record her CD?" she said, unable to keep the disbelief from her voice.

"Yes. I think it makes sense to see as many people personally as possible who might have played some role in this situation."

Her eyes couldn't have opened wider. "Do you think that Sally Prentice might have killed Mr. Marker?"

I laughed, and waved away that thought. "Don't rush ahead of me, Cyndi," I said. "I'm not saying anything of the kind. It's just that there are other individuals who were close to Marker, and I want to find out what they know. Your former landlady, Mrs. Granger, is taking me as her guest. She's a friend of the studio's owner, and knows one of the musicians."

A pout crossed her pretty young face. "I wish I could go, too," she said.

"I'll give you a play-by-play as soon as I get back. In the meantime, how about ordering up some dinner?"

Chapter Eighteen

Lynee Granger drove a vintage green Jeep with a soft top and a stick shift. I climbed into the passenger seat—there were no backseats—and she shoved the gearshift into first gear and peeled away from the hotel, pressing me against my seat back. I felt like an astronaut during blastoff.

"Had dinner?" she asked as she went through the gears, almost sideswiping a car and cutting off another.

"I did," I said, aware of the catch in my throat.

"Good. Oh, almost forgot."

She reached behind her, came up with

a large white Stetson cowboy hat, and handed it to me.

"What's this?" I asked.

"It's for you, darlin'. Got to look like you belong here in Nashville."

I put it on and checked myself in her rearview mirror.

Lynee gave me an assessing glance. "Now you're a proper Nashville lady."

"I wouldn't want to look like anything else," I said through a laugh.

BIGSound Studios occupied an impressive, one-story brick building. Like several other studios I'd passed since arriving in Nashville, this one had a huge statue of a guitar at its front entrance. I mentioned it to Lynee.

"Guitars in Nashville, Jessica, are like sand on the beach. Probably got more guitars in town than telephones."

The lobby floor was pink-and-white marble; large color photos of performers who'd recorded there lined the walls. A young woman came through a door, flashed a big smile at Lynee, and hugged her. "You look younger every day," she said.

"You forgot to take your truth serum today, Bobbie," Lynee retorted. She pointed her thumb at me. "Looky who I brought with me. This here's Jessica Fletcher," she told Bobbie. "She's a famous mystery writer; she wants to catch the session."

"Oh, I know who you are," Bobbie said, shaking my hand. "Everybody knows who you are from the newspaper."

I smiled, but said nothing.

"Well," said Bobbie, "you're welcome to be here as long as you're with Lynee. Let's just go ahead on back."

We walked down a long hall with framed gold and platinum records hanging on the walls on either side, leading to the control room, a dark, cavernous space painted black. The only lights were pin-spots in the ceiling that were trained on the huge console that spanned the expanse of glass separating the control room from the studio, and on a long, narrow, dark wood table up one level from where the console was situated. Lynee and I took seats at the table.

"Pretty fancy," I said, swiveling in my white leather chair.

"It's one of the biggest studios in Nashville," she told me. "Lots of megahits have been recorded here. I mean *really* big hits. Only the top singers get to record here."

"They must think that Ms. Prentice will be one of those stars," I said.

"That's the talk around the business," Lynee said. "Once a buzz develops, things really start to happen. The publicity machine cranks up and it's what you call—um . . ."

"A self-fulfilling prophecy."

"Exactly what I was thinking."

I turned my attention from the console and the two young men working at it to the studio beyond the glass. Musicians had begun filing in; a drummer was setting up in what was almost a separate room surrounded by noise baffles. A grand piano was being positioned, and two technicians were busy placing microphones at the various instruments, four of them on the drums alone.

"Quite a production," I said as I watched with fascination.

"Takes a lot to put a song on a CD, Jessica. See, the first thing that happens is—"

I held up my hand to stop her. What had diverted my attention was Wally Brolin, who'd entered the studio carrying his guitar. "That's Wally Brolin," I whispered.

"Sure is. Looks like he got himself a gig with Sally."

"He mentioned he was hoping for that."

My eyes went back to the studio. Sally Prentice had arrived wearing a patchwork skirt, denim jacket, and green cowboy boots. Her clothing wasn't what interested me, however. She crossed the studio, passing the other musicians, went directly to Brolin, and threw her arms around him.

"Wally and Ms. Prentice seem fond of each other," I said.

"Looks that way, don't it?"

A few minutes later, Sally Prentice entered the control room and greeted the technicians at the board. She waved at Lynee and me. "Hi, y'all."

"Ms. Prentice," I said, standing and approaching her. "I wonder if I could have a word with you."

"Sure thing. You want my autograph?" She nudged one of the technicians and giggled at her own joke. "Just kidding. What did you want?"

"I'm Jessica Fletcher." I said, extending my hand.

She took my hand tentatively. "How do, ma'am. Do I know you? You look familiar."

"She should," Lynee put in. "Her face was all over the newspaper this morning."

I ignored Lynee's comment. "I'm here in Nashville helping Cyndi Gabriel fight the murder charges against her," I said. "I know you were close to Mr. Marker. I saw you sing at his memorial service this morning."

Her face fell. If she'd thought at first I was a member of the press after a story about this rising young star, she now understood that I was something else altogether.

"What do you want from me?"

"Just a few minutes of your time. I have some questions for you and—"

"Excuse me," she said, and turned to leave.

"I wouldn't dream of interfering with your recording, but I would be sincerely appreciative if you'd grant me a moment to talk with you."

She struck a pose, hand on hip, her pretty red lips curled into what I can only describe as a snarl. "Look," she said, "I'm not interested in your friend Ms. Gabriel and whether she goes away for life. She deserves it. She killed Rod in cold blood and—"

"You were interested enough in her to steal her song!"

She jerked her head, setting her platinum hair in motion. "How dare you?" she said.

"But it's true, isn't it?" I said. I was aware that the engineers seated at the console had stopped adjusting their equipment and were taking in our confrontation. "Cyndi wrote 'Talkin' Through the Tears.' You didn't, yet your name will appear on it as a co-writer. That doesn't strike me as fair."

I hadn't realized that Wally Brolin had entered the room. "Is there a problem, Sally?" he asked.

"You bet there is," she said. "This—this person is accusing me of stealing a song by . . . by . . . by that girl who killed Rod."

Brolin faced me. "I don't know what you're doin' here, Mrs. Fletcher, but this is not the time to air your theories on who killed Rod. We're workin' here. You want to watch, fine, but don't go riling up Ms. Prentice, 'cause she had nothing to do with that."

"Maybe we should have this conversation in less public circumstances," I said.

I looked at Lynee Granger, who motioned for me to take my seat again.

"Get her out of here," Sally said, stamping a foot. "I want her to leave."

When I didn't budge, they both stormed from the room.

"You always rub people the wrong way like that?" Lynee asked, her eyes merry and her voice hinting that she wasn't being accusatory or critical.

"I try not to," I said.

A voice through a speaker in the control room said, "Are we set in there?" I recognized it as belonging to Wally Brolin.

"Anytime you are," an engineer replied.

I turned my attention to the studio, where Brolin seemed to be in charge of the other musicians. "Can we get Sally to do a scratch track?" he asked.

Sally walked up to a microphone.

"Hey, you okay, doll?" Brolin asked.

"I'm just fine," she replied in a hard voice that didn't support what she'd said. "Let's do it."

"Take One," an engineer said, "'Talkin' Through the Tears.'"

Sally talked the lyrics more than sang them, consulting a sheet of paper on a music stand.

It was distressing to hear that song being rehearsed and featuring someone other than Cyndi Gabriel. I thought back to that

night in the Cabot Cove High School auditorium when, as Cindy Blaskowitz, she
brought down the house with her rendition
of it, playing and singing alone onstage, her
voice plaintive and sincere, the chords from
her guitar rich and raw. Janet Blaskowitz
had once told me that Cindy sometimes
practiced the guitar for such long stretches
that her fingers bled. I'd heard Sally's playing that morning at the memorial service.
She was competent but uninspiring. I hoped
that she would give more to the song she
was claiming was hers.

A man entered the control room and
motioned for Lynee to join him outside.
When she returned, she whispered to me,
"That's Hal. He owns the place. He wanted
to know what was wrong. I told him there's
nothing wrong, just a slight misunderstanding."

"I can stay?"

"Long as you don't get into another fracas with somebody. 'Course, I don't mind
if you do. I'm having me a good time."

After the first run-through of the song,
Brolin made suggestions to the other musicians about changes he wanted made. I
kept my eyes on Sally Prentice, who'd taken

a stool and looked bored. Brolin gave the downbeat and the musicians played without Sally's participation. A third take included her. This time she did more singing than talking, and I had to admit that her voice was pleasant with a thick Western twang that added color. But of course I was biased in favor of Cyndi; as far as I was concerned, any singer I heard would pale in comparison.

I sat silently next to Lynee—I didn't dare open my mouth and risk expulsion again—and took in the remainder of what I assumed was a rehearsal. But when the band called it quits, Lynee informed me that the musicians had recorded what would probably be the final track, and that Sally Prentice would return at another time to add her voice to "Talkin' Through the Tears."

"That's how it's done?" I said.

"Yes, ma'am. Used to be that the musicians and singer would record at the same time, but all this techie stuff changed that. They overdub the vocals after the music tracks're finished. Gives the singer a chance to play with the music without holding up a roomful of musicians. They mix it together later for the master."

The lights came up in the control room as the musicians, followed by Wally Brolin, came in to hear a playback. He watched me from the doorway. I waved. He half-heartedly returned it and lingered there, as though not sure whether to continue into the room, or back out of it.

"Hi again," I said, getting up and going to him.

"I didn't know you were goin' to be here."

"I came with my friend Lynee."

"Oh." He looked past me and returned Lynee's greeting.

"You've recorded Cyndi's song."

As I said it, Sally Prentice came up behind. "It's not her song," she snapped. "I'm the one who'll make it a hit, not her. Besides, she's getting a writing credit. That's more'n she deserves."

"I'm not here to cause a problem, Ms. Prentice, but a talented young girl's life is at stake. All I'm asking is that you spend some time helping me understand what went on after she arrived in Nashville. Is that asking too much?"

She drew a deep, exasperated breath and turned her back to me.

"What about you, Wally?" I said. "I need

to know what role having Cyndi's song given to Ms. Prentice might have played in Roderick Marker's death."

"If it played any role at all, it gave her a motive to kill him."

"I thought you believed in her innocence."

"You ready for playback, Wally?" asked an engineer.

"Look, Mrs. Fletcher," he said in a conspiratorial voice, "I have to listen to what we just laid down. How about we meet up later?"

"Anytime you say."

"Give me an hour. I'll come by your hotel."

"One hour? I'll be waiting."

"Pallin' around with you sure is excitin', Jessica," Lynee said, putting the Jeep in gear and roaring away from the studio. "Sure beats my quiet life. Only thing happens to rattle my cage is I get cheated by a tenant. Not much to chew on there."

"Oh. Who cheated you?"

"Miss Alicia Piedmont. Never did trust that girl. Packed up and left. Owes me a week's rent, too."

"Not very considerate of her."

She sighed. "Jilted my nephew, too. He

thinks I don't know he was stepping out with her. But not a lot gets past me. I told him early on not to waste his time. She's just looking for whoever can get her ahead. A manipulator. Just foolin' herself, that's all. She wasn't going nowhere. Back home, they're all big fish in a small pond—you know what I mean?—the best singer in their school chorus and all that sorta thing. But this is the big time, Jessica. Bein' the star in your high school musicals doesn't cut it here."

Her assessment was hard-nosed and callous, and probably accurate. This was a woman who'd been around and had gone through the hoops. And I admit I wasn't surprised that Alicia had vacated her room without paying. To be as candid as Lynee, I didn't particularly like the girl either based upon our brief, disconcerting meeting.

"Don't let Wally keep you out too late," Lynee said when we pulled up in front of the hotel.

"I was surprised to see him at the recording session," I said. "He and Ms. Prentice obviously work well together."

It was more a snort than a laugh from

Lynee. "Wally, he's like so many dudes in Nashville tryin' to make it big. Of course, take it from me, it's easier as a musician than a singer, more opportunities to perform provided you've got what it takes. Wally's a hustler, Jessica. You've got to be to survive in Music City." Another snort preceded "Music City." "I suppose I shouldn't be so cynical, huh? Here I am still tryin' to make it with the songs I write with my partner up there in Rhode Island. I've still got the dream, Jessica, still think I've got what it takes to turn Nashville on its ear. I suppose I'll meet my Maker thinkin' that."

I reached across and patted her arm. "I don't doubt that when you meet your Maker, you'll be carrying a gold record under your arm," I said. "You're a good person."

"Thanks, darlin'. You're a pretty nice gal yourself."

I thanked her for bringing me to the recording session, and promised to stay in touch.

Instead of going up to the suite while waiting for Wally, I decided to stretch my legs. It seemed to me that even though I'd been moving from one place to another, I'd been sitting all day. My usual workout routine had been abandoned ever since I got to Nashville, and I was feeling stiff and eager to loosen my muscles. It was a pleasant evening; a short walk would accomplish two things: It would help me stay fit and would give me the chance to clear my brain and let me reflect on my experience at the recording studio that night.

I walked downhill from the hotel, breathing in the night air, reaching my arms overhead and out to the side before letting them swing naturally. I turned the corner, setting my steps in the direction of Broadway. The streetlights provided ample illumination, but the sidewalks were empty of other pedestrians with one exception. I passed one couple, clearly tourists, judging by their apparel; they smiled at me, their eyes raised, and I realized I was still wearing the Stetson Lynee had given me. I put one hand on top of the hat and snugged it down. *When in Rome,* I said to myself, pleased that I might pass as a native.

My thoughts turned to Wally Brolin. During my first meeting with him, he'd painted himself as sort of an outsider, not as wired into the music scene as he'd like to be. Yet on this evening, it was apparent that he was the leader of the band accompanying Sally Prentice, a far cry from the image of a struggling musician. Too, he'd had full command of the song "Talkin' Through the Tears," Cyndi's song, as though he'd been working on the arrangement for a while. And there was his closeness to Sally that caused me to wonder. I had the feeling that Wally and Sally were intimately familiar with Cyndi's song, that they'd probably been working on it together prior to the recording session. And he'd referred to Marker by his first name. That seemed to indicate he knew the man better than someone who'd simply "met him a few times," as he'd told me.

I stopped at a traffic light at the next corner and became aware of an older, faded blue sedan standing several yards behind me in the street. Since there wasn't another car at the light, it struck me as strange that the car would stop so far back. I entered the crosswalk and heard strains of music in the distance. A crowd was gathering on the next corner. As I approached, I saw that a group of older musicians in tight-fitting gray suits, snakeskin boots, string ties, and white cowboy hats were tuning up for an impromptu concert. There were five of them, two guitars, two bass guitars, and a fiddle. As I approached them, they broke into a song, their voices melding together beautifully and filling the previously silent street. Evidently they had played together for a long time, the band effortlessly featuring first one then another musician until each had had a chance to show off his skills in a solo. A soft round of applause greeted the end of the song. I stopped to listen, joining their temporary audience, until a police cruiser pulled alongside and encouraged the musicians to move along. The musicians and the crowd dissipated and I found myself alone on the street again, with several tall dark buildings ahead of me.

Instead of crossing the street as I'd initially intended, I turned the corner, aiming to circle around the block and head back to the hotel. Wally would be there soon, and I didn't want him looking for me or going up to the room unannounced and seeing Cyndi without my being there.

There was no traffic, but the car I'd seen earlier made the turn, too, pulled up to the curb, and stopped, leaving the engine running. I looked around. The police car was at least a block ahead of me, and all the people I'd stood with listening to the musicians had drifted off in other directions. Cautiously, I walked past the car, noting that the man behind the wheel also wore a cowboy hat—hardly unusual in Nashville—but I couldn't make out any other distinguishing features. I continued down the block, but had the uncomfortable feeling that the driver's eyes were on my back. Increasing my pace, I groped in my shoulder bag for the flashlight I always carry. It was not much of a weapon, but it would do in a pinch.

What were you thinking? I chided myself. *You're all alone in a strange city. It's after dark and you're walking along a deserted street. What is this man doing? It feels like he's following me. Why is he following me?*

I reached the corner and turned right, walking uphill as swiftly as I could. This street was much darker than the broader boulevard I had walked down. I debated turning around and retracing my path on the streets with better lighting, but decided against it. I glanced over my shoulder. The sedan had also made the turn and was parked at the base of the hill. The glare of the headlights kept me from seeing the car itself, not that I was familiar enough with brands of automobiles to have been able to identify this particular one, should the need arise.

By now, my breath was coming fast and my heart rate had reached the level of a good cardiac workout. I hurried across the street, still walking uphill as fast as my tired legs could carry me. I gained the next corner and could see the bright lights of the hotel entrance halfway down the block. I took a deep breath and slowed my pace, figuring no one would try to wrestle me into a car in full view of the Renaissance doormen. Well, I'd wanted exercise and I'd gotten it. And I'd exercised my brain as well. Now that I felt secure approaching the hotel, I began to think my reaction to the blue car had been foolish. I'd been concerned for no reason. A man can drive a car without being a threat to a woman. Why would anyone want to kidnap me anyway? *Unless it has to do with the murder, or with your notoriety, thanks to the newspaper column.*

I removed the cowboy hat and fanned

my damp face. Convinced my apprehension had been the product of an overstimulated imagination, I looked back in the direction I'd come from. The sedan was perched at the top of the hill facing me. The lights were off.

I lingered in the hotel lobby until I spotted Brolin pulling up in his pickup truck. I got in and he drove away without saying anything. There was a faint aroma in the cab of the truck that I recognized, that hadn't been there the first time I'd ridden with him. Since he wore a beard, he was unlikely to use aftershave, and I hadn't noticed that he was wearing cologne earlier in the evening. I leaned toward him and sniffed the air.

"You got a cold?"

"No. Just admiring the scent you're wearing. What's the name of it?"

"I don't wear no perfume," he answered, eyes straight ahead. "You're imagining things."

"Where are we going?"

"A little place I know."

"A bar?"

"Yes, ma'am, a bar."

Twenty minutes later, he pulled into a

small strip mall and stopped in front of a
narrow storefront. A crude sign over the
door read DOWN HOME. A couple of men in
cowboy clothes, including the requisite
Stetson hats, stood with some young
women similarly attired, all of them smoking
and laughing. Wally got out and brusquely
walked into the place, seemingly oblivious
that I was with him. I followed.

There was obviously no need to go outside for a cigarette. The air inside was
heavy with the blue haze of cigarette and
cigar smoke, and I remembered what
Wally had told me, that under Tennessee
law if an establishment didn't allow customers in under the age of eighteen they
could allow smoking.

An older man with a scraggly red beard
and wearing a greasy once-white cowboy
hat sat at a microphone playing his guitar
and singing in a deep, whiskey-and-nicotine-
influenced voice. There were about a dozen
customers, none of whom seemed to pay
attention to him as they talked in loud voices
at the bar and at the few tables that were occupied. We took a vacant table in the far recesses of the long, narrow room. A pretty
young brunette wearing short shorts and a

tight T-shirt took his order of a beer. I decided to have the same—*when in Nashville*—and was pleased that the Stetson Lynee had given me helped me to blend in with the other customers.

"Okay," he said once we'd been served, "what made you decide to make the session tonight?"

"I was interested, that's all."

"Interested in *what*, how a CD is cut, or interested in me?"

I smiled and took a tiny sip of my beer. "I'm interested in everyone and everything that might bear on Cyndi's predicament, Wally. Right now, I'd like to better understand how Cyndi's song, 'Talkin' Through the Tears,' got from Roderick Marker to Sally Prentice."

"He gave it to her. Pretty simple. Happens all the time."

"What happens all the time?"

"People taking other people's songs. Ever heard of 'bein' in the room?'"

"No."

"A performer or a musician happens to be in the room when some songwriter is working out a tune. You hear it, you like it, it sticks in your head, and you end up putting some finishing touches on it, and you get a share of it; it's yours. You just happened to be in the room."

I shook my head. "You make it sound so normal and legitimate. It isn't."

A twisted smile could be seen behind his beard and mustache. He drank and wiped his beard with the back of his hand.

"Maybe you can educate me about the Nashville music business," I said. "You seem to have gotten what you claimed you wanted, to play on Sally Prentice's CD. It looked to me as though you were the leader of the band. How did that come about?"

He sat back and narrowed his eyes, which were surprisingly small for such a large face. "I got the gig because I'm good."

"Had you been close to Ms. Prentice before? You seem to be, well, how shall I say it?—you and she seem to be very close friends."

"You know," he said, coming forward and placing his elbows on the table, "I'm beginning to resent your questions. They sound more like accusations. Okay, I know you mean well where Cyndi's concerned. I really like her and I hope she comes out of this okay. But I gotta tell you something else. How you want things to be don't necessarily mean they'll end up that way. Between you and me, I think that Cyndi did kill Rod because she was angry at him over her song. I hate to say that, but that's how it looks to me."

"You don't sound as though you hate to say it, or hate to think it. That's quite a switch from when we first talked."

"I'm just trying to be realistic, that's all. Maybe you should be, too."

"Realistic in the sense that I should give up trying to prove Cyndi's innocence?"

He shrugged, finished his beer, and motioned for another. Mine sat virtually untouched.

"Wally," I said, "when we first spoke at that Irish pub, you said that another woman had introduced you to Cyndi. At that point, she'd only been in Nashville for a few days and wouldn't have known many people. Who was it that introduced you to her?"

"I don't even remember," he said in such a way that I didn't believe him.

"I'm guessing that it was a young woman from Lynee Granger's boardinghouse who made the introduction. You know Alicia Piedmont, of course."

He feigned puzzlement. "I've heard the name."

"Did you know that she's moved out of her rooming house?"

"Really? No, I didn't know that."

"Skipped out owing a week's rent to Lynee."

"No kidding?"

We were interrupted by the old singer, who'd completed his set and staggered to our table. "Hey, Wally, you ol' coot," he said with a deep twang. He noisily pulled up a chair from an adjoining table and sat next to me. A pungent smell of alcohol came with every word. "Leave it to you to be with some fine-lookin' chick," he said, leaning against me. "This gal is more my style than yours. Whaddya say, darlin'? Wanna do a two-step with me? I'm a purdy good dancer, Wally can tell ya. Bet you are, too."

"I think it's time I left," I said, standing.

"Just when we're about to get a real nice party goin,'" he said.

I looked at Wally, who hadn't moved.

"Will someone call a taxi for me?" I asked, looking around.

"You don't have to get a cab," he said, disgusted. He threw a few bills on the table and stomped outside, leaving the drunken cowboy listing in his chair.

"You get the answers you wanted from me?" he asked as we exchanged the smoky air inside for smoky air outside.

"Frankly, no, but I thank you for your time."

"Well, I just don't think you should be snoopin' around like you do and getting people all riled up."

We walked to where he'd parked the truck; he held open the passenger door, and I climbed in.

"It's certainly not my intention to rile anyone up, Wally," I said, as he started the engine, "but Cyndi's defense depends on the answers to these questions. You do want to see Cyndi go free, don't you?"

He seemed stunned by the question. He stuttered a bit before agreeing. "Well, um, o'course. Sure." He put the truck in gear.

But I wasn't so sure he was sure. And it gave me something to think about.

We were about halfway to the hotel when

I noticed Wally glance in the rearview mirror several times. He pushed his boot down on the accelerator and the truck sped down the empty streets of Nashville.

"What are you doing?" I asked, grabbing the top of my hat as he took a corner on what felt like two wheels.

"We've got a tail," he said. "Anyone threaten you lately?"

"Not that I'm aware of, but I have the hotel screening my calls." I turned in my seat and tried to see around the gun rack to who might be following us. "Is it a car? What's it look like?"

"Light blue. An American model, maybe a Ford, ten, twelve years old."

"Sedan?"

"Yeah. Know it?"

"I think he was following me earlier tonight."

"Well, he's back. Let's see if we can lose 'im," he said, careening around a corner down a one-way street.

"You don't have to do that," I said, thinking the person in the car behind us knew very well where I was staying. "Please, Wally. Slow down. Let's get there in one piece."

But he wasn't listening. "This sucker doesn't have a chance," he growled. "Hang on, ma'am. Now you'll see what good Tennessee drivin' is all about."

Wally accelerated even faster while I frantically grappled for a nonexistent seat belt. We roared down one street after another; the blue car had no chance to keep up.

"He's gone, Wally. You can slow down now," I shouted over the gunned engine.

"Havin' too much fun," he yelled as the truck dipped into a pothole in the pavement and I bounced off the seat, the crown of my cowboy hat hitting the roof.

I grabbed a hook on the gun rack with one hand and pulled off my hat with the other, crushing the brim with my fist. "Wally, please stop! This is dangerous."

The sound of a siren cut through the air, loud enough to override the engine's growl. I risked a look behind and saw flashing lights. "Wally, it's the police. You have to stop."

"I boosted the horsepower on this baby. She can whip those guys any day."

"I don't care about that," I yelled. "What I do care is that I get out of this truck alive."

"Aw, yer a sissy," he said, grinning, as the patrol car drew alongside us.

A voice came over the loudspeaker: "Pull over immediately and turn off the engine. Do not exit the truck. Roll down the window. I want to see both hands on the wheel."

Wally did as instructed and I heaved a sigh of relief, collapsing back in the seat to catch my breath.

"Have yourself a good time there, boy?" the officer said as he approached the open window.

"Just showing this lady what a souped-up Chevy can do," Wally said, chuckling, his daredevil driving apparently having released a good dose of adrenaline to course through his veins.

The officer peered over at me. "You all right, ma'am?"

"I think so, Officer, but I'd like to get out of the truck."

"Don't worry. He's not going anywhere with you. C'mon, son, I want to see if you can walk a straight line."

"Only had one or two beers," Wally whined as he jumped down from the truck. "I ain't drunk."

"That remains to be seen," the policeman said, holding up a Breathalyzer. "I'm betting you know how this here thing works."

To my amazement, Wally passed the Breathalyzer test, barely, but there was no way I would allow him to drive me back to the hotel. The officer gave me permission to climb out of the truck while he ticketed Wally for several moving violations. "If I see you again," he said, poking a finger in the younger man's chest, "I'll haul you in, test or no test. You hear me?"

"Yes, sir," Wally said, working to put on a serious face. But he was clearly delighted that he'd not only made it through the alcohol test, he'd terrified an annoying woman who'd been a thorn in his side.

"Seems to me, ma'am, that you could use a lift to wherever you're going," the officer said.

"That would be very much appreciated," I said.

During the ride to the hotel the officer asked what I'd been doing in a truck with a young guy who was close to being arrested on a DUI.

I laughed, more from nerves than in

reaction to anything funny. "I suppose I just wanted to see another side of Nashville," I said.

"Mind a piece of advice?" he asked.

"Not at all."

"Stick to the side of Nashville where you belong. We've got a nice, safe city here, but things do happen."

"I'll certainly keep that in mind," I said. "Thanks for the ride and the advice."

Chapter Nineteen

I was surprised to find Jamal Washburn at the suite when I returned. He was dressed casually in tan chino pants, a blue button-down shirt, and a multicolored, patchwork V-neck sweater, and he sat on the couch while Cyndi performed.

"Hi," he said when I walked in. "I've been treated to my own personal concert."

"Lucky you," I said, taking off my cowboy hat and fluffing my hair. "Is everything all right on the legal front?"

"Sure," he said, turning away from Cyndi so she couldn't see his face. He gave me a small smile, but it was apparent he preferred not to discuss in front of Cyndi whatever it was that had brought him to the hotel so late.

Cyndi put down her guitar and stifled a yawn. "I can't believe I'd ever say this, but I'm too tired to play anymore. Would you excuse me? I can barely keep my eyes open," she said sweetly.

"Of course," I said, looking at my watch. "It's late. But before you go to bed, I wanted to ask: Do you remember who introduced you to Wally Brolin?"

"I think it was Alicia. Alicia Piedmont, from the rooming house. That's right. We were at Douglas Corner Café and he walked in with some friends. That's where I met him. Why did you want to know?"

"No special reason. Just curious. Sleep tight."

When she was gone from the parlor, I took a seat opposite Washburn. "This is pretty late for a visit," I said. "You must have something important on your mind."

"I told Cyndi that you and I needed to discuss her next court date, but that wasn't true," he said. "I'm here because I had a strange call this afternoon."

"Oh? From whom?"

"Marker's son."

"Jeremy," I said.

The attorney's eyebrows rose. "You know him?"

"I haven't met him, but he spoke at his father's memorial service. Why did he call you?"

"He read my name in the paper, in some article that mentioned I was the lawyer defending Cyndi. Said he wanted to talk, that he had important information that might help my client."

"And did he?"

"Maybe. He came to my office, stayed about a half hour. He's a strange young guy, very full of himself in a superficial sort of way, but it's a show. He's like other kids I've met who live off a parent, unsure of themselves and of who they are. Anyway, he told me he suspected that Marker's wife, Marilyn, his stepmother, killed his father."

"Ooh," I muttered. "Does he have any proof of that?"

"Well, he claims that he wasn't entirely truthful to the police when they questioned him."

"Detective Biddle said they spoke to Jeremy in the hospital waiting room before

Marker passed away. What did he say that wasn't truthful?"

"Apparently Marilyn claimed she was home at the time of the attack on her husband. That's what she told the cops when Jeremy was standing right there. He didn't contradict her. But now he says he was home Friday night around that time, and that Mrs. Marker wasn't there. He says he knows that because her Jag wasn't in its usual parking spot in the circular driveway, and that he saw her pull in at around six thirty that evening, later than what she'd led the police to believe."

I fell silent as I processed what I'd just heard. Finally, I said, "It's my understanding that Jeremy wasn't close to his father but didn't get along with his stepmother at all. Do you think he's saying this to get even with her, to hurt her?"

Washburn shrugged and smiled. "I'd like to think he's telling the truth," he said. "It'd be good for Cyndi if the police had another suspect to go after. I don't really know the kid, Jessica, so I can't say whether he's being truthful or not. He's not the sort of guy you automatically believe. Then again, all we need is a reasonable doubt."

"How will you follow up on it?"

"I'm not sure. I suggested that he go to the police and correct his statement."

"Will he?"

"He didn't commit to it. I told him that I'd give him a day to do that before I mentioned it to them myself."

I was silent again for a moment. "It seems to me, Jamal, that the only motivation he would have to put himself in possible jeopardy for having lied to the police is to hurt Marilyn Marker. Otherwise, why bother? They accepted his original statement."

"I don't care if he's just getting his jollies by accusing his stepmother. If it's the truth—"

"You're right," I said. "He can't simply be written off. Have you told Cyndi about your conversation with him?"

"No. Didn't want to get her hopes up. She's a charming young woman, Jessica, if a bit naive. Also very talented. It would be a terrible waste if she's convicted."

"A waste in so many ways."

"And how's your investigation coming? I'm sorry I've been tied up in litigation. I came to see you earlier but you were out. What's happening? Do you have anything else I can follow up on?"

"I just came from meeting with Wally Brolin for the second time," I said. "He's the musician who sheltered Cyndi when the police were looking for her."

"Find out anything useful?"

"Maybe." I gave him a rundown of my talks with Brolin and told him of having attended Sally Prentice's recording session, and my surprise at seeing Brolin there leading her band. "I have this nagging feeling, Jamal, that he's involved more than by having provided her with a place to stay. I find it interesting that he refers to Marker by his first name when he'd told me originally that he barely knew him, and had bad things to say about him. Now, he's 'Rod.'"

Washburn stood, stretched, yawned, and rubbed his eyes. "Cyndi's not the only one who's sleepy. It's been a long day. Want me to follow up on Brolin in some way?"

"I can't think of anything at this moment. But you can do something else for me."

"Name it."

"Can you gain access to records of parking tickets issued over, say, the past two weeks?"

"Sure. If the Traffic Violation Bureau

won't cooperate, I can have the records subpoenaed. Why?"

"Marilyn Marker has a reputation for getting parking tickets."

"She does? How the devil did you find that out?"

"I have my sources," I said, smiling. "Anyway, I'd like to know if she received any summonses on the day of her husband's murder."

He returned my smile. "I'll take care of it first thing tomorrow."

"Thanks, Jamal. Call me when you have the information?"

"Shall do. Get some sleep. You look beat, too."

He was right. A wave of fatigue had swept over me while we were talking, and the idea of climbing between the sheets was compelling.

But I didn't go to bed right after he left. I sat by the window in the parlor and stared down for a long time at this place called "Music City." Out there were thousands of songwriters, singers, and musicians, some more talented than others, and each clawing for fame and recognition, seeking success and the riches that follow. Chasing that gold ring was certainly exhilarating, but failing to grasp it could be equally depressing. Was it worth it? Who was I to judge? Pursuing a dream, no matter how elusive, was what made life exciting and fulfilling. It didn't have to be the dream of success in show business, or writing, music, or art. Every dream matters, regardless of the arena in which it flourishes.

I thought of Cyndi sleeping in the next room and of the man she thought to be her friend. The prosecution would argue that she'd wanted so desperately to capture her dream that she'd lost her balance. And Wally, who'd originally given her a place of refuge, had suggested just that. But I didn't believe it. Even considering for a moment that she might be guilty of killing Roderick Marker was a breach of my belief in her.

But *someone* murdered Marker.

I went to my room and read through the notes I'd been making ever since I'd arrived in Music City, and added the day's events to the tally. For the first time, I fell asleep that night feeling that I might finally be making progress in determining who the murderer was.

Chapter Twenty

Although I'd gone to bed feeling some-
what more confident that progress was
being made, I awoke groggy and out of
sorts. I slipped on the robe provided by
the hotel, and slippers I'd brought with me
from Cabot Cove, and padded into the
parlor. Cyndi was still asleep, which suited
me. I wanted some time alone to clear my
head and to plan the day.

At my request, a copy of the *Tennessean* was now left outside the door each
morning, and I retrieved it. Before starting
to read, I called Room Service and ordered
up a basket of breads and muffins, some

fruit, juice, and coffee, figuring Cyndi would also be hungry when she woke up. While waiting for our meal to be delivered, I settled in a chair by the window and scanned the front page. There was nothing there about the Marker murder—a blessing—and I went on to page two. Nothing there either. But when my eyes moved to page three, a photo stopped me cold. It showed me getting out of Lynee Granger's car outside the BIGSound Studio, and the caption below the picture said: "Mystery author Jessica Fletcher traded her typewriter for a Stetson. The Nashville newbie is getting her country on while in town to defend a hometown young'un accused of murder. Next thing we know, she'll be eating roasted possum with sweet potatoes." The picture ran above a column by Brian Krupp, who wrote what amounted to a speculative piece about my movements in Nashville, and what they might mean to the Marker murder case.

"Last night, this reporter decided to see what famed mystery writer Jessica Fletcher was up to in Music City. As readers of this paper know, Mrs. Fletcher has traveled to Nashville to help exonerate Cyndi Gabriel, a young singer from Cabot Cove, Maine, who came here seeking fame and fortune as a songwriter and performer. Not long after Ms. Gabriel arrived, she was arrested and charged with the murder of Roderick Marker, a well-known music publisher and a partner in the firm of Marker & Whitson.

"General Session Court Judge Candice Grimes surprised everyone by releasing Ms. Gabriel into Ms. Fletcher's custody without posting bail, and she's been living with Ms. Fletcher in the writer's suite at the Marriott Renaissance Hotel in downtown Nashville. Nice digs for an accused murderess.

"Ms. Fletcher also has managed to get herself a place on Ms. Gabriel's legal defense team headed by a court-appointed attorney, Jamal Washburn. In other words, this famed writer of murder mysteries, who hails from Ms. Gabriel's hometown in Maine, has found herself smack dab in the middle of a *real* murder mystery, and apparently not for the first time. Besides writing best-selling books, Jessica Fletcher has been known to involve herself in real crimes, sometimes to the annoyance of local law enforcement officials. So far, however,

Nashville's finest don't seem to mind; a recent query elicited a 'no comment.'

"To see how a famous mystery author would go about trying to solve an actual murder case, this reporter took it upon himself to join Mrs. Fletcher on her jaunts last evening, although from a distance.

"Mrs. Fletcher's first outing was to BIG-Sound Studios. She was driven there by Lynee Granger, a local songwriter who also owns the boardinghouse where the accused had been staying prior to her arrest. Although I wasn't in the studio to see what transpired, sources who were there tell me that Mrs. Fletcher had a heated confrontation with up-and-coming songstress Sally Prentice, who was recording a song allegedly written by Ms. Gabriel, and given to Ms. Prentice by none other than the late Roderick Marker. The 'theft' of her song is what police say was Ms. Gabriel's motivation for killing him. My sources also inform me that Mrs. Fletcher was particularly interested in the musician in charge of the band, Wally Brolin, a veteran Nashville guitarist, and that they made a date to meet later that evening.

"Sure enough, Mrs. Fletcher was picked

up by Mr. Brolin back at her hotel and driven to Down Home, a venerable club frequented by local musicians. After a few beers, the couple took off in Mr. Brolin's pickup, perhaps to another watering hole. This reporter tried to get a comment from Mr. Brolin, but efforts to reach him were unsuccessful. Should he return my call, I'd like to know what role he has played in this intriguing murder case that has all of Nashville talking and speculating. Will Jessica Fletcher solve the crime, absolve her ward of guilt, and have yet another bestselling story to write?

"More tomorrow."

"How dare you?" I said aloud.

There was a knock on my door. I opened it and my breakfast was wheeled in. I signed the receipt, poured coffee, and read Krupp's column again, my anger rising with each paragraph.

The phone rang.

I picked up quickly, not wanting to awaken Cyndi. "Hello?"

"It's Wally. What are you tryin' to do to me?"

"Oh, yes, Wally. I assume you've read today's paper."

"That's why I'm calling. I don't know how I got into the middle of this mess that Cyndi caused, but I want out."

"I don't believe that Cyndi caused any 'mess,' as you put it, but I am sorry that your name appeared in the paper, and I'm sorry mine did, too. I might add that I'm furious at the thought of being followed by the press."

"Now I'm gettin' all sorts of messages on my machine in addition to his."

"Have you called him?"

"No, and I don't mean to. He must've been the guy followin' us last night, the guy I lost."

"I'm sure you're right."

"Yeah, well, I don't appreciate being drug into this."

"Now, wait a minute, Wally. You became involved when you helped Cyndi avoid the police. I'm sure you didn't think what you did was wrong. It was purely an act of friendship, isn't that so? But nobody made that decision for you."

"You have an answer for everything, don't you, just like you have a question for everybody."

"And I intend to keep asking questions

until Roderick Marker's real killer is identified and apprehended."

The *click* on the other end loudly proclaimed that the conversation was over.

Cyndi came from her bedroom. "Who was that?" she asked sleepily, covering a wide yawn with the back of her hand.

"Your friend Wally Brolin."

"Did he want to talk to me?"

"No, Cyndi. Maybe this will explain." I handed her the newspaper.

When she was finished reading Krupp's column, she looked at me with an expression that demanded an explanation. "Is Wally in trouble?" she asked.

"I don't know," I said. "What I do know is that someone isn't telling the truth."

"Why would Wally lie, Mrs. Fletcher? He had nothing to do with any of this. I just showed up at his place after I left Marker & Whitson. He could hardly turn me away from the door. I knew I was in trouble and that I ran away. He let me stay. I'm the one who made the mistake. It would be terrible if he got in trouble just for helping a friend."

"You told him what had happened. If he thought the police were looking for you, he becomes culpable, too," I said. "It just dawned on me that he hasn't informed the proper authorities about that, nor have I made them aware of it."

"Please don't do it, Mrs. Fletcher," she cried. "He was just helping me. Oh, I never should have gone there. Now the police will arrest him, too."

"Cyndi," I said, "it's time for you to do a little growing up. You've been charged with murder. If you're convicted, you could be facing many years in prison. Trying to protect people who may know something that could contribute to this case isn't in your best interest, nor is it very smart. Someone murdered Roderick Marker, and unless I can get to the bottom of it—and do it fast—your dreams of becoming a country music star won't end with you singing your songs. It will end with a cell door slamming shut behind you."

I hadn't intended it to sound quite so harsh, but Cyndi was getting in the way of her own defense. It was time to acknowledge reality, that she couldn't protect anyone but herself, that she wasn't simply an innocent victim, that her actions after she had discovered Marker had contributed to her predicament. And if someone who helped her didn't want to be involved now, it was too bad. The truth had to come out. And I needed her to take a role in the investigation in any way she could. She was luckier than most accused killers; she wasn't confined to jail, but she had a responsibility to stop feeling sorry for herself and to help those who were working hard to get her out of trouble.

Cyndi stared at me for a few seconds before slumping back into the couch's deep cushions, fighting back tears. My temptation was to go to the couch and hug her, but I resisted the urge. I'd meant what I'd said. She was living in a cloistered, unrealistic dream world, ensconced in this spacious, nicely appointed suite, with nothing to do but write and perform her songs and hope all the bad things would miraculously disappear so she could get on with her career. But I knew that it wouldn't work that way; it never does.

"I'd better get showered and dressed," Cyndi said.

"Good idea," I said.

I picked up the ringing phone as she disappeared into her room.

"Jessica. It's Jamal. Guess what? Marilyn

Marker had a parking ticket from in front of her husband's office building the day of his murder."

"What time was it issued?"

"Five thirty."

"Where are you?"

"My office."

"I'm going to call Detective Biddle, make him aware of this, and suggest we pay Mrs. Marker a visit. Are you free to come with us?"

"I'll make myself free. Get back to me with the time."

My call to the central precinct did not produce the hoped-for result. It was Biddle's day off and he wouldn't be back until tomorrow. I left a message for him and called Jamal again. "Biddle's not available," I said, "but why don't you and I go to Marker's house. If we learn anything new, we can always ring him in later."

He agreed.

I left a note for Cyndi telling her I'd be out for a while, and a half hour later Jamal and I were on our way to visit Marilyn Marker.

Chapter Twenty-one

The Marker home was a sprawling, white-brick, one-story house that was similar to others on the winding street. Brentwood was an upscale neighborhood, although the house didn't seem especially lavish. For some reason I expected a more ostentatious home.

We pulled into the driveway and parked behind Marilyn's shiny silver Jaguar. Jamal was poised to knock when the door was opened by Jeremy Marker, Marilyn's stepson. He looked at us without saying anything.

"I'm Jessica Fletcher," I said, "and this is

Jamal Washburn, attorney for Cyndi Gabriel."

Marilyn Marker came up behind him. "What do you want?" she said.

"We were hoping that you'd give us a few minutes of your time," I said. "It's important. You see, we're helping Cyndi Gabriel and—"

"I know who you are. Get out of here," she said. "I have nothing to say to you."

Jeremy's response was to flash a smile, step back, and say, "Come on in. I'll put on some coffee unless you'd like something stronger."

His stepmother's face was a mask of shock and anger. She spun around and disappeared into the recesses of the house. Jeremy bowed from the waist and extended his hand toward the interior, like a courtly manservant. Jamal and I glanced at each other, shrugged, and followed him inside.

He led us to a large living room furnished almost entirely in white—white carpeting, chairs, and couch. A stainless-steel bookcase spanned one wall and reached the ceiling. It was decidedly modern, something we don't see much in Cabot Cove.

"Have a seat," he said.

Marilyn emerged from the kitchen. "I want them out of my house."

"Hey," Jeremy said, pointing a finger at her, "don't tell me who I can invite in. Remember, this was dear old Dad's house, not yours."

"You're despicable," Marilyn hissed.

Jeremy laughed. "Just another loving family," he said. "Coffee?"

"If you don't leave this instant," Marilyn said, pointing at me, "I'll call the police."

I wondered whether we were on shaky ground being there, but Jamal stepped in with, "That'll be fine, Mrs. Marker. You're welcome to call the police. We've already informed them that we were coming here. You can save yourself some grief by talking to us, but I can formally depose you, if you'd prefer."

"Depose me?" she shouted. "I have just lost my husband, a man I loved very much, and—"

"Ooh, it's getting good now," Jeremy said, going to the kitchen.

"I have every right to depose you," Jamal added, "as part of my defense of Ms. Gabriel."

Some of the steam went out of Marilyn's

voice and demeanor as she said, "How can you possibly defend that vile young woman?"

"Because she's entitled to a presumption of innocence," Jamal said. "Look, we won't be here long, but there's a question we need to ask you."

Marker's wife drew a series of deep breaths before saying, "All right, go ahead with this question you have."

Jamal looked at me.

"Mrs. Marker," I said, "I am truly sorry for your loss. You have my deepest sympathies, and the last thing I want to do is intrude on your period of mourning. But the question is important."

She challenged me silently with her eyes.

"Where were you when your husband was killed?" I asked flatly, keeping any hint of accusation from my voice.

"Are you suggesting that I might have killed Rod?"

"I'm suggesting nothing of the kind," I replied, "but we need to know where you were."

She said nothing.

"You're going to have to answer this under oath," Jamal reminded her.

"I was—I was here at home."

"What time are you referring to?" I asked.

"I don't know," she said, exasperated. "Maybe five, five thirty."

"No you weren't, Ma-má," Jeremy said, having returned.

"Don't call me that," she snapped.

"I was here and saw you drive in." He turned to Jamal and me. "Must have been about six thirty."

"You don't know what you're talking about, Jeremy. I was here all afternoon."

He shook his head.

"How would you know?" she countered. "You weren't here that day. I remember it well. You arrived the previous day, threw your things in your room, and disappeared."

Jeremy forced a gleeful laugh. "Great technique, Marilyn, lie to cover up your own lies."

I wondered when Jamal would break the news to her about the parking ticket. He didn't, so I raised it.

"Mrs. Marker," I said, "we know you were

at your husband's office building at the time of his murder."

"Prove it!"

"That's easily done," Jamal chimed in. "You were issued a ticket for blocking a fire hydrant in front of the building at five thirty that evening."

It was as though someone had undone a twist tie on a plastic bag filled with air, and she collapsed into herself. But she recovered quickly. "Oh, yes," she said, "now I remember. I had to run in for a few minutes, no more than five, to pick up something I'd left there."

"What had you left?" Jamal asked.

"Some papers. I'm not even sure."

"Did anyone see you?"

"No. Edwina was gone by then."

"Did you come in the main entrance?" I asked.

"Yes."

"But you have a key to the back door, the one that empties on to the parking lot."

"Do I?"

"And you didn't see your husband when you—when you ran in to pick up those papers?" I asked.

"No. I've had quite enough of this inquisition. The next time we talk it will be with my lawyer."

"Fair enough," said Jamal. "I'll arrange for you to be deposed in the next few days. Thanks for your time." He stood to signal the end of our visit. Jeremy, who'd been sitting in a chair, one long leg flung over its arm, got to his feet and escorted us to the door. We'd stepped outside when I turned and asked, "*Were* you here that evening, Jeremy?"

His artificial gaiety now abandoned, he gave me a hard look and forcefully closed the door.

Chapter Twenty-two

We were halfway back to the hotel when my cell phone rang.

"Mrs. Fletcher, Detective Biddle here. I understand you called."

"Yes, I did. Thanks for getting back to me. Cyndi's attorney and I have just come from Mrs. Marker's home. I was hoping you'd be able to come with us, but they told me it was your day off."

"It *was* my day off. Why did you go to Marker's house?"

"Because we discovered that she lied when she said she wasn't at her husband's office building the evening he was killed."

Biddle grunted before asking, "And what leads you to that conclusion?"

"A parking ticket."

"Huh?"

"A parking ticket. Marilyn Marker was issued a parking ticket in front of the building at five thirty that night."

I waited for a response. There wasn't one.

"Detective Biddle? Are you still there?"

"Yes, ma'am, I'm here. I think we ought to have a little talk, Mrs. Fletcher."

He sounded irked.

"I'm all for that," I said.

"Where are you now?"

"Heading back to the Renaissance Hotel with Mr. Washburn. We should be there in a few minutes."

"I'll meet you there in the Bridge. Know it?"

"The upstairs bar and restaurant? Yes, I know it. But I hate to interrupt you when you're off duty."

"One of these days I'll get smart and not call in for messages." He signed off.

I told Jamal what had transpired during the brief conversation, and suggested that he be there when I meet with Biddle.

He agreed, with the caveat that if we sensed that the detective didn't want him present, he'd make his excuses and leave.

Jamal went directly to the Bridge while I made a brief stop in my suite, staying just long enough for Cyndi to tell me that she'd spoken with her mother, who was home from the hospital. While Janet was feeling better, she was under doctor's orders to take it easy for at least two weeks, and advised not to travel.

"I also talked to that newspaper writer, Mr. Krupp."

"He called you?" I said, unable to hide my pique.

"Not really. He called *you*. I only answered the phone because Mama said Emily wanted to talk to me and would call back. He asked for you, but when he knew it was me, he started asking all sorts of questions."

"I hope you didn't tell him anything, Cyndi."

"I didn't. I said I thought it was probably wrong for me to be saying anything to a newspaper reporter. I didn't want to be rude and hang up on him, but I did."

"Rude or not, it was the right thing to do," I said, greatly relieved.

While I had asked the hotel to screen our calls and given them a list of those allowed to be put through, slipups were bound to occur. I was tempted to call the newspaper to insist that our privacy be respected, but that would have been an exercise in frustration. Whether I liked it or not, the media were always going to pursue a story. Besides, I didn't want to keep Detective Biddle and Jamal waiting. I told Cyndi where I'd be in case anyone needed to reach me, and went to the Bridge, where Detective Biddle and Jamal Washburn had taken a table that afforded a clear view through huge windows of a portion of downtown Nashville. In the distance was the landmark AT&T building, affectionately known as the "Batman Building" because of its unusual architectural design. Biddle was dressed befitting a scheduled day of leisure—jeans, loafers, open white shirt, and blue cardigan sweater.

"Mr. Washburn was just telling me how he got the parking ticket logs from the Traffic Violation Bureau," Biddle told me after I'd taken my seat. "What prompted you to suggest that?"

"A fellow I met at Marker & Whitson—

his name is Buddy—told me that Mrs. Marker spent more in parking tickets than he made each month. It was a wild chance, but I thought it would be worth knowing whether she happened to have gotten one on the night her husband was murdered. And she had, for parking at the fire hydrant in front of his building."

"Are you suggesting that *she* might have killed him?" Biddle asked.

"I don't know *who* killed him, but I'm finding more and more people with possible motives. I do have a question for you, however."

"Shoot."

"When your officers picked up Cyndi a few days after the murder, did she have her cell phone with her?"

Biddle thought for a moment. "I don't recall, but it's easy enough to check. We did have her number. Marker's secretary, Ms. Anderson, gave it to us."

"I thought she'd gone home for the night."

"She did, but the security guard had *her* home number. We asked her to return to the office but didn't tell her why."

"It must have been a terrible shock for

her," I said, feeling sorry for the woman despite her rudeness toward me.

"She handled it pretty well. She was the one told us about seeing Cyndi coming in as she was going out. She had a picture of your girl on file with her cell phone number, so we put out a BOLO on her."

"A BOLO?"

"Stands for 'be on the lookout' for someone. All our patrol officers have MDTs in their vehicles—that's mobile data terminals. We can get information out pretty fast. Anyway, we ran a check on her cell phone to see if she'd called anyone that day or night, figuring it would help us track her down. Nothing came up. Now I have a question for you."

I smiled. "Shoot," I said.

"Who's this guy Wally Brolin?"

"He's the fellow who—" Biddle's hard stare caused me to pause. "I realize that you didn't know about him, and that I should have told you the minute I got his name, but—"

"Mrs. Fletcher," Biddle said, "I've been pretty easygoing with you since you arrived and started your own investigation. You agree?"

"Yes, and I've appreciated it."

"I sat down with you and we agreed to exchange information that might be helpful to the attorney here and his client, and might also help the department solve this case. I've taken a lot of ribbing from my colleagues, and some criticism from the higher-ups. I don't like being kept in the dark. It puts me in an awkward position, Mrs. Fletcher, and makes me think I made a mistake not keeping you far away from Metro Police in general, and from this investigation in particular."

"I understand why you feel that way, Detective, and I assure you I haven't deliberately withheld Wally Brolin's name from you. Cyndi was hiding at Wally's place when you were looking for her. I knew that she'd refused to tell your officers where she'd spent those few days. When we convinced her to confide in us, I made a point of contacting him, but I neglected to tell you about it. It was my error, and all I can say is I'm sorry."

"Yeah, yeah, yeah," he said, shaking his head and sipping the Coke he'd ordered. "All right. So now that you've ID'd this guy Brolin, tell me what you've learned from him."

I took a deep breath. "Not very much," I said, "except that I'm not sure he's been totally honest with me. I get the feeling he knew Mr. Marker better than he let on at first. I also suspect he might be involved in some way with the song that Cyndi wrote and that Marker gave to Sally Prentice to record. Having someone else record that song was a great disappointment to Cyndi, but I think that giving Sally a cowriting credit was even more hurtful."

"And a motive for murder."

"Except that she didn't kill him."

He crossed his arms and stared at me.

"Are you going to follow up on Brolin?" I asked

"Already sent officers to his house to question him. The girlfriend was there, but he wasn't. Know where he might be?"

"What girlfriend?"

Biddle shrugged. "Some girl who was there. Said he wasn't home."

"I have no idea where he might be," I said. "Have you checked *his* cell phone records?"

"All in good time, Mrs. Fletcher." He was silent for a moment. "Krupp at the

Tennessean wrote that this guy Brolin led the band at the session last night."

"That's right. They were recording the music for an album with Sally Prentice."

"We'll check the union to see what other jobs he has scheduled."

"Good idea."

"Anything else you haven't told me?" Biddle asked.

"Good heavens, I hope not."

Biddle frowned.

"I mean, I don't believe so. Oh, but Cyndi did tell me there was music playing in Marker's office, which was why she couldn't hear whether he was arguing with someone on the phone or in person. She said she'd forgotten that and only remembered it when I jogged her memory."

Biddle sighed.

"I promise I'll read through my notes to see if there's anything else I haven't discussed with you. If there is, I'll call right away."

Biddle turned to Jamal, who'd sat in silence throughout my conversation with the detective. "You have notes, too?"

He shrugged. "I don't have anything," he

said. "Mrs. Fletcher has ended up my chief investigator. I'm just her sounding board."

"And occasional accomplice," Biddle added, tearing at the wrapper of a Goo Goo Cluster he'd taken from his pocket. He didn't offer one to us.

"That reminds me," I said, "what about the background check you said you were going to do on Edwina Anderson?"

"Waste of time," Biddle said. "We did some checking. She's one of these slaves to routine. Leaves the office every day at five, arrives home at five thirty, eats dinner, watches *Jeopardy* and *Wheel of Fortune*, in bed by nine thirty. She visits her great-aunt in a nursing home out in Franklin once a week and brings her a gluten-free brownie from the Bonefish Grill. Not exactly a thrilling life. Satisfied?"

"I just thought that it made sense to look into everyone who had a close relationship with the victim," I said, not pleased with my defensive tone. "There was nothing in the report about her life before she came to Nashville?" I said, thinking of Buddy and the gossip he passed along.

Biddle gave me an odd look. "You sure

do get around," he said, shaking his head. "She was cleared of manslaughter in a parking lot accident that took place thirty years ago in Arizona. You think that's relevant?"

"Perhaps, but I don't know the details. I do know that she has a key to the back door, even though she claims she never uses it."

"That list of key holders we got from the building doesn't shed any light on the case for me. Only the principals, Whitson and Marker, were issued keys, but they obviously made their own duplicates because Anderson wasn't on the list."

"Or she had the keys made for them," I put in. "You could ask her. I don't think she'd respond to me."

"It's nice to know I have some function in this investigation," Biddle quipped with a wry smile. He downed what was left of his Coke and pushed back his chair. "I think I'll go back home and try to salvage what's left of my so-called day off. Sure there's nothing else you've come up with that I should know?"

"I can't think of anything at the moment,"

I said. "You will let me know the results of your check on Wally Brolin's phone records for the night of the murder?"

"Oh, sure, Mrs. Fletcher," he replied. "I'd hate to leave you in the dark about anything. Good seeing you, Counselor. Maybe you ought to hire Mrs. Fletcher as your full-time investigator and get her to move down to Nashville."

Washburn grinned and shook Biddle's hand. "If I thought there was a chance that she'd accept the offer, I'd have made it days ago. Good seeing you again."

Jamal and I lingered over what was left of our soft drinks after Biddle was gone.

"He's a good guy," Jamal said.

"I agree," I said. "I just hope we can come up with Marker's killer before he runs out of patience with me."

"What's next on your agenda, Jessica?"

"I'm not sure. I wish I had more facts to support these gut feelings I have about certain people. For instance, I've never really gotten a handle on Marker's partner, Lewis Whitson. Maybe I should—"

The arrival of someone else at the table put a stop to my reflection. I looked up into a vaguely familiar face, although I couldn't put my finger on why I knew him.

"Mrs. Fletcher," he said. "Brian Krupp." He pulled out a chair and sat down, dropping his cowboy hat on an empty table behind him.

Of course. His picture accompanied his columns in the *Tennessean*.

"Sorry to bother you," he said, "but I called your suite and Ms. Gabriel said you were here in the Bridge. Hope I'm not interrupting anything."

"As a matter of fact, you are," I said. "I was just having a conversation with Mr. Washburn."

"The attorney for Ms. Gabriel," Krupp said. "How's the case going?"

Washburn didn't respond.

"Look," Krupp said, "I know you don't want to talk to me. It's an ongoing case. Yadda. Yadda. I understand all that. But maybe talking to me would be beneficial to Ms. Gabriel and your case. That's something to think about. Right?" He raised both hands. "See? No tricks up my sleeve." He pulled open his jacket to reveal a plain white T-shirt. "No wires, no nothing. Just give me ten minutes. I won't ask any questions, but I will share some information that I've dug up that might interest you. If it does, and you want more, I have a proposal for you. It's no commitment on your part until you hear me out. Deal?"

I was poised to tell him no, but there was something about his directness that kept me from doing it. Maybe it was his youthful, almost boyish face that won me over despite my inherent caution when it comes to being open with a reporter when something sensitive is involved. I know they have their job to do, and it's an important one in our society. But there have been a few instances in my career when they weren't as forthright and, well, honest in their reporting as I would have hoped.

"I'm listening," I said.

Washburn immediately stood. "I have someplace I have to be," he said. "Nice seeing you, Mr. Krupp, and thanks for spelling my name right." To me: "Give me a call later, Jessica. I'll be in my office."

"Looks like I scared him off," Krupp said, pulling his hat from the other table and dropping it in the chair Jamal had vacated.

"It wouldn't look right for him to be sitting

with a reporter in a bar in the midst of the case," I offered. "So, Mr. Krupp, I'll take you at your word. Ten minutes without questions from you while I listen to what you have to say."

"Then we talk deal," he said pleasantly. "What do you know about Lewis Whitson, Roderick Marker's partner?" he asked.

"You've already broken your promise," I said. "You asked a question."

He laughed. "Just my way of leading in to what I have to say. Won't happen again—I think. Okay, I don't know if your young friend Cyndi Gabriel, aka Cindy Blaskowitz, killed Marker or not. But if she didn't, that means somebody else did."

"A logical assumption."

He ignored my sarcasm and said, "The thing is, this little girl from out of town stepped into a real pit of vipers at Marker & Whitson. There have been rumors floating around about that firm for years."

I had a feeling I wasn't the only person to whom Buddy had talked so freely.

"You know, Nashville may be a big city, but at heart it's really a small town," Krupp said, signaling to a waitress. "Got any local brew, Blackstone Ale?" he asked when she arrived at the table. "No? Okay. Let me have a Sam Adams." He turned to me. "What about you, Mrs. Fletcher?"

"I'm fine as I am," I said, marveling at how he was going to turn "ten minutes" into an extended conversation by ordering a beer.

"Where was I?" he said. "Oh yeah. Small town. In the music industry, everybody knows everybody. It's hard to keep a secret here. We know who the good guys are and who the bad guys are, although sometimes they switch places. So the way I see it is if it wasn't Cyndi, it had to have been someone closely involved with Marker, not some stranger. Also logical?"

I nodded.

"I did some checking around about Whitson. To put it simply, he and Marker weren't bosom buddies. In fact, sources tell me that they were about to split up the partnership."

My raised eyebrows said that he'd captured my interest, although a breach between the partners didn't come as a complete surprise. Whitson had moved into Marker's office with unseemly haste, in my view, even before its previous occupant had been buried.

"A couple of months ago," he continued, "Whitson and Marker actually got into a shoving match at a local bar. According to someone who was there, Whitson—he's bigger than Marker—knocked his partner down."

"Were the police called?"

"Yeah, they were, but neither of them brought charges. But my informant says Whitson accused his partner of skimming funds from the company and potentially putting it in hot water with the IRS. Once they'd officially parted, Whitson would have been left holding the bag." Now Krupp's eyebrows were raised. "Motive for murder?"

"Yes."

"And—" He paused when the waitress came to the table and set down his bottle of beer. "As I was about to say, there's more to the bad blood between Marker and Whitson than business dealings. I pick up on scuttlebutt around town—that's my job, been doing it a long time."

"Which I understand you're very good at," I said.

"I have my moments. Anyway, rumor has it that Whitson and Marker's wife, Marilyn, are—how can I put it delicately?"

"You don't have to put it delicately," I said.

"Okay. Whitson and Mrs. Marker have been having an affair, which Marker learned about." He took a sip of his drink, his eyes never leaving mine. "Interesting?" he said.

"So far. Go on."

"On top of that, Marker was an inveterate groper."

"Groper?"

"Liked groping pretty young women. The guy is a serial adulterer, according to those in the know. He's had a number of extramarital affairs, including—"

"Including?" I urged, wondering if his tabloid snapshot of Nashville matched Detective Biddle's suspicions.

"Well, there's talk about Nashville's up-and-coming country music star, Sally Prentice, but she adamantly denies it. Methinks she doth protest too much. And Whitson was the one who introduced her to Marker."

He sat back, took a long swig of his

drink, and smiled smugly, as though he'd just delivered a knockout blow.

"This is all very interesting," I said, "but it doesn't point a finger directly at Whitson as a murderer."

He came forward again. "If I were looking for who killed Marker," he said, "I'd put my money on a greedy business partner."

I chose to file away his conclusion and asked whether he had information about anyone else closely associated with Marker.

"Isn't this enough?" he said.

"That's another question," I said.

He snorted. "Sorry."

"What you've told me is interesting, nothing more. Just how do I apply it to solving Marker's murder, and exonerating Cyndi Gabriel?"

"That's your problem," he said.

He was right. It *was* my problem, and Cyndi's.

"Let me ask *you* a question," I said. "Why did you decide to share this with me?"

"Because, I happen to know you're an honorable woman—I've done the research—so if you use what I've given you to break this case open, I figure you'll owe me first crack at writing about it."

"That seems fair enough, Mr. Krupp."

"My friends call me Brian."

I smiled. "All right, Brian, you'll be the first to know if I accomplish what I've set out to do. The first reporter to know, that is."

He insisted upon paying, grabbed his hat from the chair, and we went to the lobby.

"Thanks for your time," he said, shaking my hand.

"And thank you for the information. Oh, since you seem to have learned a great deal about the victim, Roderick Marker, what have you uncovered about others at the firm, a fellow named Buddy, or Mr. Marker's secretary, Edwina Anderson?"

His grin was devious. "Buddy? Where do you think I got a lot of this information? Buddy's a character, loves scandal and juicy, inside stuff. He's been fueling my column for a long time. As for Eddy Anderson, she's harmless enough unless you believe Buddy's story about her."

"The accident in the parking lot?"

"My, my, Mrs. Fletcher. You're in the wrong field. Ever considering writing for a newspaper? What did Buddy tell you?"

"What did he tell *you*?"

He shook his head. "I heard it years ago. Supposedly, she's related to Marker in some second- or third-removed sort of relationship. Cousin? Sister-in-law? Not sure. She got into a messy legal jam somewhere out west—California, Oregon, someplace like that. Seems she killed some guy—I think she was charged with manslaughter—but beat the rap. Another guy here in town who was writing for one of the tabloids—the *Star*, I think—tried to nail it down but hit a brick wall, records sealed—unclear why—and dropped the story. She moved home to Nashville and when Marker and Whitson opened, the family prevailed upon him to give her a job. That's all I know except that she's a little weird."

"Well," I said, not anxious to add my own evaluation of Edwina Anderson to his tabloid view, "thanks for sharing all this with me."

"I hope you succeed in coming up with Marker's killer, Mrs. Fletcher—even if it turns out to be Cyndi Gabriel. It'll make a great story."

Chapter Twenty-three

I was tempted to stay at the Bridge, sit by myself in a secluded corner and gather my thoughts over a quiet glass of wine. My adrenaline level had risen after talking with Brian Krupp and Biddle, and I felt a need to slow things down, at least for the moment.

Instead, I boosted my energy level by stopping at a Starbucks just off the lobby and ordering a "Grande Latte"—I'll never understand why they don't just call their drinks small, medium, and large—and carried it up to the suite. As I fumbled for my card to open the door, I heard two voices from inside, one female, one male. The female was obviously Cyndi. Had Washburn decided to return to spend time with her?

I opened the door. Before I took one step into the suite, the source of the male voice was visible. It was Wally Brolin, who sat with Cyndi on the couch. He tensed as I walked in, and stood.

"I'm surprised to see you here," I said.

"Oh, how do, ma'am. Just stopped up to see Cyndi."

"I thought you understood that it wasn't a good idea for you to come here."

"I know, but—"

"I'm happy he came," Cyndi said. "I can't go anywhere or see anybody."

"I understand that, Cyndi," I said, "but you're in a very precarious situation."

Brolin went to where he'd tossed his jacket on a chair, picked it up, and started for the door.

"As long as you're here," I said, "I need to speak with you. Please sit down."

"Were you with that newspaper reporter?" Cyndi asked. "Wally is upset at what he wrote about him in the paper."

"I just left him," I replied. "I know he'd like to interview you, Wally."

"I have no interest in seeing the guy," was his response.

"I wouldn't worry so much about him," I suggested. "However, the police are looking for you, too. They went to your house and—"

"They did? When?"

"Earlier today. A woman there told them that you weren't home."

Cyndi shot Brolin a questioning look.

"Must have been a neighbor," he said weakly. "They borrow stuff sometimes."

"Maybe it was," I said. "You know, Wally, when we first met you gave me a primer on how the Nashville music scene works. I appreciated the education, but I obviously have a lot to learn. I still don't understand how Cyndi's song ended up being recorded by Sally Prentice, and how she receives credit as a cowriter. You told me that there's this 'in the room' notion, that if someone is present when a song is being composed and makes a suggestion, it's not unusual for that person to claim a writing credit."

Brolin nodded. "That's right," he said. "I told Cyndi about that when we first met."

"He did," Cyndi chimed in, obviously

eager to provide positive reinforcement for him.

"Is that how Cyndi's song, 'Talkin' Through the Tears,' ended up with Ms. Prentice?"

"I—I don't know exactly. That's something you would have had to ask Rod."

"Just how friendly were you with Roderick Marker, Wally?"

His shrug was exaggerated. "Not friendly exactly. I mean, I knew the guy and—"

"I suppose what I'm trying to figure out is why he would do that, take Cyndi's song and give it to someone else. Cyndi wrote it by herself. Sally Prentice wasn't even 'in the room.' Was he doing a favor for a singer he'd already signed? Everyone says she's about to become a star. Do you think that was his motivation?"

He nodded three or four times, another exaggerated response. "Yeah, that's probably it."

"I imagine that many people would try to get close to an emerging star like Ms. Prentice, impress her, you know, provide her things to help her career."

Brolin became overtly uneasy, fidgeting in his chair and playing with his fingers.

I continued. "I remember you telling me that you hoped to get a gig with her band. Remember?"

"Yeah, sure."

"And you certainly succeeded. It looked to me as though you ended up *leading* her band."

"Yeah, well, I got lucky I guess. I think I'd better go. I've got a gig."

"With Sally Prentice?" I asked.

"What? No. Just some local group. Look, I'm sorry I came here when you said I shouldn't." He put on his jacket. "I just wanted to make sure that Cyndi was all right."

"That was thoughtful of you," I said, hoping that the edge in my voice wasn't too apparent. "I'll walk you down to the lobby."

"No, that's okay, I—"

"I need the exercise anyway," I said.

"Goodbye, Wally," Cyndi said. "Thanks for being such a good friend."

"Yeah, well, you take care, Cyndi. I'll be in touch."

As we rode down in the elevator, that same perfume that I'd smelled in Wally's truck permeated the small space. It was on his clothes.

"Is Alicia staying with you, Wally?" I bluntly asked as the doors slid open at the lobby level.

"What? Alicia?"

"Yes, Alicia. I asked if she's staying with you."

"No, of course not. You said she'd skipped town."

"No, Wally. All I said was that she'd left the rooming house. I'm asking because I recognize the perfume that Alicia sprayed herself with in Cyndi's place at the rooming house, and that was missing when I went back there to collect Cyndi's things. It's all over your clothing. Was she wearing your jacket?"

"That's ridiculous."

"Then I take it that the woman the police said was at your house isn't Alicia."

Up until that moment, he'd maintained a pleasant facade, nervous to be sure, but pleasant. Now his face turned hard and his lips curled beneath his mustache. He said, "You're nothing but a busybody and a troublemaker, Mrs. Fletcher. All you want to do is make trouble for everybody. I'll give you some advice."

"I'm listening."

"Pack up and go home. Let Cyndi's attorney handle things for her. I'm just a guitar picker trying to make a living, and you're doing everything you can to foul things up for me. You don't know zilch about how things work here in Nashville, zippo, how tough it is to make your mark and go after the gold. Go back to your pretty little town in—where is it, someplace in Maine?— and write your books. Just leave me alone!"

I watched him storm through the door and out onto the street. It was okay that I'd angered him. I'd intended to. I felt it was time to put pressure on those people who'd been involved with Cyndi and Roderick Marker. When people feel pressure, they tend to do irrational things, and I was hoping that would be the case with Wally Brolin.

"I know he wasn't supposed to come here," Cyndi said when I returned, "but it was so sweet of him to do that. Like I told you, he's really the only friend I have here in Nashville, except you, of course, and Mr. Washburn. But Mr. Washburn's my attorney, so he's supposed to be a friend."

I saw nothing to be gained in challenging her assessment of Brolin. But the truth was that I'd come to the conclusion, albeit reluctantly, that he was involved in the misfortunes that had befallen her since coming to Nashville. But how? What had he done?

I went to my bedroom, put my feet up, and picked up where I'd left off in that day's newspaper. Again, it was an item on the entertainment page that caught my eye. Sally Prentice was performing that night at a place called the Douglas Corner Café. I seemed to remember Cyndi telling me that it was where she'd been introduced to Wally Brolin shortly after arriving in Nashville.

"Cyndi," I said, "what was the name of the club where you met Wally?"

"Douglas Corner. Why?"

"I see in the newspaper that Sally Prentice is appearing there tonight."

A shadow of anger fell across her pretty face.

"I know how you must feel about her," I said, "but I think I might go."

"I envy her," Cyndi said. "Douglas Corner is, like, one of Nashville's top places to perform. They do songwriter nights when they don't have a live band. That's the night I was there, one of the songwriter show-cases. It's sort of like the Bluebird Café. Lots of writers and singers have launched their careers there."

"Maybe that's where you'll launch *your* career," I said.

"I don't think I'm ever going to have a career," she cried. "I'll just stay cooped up here in the hotel and probably end up in jail for the rest of my life." She took a pillow from the couch and buried her face in it.

I sat beside her and put my arm around her shoulder. "I don't want to hear you talk like that, Cyndi."

She sniffled, and I pulled her closer. "I know how difficult this is for you," I said, "but things will work out. I wouldn't be here if I didn't believe that. You're innocent. I know that and I intend to prove it. But some-times these things take time. As hard as it is, you need to be patient, and to trust me."

"I do," she said. Her face was red and her eyes were wet. "It's just—"

"I know."

I waited for her to stop crying before re-turning to my bedroom. I'd put on my most positive persona for her, but now that I was alone I allowed my own pessimistic feelings to surface. As confident as I was that I was getting closer to the answer, there was a parallel sense of dread that was never far away. *What if I failed?* I'd steadfastly refused to ask myself that question out of fear that the answer was too shocking to consider. I knew that if I failed, what Cyndi had just expressed would become reality—no career and a young life wasted behind bars.

I banished those negative thoughts from my consciousness and set about getting ready to attend Sally Prentice's performance at the Douglas Corner Café. I called and made a reservation. I'd no sooner hung up than my cell phone rang. It was Detective Biddle.

"I thought you were going to enjoy the rest of your day off," I said.

"The best laid plans and all that. I swung back by headquarters after I left you. The phone records for Wally Brolin came in."

"Oh? Anything of interest?"

"Probably not. He received a slew of calls that day. We traced the numbers back. Musicians, a couple of nightclubs, the sort of stuff you'd expect."

"What about closer to the time of Roderick Marker's murder?"

"Let's see," he said, muttering to himself as he consulted the report. "He got a call at five fifty-five that evening from a cell number assigned to someone named A. Piedmont."

Soon after the estimated time of Marker's murder, I thought. *Interesting.*

"He called that number back a couple of times, at six twenty-one and seven forty-two. This other party, Piedmont, called him at nine oh five and nine sixteen. Brolin made two more calls to that number later in the evening."

"Thank you, Detective."

"I don't know what you're thanking me for, Mrs. Fletcher. I'd be more interested in these calls if they involved Ms. Gabriel."

"Frankly, I'm glad they didn't," I said. "I really appreciate you calling to tell me about this."

"Hey, listen, I've let you get involved to this extent, might as well bring you in all the way. You have yourself a good night. I

intend to. There's a good game on TV tonight and I've got myself a new plasma
TV. Nothing'll drag me away from it."

I jotted down the times the detective
had given me and reviewed them. While
they didn't constitute direct evidence, the
picture was beginning to form.

Cyndi and I had dinner sent up before I
dressed for the evening. Although I seldom
wear jeans, I'd brought a pair with me to
Nashville, and put them on. I'd also packed
a light blue shirt, hardly of the Western va-
riety, but better than the print blouses in my
traveling wardrobe. When Cyndi saw what I
was doing, she gave me a red bandana to
wear with the shirt, and offered her cowboy
boots. I tried them on, but they were too
small; I didn't want to be limping around
Nashville all evening. My flat black shoes
had to suffice. My final preparation included
wearing heavier makeup than usual, including bloodred lipstick. To top off my Nashville outfit, I donned the white Stetson Lynee
Granger had given me. When I presented
myself to Cyndi in the parlor, the sight of
me brought forth a rare burst of laughter
from her. "You look like you belong in Nashville, Mrs. Fletcher," she said, still giggling.

"I wouldn't go that far," I said, "but maybe I look a little less alien. I'll try not to be late. And, Cyndi, no visitors. Right?"

"Right. Don't worry about me. I'll be a good girl."

The taxi driver dropped me off in front of the redbrick building housing the club. Neon beer signs created the appearance of a neighborhood bar. Across the street was a comedy club called Zanies, according to its sign. I paid the driver, pulled my Stetson down low over my forehead, and entered.

"Hi," a waitress said. "Do you have a reservation?"

"Yes," I said. "I know I'm early for the show." I gave her my name.

"Better to be early," she said. "We're expecting a crowd. Sally Prentice is developing a big following."

I chose a small table wedged into a corner near the bar at the rear of the room despite the waitress's warning that it wasn't the best vantage point from which to catch the act. As I sat and nursed a ginger ale, other tables began to fill up, as did the bar. I was halfway through my drink when Lewis Whitson entered the club, accompanied by

Marilyn Marker. I kept my hat low as they passed and were shown to a prime table directly in front of the bandstand.

Minutes later, the musicians started arriving. As I suspected would be the case, Wally Brolin was among them. He and two other musicians went about their business rearranging the stage, plugging their instruments into amplifiers, and testing microphones. If my confrontation with Brolin earlier in the day had unnerved him, he didn't show any signs of it. He seemed in good spirits, and exchanged jokes with the musicians, laughing loudly at their offerings.

Finally, almost an hour after I'd arrived, Sally Prentice walked in. She was dressed in a silver jumpsuit, her ample platinum-blond hair piled high on her head. Whitson stood as Sally approached his table and gave her a cursory kiss on the cheek. Marilyn offered her hand, which Sally took but dropped quickly. She left them and climbed up on the stage, where she gave Wally a prolonged hug and kissed the other musicians.

The lights were dimmed, and a young man wearing the requisite jeans and Stetson hat took the microphone.

"Hey, all you music lovers," he said with a wide smile, his voice reverberating from large speakers, "nice you all decided to stop by because we have got one special, boot-scootin' treat for you tonight. This little lady—and ain't she a beauty?—is about to turn the country music business upside down. I mean really turn it upside down! She's recording her first CD right here in Music City, USA, and from everything this ol' boy hears, it's gonna knock everybody's socks off—assumin' you wear 'em. So come on now, let's give her a real Douglas Corner welcome, Miss Sally Prentice!"

The room erupted in applause and whistles as Sally counted off her first number and the band launched into a spirited intro to her song. I listened intently. Although my exposure to country music was admittedly limited, I thoroughly enjoyed her performance. She was vivacious on stage, appearing to be singing directly to each person in the room. Wally Brolin played a chorus that blended country, rock and roll, and the blues, and Sally jumped in after it and ended the song to an enthusiastic response.

But my enjoyment of her opening number was dashed when she said into the mike, "Ah'd like to do a song for you now that I recently wrote especially for mah new CD. It's a sad song, but the beautiful words say that somehow things'll end up just fine. It's called 'Talkin' Through the Tears,' and I want to thank this here big hunk of a mountain man, mah favorite guitar picker, for encouraging me to put it on mah CD." She mussed Wally's hair. "Come on now, take a bow, Wally."

He remained seated, grinned, and waved his hand to the crowd, which had now filled Douglas Corner to capacity, and beyond. Every seat was taken, and men and women clogged the aisles between them, making service tough for the waitresses. The air was thick with smoke.

I didn't join in the applause. All I could see while she sang "Talkin' Through the Tears" was Cyndi standing on the stage back home singing the song for her friends and family. Sally Prentice's rendition, while professional, seemed to me to miss the heartbreak inherent in the lyrics and melody. Cyndi's version would have been more low-key: a wistful, vulnerable girl trying to save a love affair by talking it out with her boyfriend despite the tears that kept getting in the way. I was also angry that Prentice had taken sole ownership of the song in front of all those people with not a word of credit to the person who had actually written it, Cyndi Gabriel, aka Cindy Blaskowitz from Cabot Cove, Maine.

The rest of the first set flew by with little attention from me—my mind was a jumble of conflicting thoughts—but lots of cheers and foot stomping from the enthusiastic crowd. Prentice eventually announced that they were taking a short intermission but would be back soon. The management played a country CD over the PA system, and I took that as an opportunity to get some fresh air.

I didn't want Lewis Whitson, Marilyn Marker, Sally Prentice, or Wally Brolin to see that I'd been in the audience and waited until I was confident I could make my exit without being noticed. I snaked my way through the maze of people and blue haze of cigarette smoke in the direction of the door, stepped outside, and drew in a deep breath. It had gotten colder since I arrived, and damp, the sort of chill that goes right through you, although the crowd outside milling about, waiting to get in, shielded me from the worst of the wind.

Loud laughter and squeals of recognition greeted the arrival of more of the club's would-be patrons. Music from the sound system settled over the people's conversations like a melodious cloud, forcing everybody to raise their voices to be heard. I edged toward a clearer area on the sidewalk, dodging knots of country music fans. It was then that I noticed Wally's pickup truck. It was stopped in the driveway, facing nose-in to a parking lot next to the club, the motor running. I ducked back against the Douglas Corner building, peered around some people, and squinted. Sure enough, Alicia was behind the wheel, and Wally stood at the open passenger-side window.

I tried to come up with a way to get close enough to the truck to hear their conversation but that proved impossible, not if I didn't want to be seen. But then Wally climbed into the passenger seat, and Alicia drove farther into the lot.

I waited to see if they would find a parking spot. The lot was full. They pulled up next to a Dumpster with a dozen garbage bags piled next to it. I waited until more people entered the lot and slowly trailed them, pulling my hat down over my brow and hiding myself behind first one and then another group of people going to their vehicles.

I could see the truck's taillights and a plume of smoke from its exhaust pipe. I walked past the truck and circled around, skirting a cluster of trash bags and crouching behind them. The Dumpster was ahead; it was only eight or ten feet away from Wally and Alicia. I drew a breath, straightened, and moved along the border of the parking lot, my back to it, hoping that they wouldn't see me. They evidently didn't. I reached the Dumpster and concentrated on my hearing. Their voices were clear, and angry.

". . . and you think I haven't stuck my neck out for you, Alicia," Wally said.

"You bet you did and for good reason," she responded in her Southern drawl. "You got me into this mess with Marker. You owed me big-time."

He uttered a string of four-letter words. Their conversation ceased. Then Alicia said in a voice that approximated the scratchy sound of a cat in distress, "You're a dirty, rotten liar, you know that. You swore Marker would do great things for me." Her laugh was sardonic. "Yeah, great things. You think I enjoyed that, Wally? How do you think that made me feel? You know what I felt like? I felt lower than pond scum. And what did I get for it? What did he ever do for me? What did *you* ever do for me?"

Now Wally's voice rose in anger. "What did I do for you?" he snarled. "I got you off the hook, that's what I did. You're like all the rest of your type, thinking you're so damn talented, thinking you can flirt your way to the top. Sally Prentice's got more talent in her little finger than you have in your whole body."

His stinging comment caused a halt in the conversation. As I waited for them to continue, I sensed something at my feet. I looked down and saw a large, greasy, black rat scurry beneath the Dumpster. The yelp that came from me was purely involuntary, and it was loud enough to cause Brolin to open the passenger door and look in the direction from which the sound came. The rat had not only caused me to shriek, I'd instinctively jumped a few feet away, just far enough so that I was now visible from the truck. I ducked back behind the Dumpster but heard the truck door slam shut and footsteps come my way. Seconds later, I was face-to-face with Wally Brolin, who didn't look at all pleased to see me. Another door was shut with force, and Alicia came up behind him. I shivered, but I wasn't sure if it was from the cold, or the rat, or the apprehension I felt facing these two.

"I don't believe this," Brolin said. "What are you doin', following me?"

"I wasn't following you, Wally," I said, forcing calm into my voice. "I came to hear Sally Prentice. You said you weren't playing with her tonight. Evidently, you have trouble with the truth."

Alicia stepped forward and stood next to him.

"Hello, Alicia," I said, still trying to override my fear.

"She heard us, didn't she?" Alicia said.

"What'd you hear, you old snoop?" Brolin asked, pushing me toward the back of the Dumpster.

"Enough to cause me to think the conclusions I've come to are good ones. Excuse me."

I tried to walk around them, back toward the street, but Brolin blocked my path.

"Don't do anything foolish, Wally," I said, mustering strength in my voice. "You're in enough of a mess as it is."

"What are you going to do about her?" Alicia demanded of him.

"What am I going to do?" he said. "You're the one in trouble, girl."

I tried to assess my situation. The street and noisy crowd in front of the club were a good forty or fifty feet from where we stood. Would anyone hear if I screamed? My eyes darted about in search of something to use as a weapon. I saw nothing.

"Do something!" Alicia insisted, stamping a cowboy-booted foot on the ground like a petulant child.

"I'll tell you what you should do, Wally," I said. "You should go to the police and tell them everything you know. You don't want to see an innocent girl spend her life in prison for a crime she didn't commit, do you?"

"What are you talking about? Are you saying that I killed Marker?"

"Don't listen to her, Wally," Alicia demanded.

"No, Wally. I don't think that you killed Marker." I looked directly at Alicia. "I think she did!"

Alicia responded by running to the truck, where she pulled Wally's shotgun from its rack. She turned and slowly approached us, the weapon pointed at me.

"Don't be stupid," Wally said. "Put it down."

Alicia pulled the trigger. But as she did, Wally brought up his arm and deflected the gun, causing the buckshot to hit the Dumpster with a series of earsplitting pings. He wrestled her for the gun and prevailed, sending her to her knees.

"Yeah," he growled. "She's the one who killed Marker."

"I know that," I said.

Alicia clambered to her feet. Panic was written all over her pretty face. She raced to the truck, threw herself in the driver's seat, put it in gear, and jerked forward, then slammed it into reverse, hit the gas, and roared backward toward us. Wally dragged me out of the way in time to avoid being crushed against the Dumpster, and Alicia roared down the row of cars and trucks.

I turned in the direction of the street.

The shotgun's discharge had gotten the attention of people who'd been congregating on the sidewalk in front of Douglas Corner. I closed my eyes in anticipation of Alicia mowing them down, but miraculously they all jumped to safety as she caromed into the street, turned, and sped away, the tires screeching.

I slumped against the Dumpster and tried to pull myself together. My white Stetson hat had flown off in the fracas and now lay squashed on the ground, a black tire tread adding a new design.

"She's crazy," Wally said, breathing hard. "She killed Marker and thought she'd get away with it, but I was going to go to the police and turn her in."

"The way you called the police to tell them where to find Cyndi?" I said.

"What are you talking about?"

I retrieved my hat, used my fist to push it back into some semblance of its original shape, and started walking toward the street. He followed. "Hey," he said, "I just saved your life."

A mass of people had gathered at the entrance to the lot; some sprinted to their cars to see if they had been damaged. The others were shortly joined by two uniformed officers who'd been summoned by the club management upon hearing the shot.

"What's going on here?" one policeman asked.

"Would it be possible to contact Detective Perry Biddle?" I asked. "I know it's late, but I assure you he'll want to know what's happened here this evening. Tell him Jessica Fletcher is here and knows who killed Roderick Marker."

As the officer made the call on his mobile phone, Sally Prentice and the other two musicians joined the crowd. She came up to Wally. "Hey, big guy. I've been looking all over for you. Get back inside," she said. "We've got another set to do."

"I don't think he'll be doing any more playing tonight," I told her.

"You again," she said, scowling at me. Her gaze shifted to Wally: "Are you in trouble?"

"No, I'm—I don't feel good. I'm cutting out."

He started to lope away, but I motioned to one of the officers and suggested that Detective Biddle would want to talk to Brolin. The officer ran after him, grabbed his arm, and informed him that he wasn't going anywhere.

Brolin came back to where I stood. "What did you tell them? You've got it all wrong," he said. "I had nothing to do with Marker's murder."

"I know that, Wally. Alicia was the one who attacked him in a rage and smashed his head with the trophy."

"That's right," he said, brightening. "She's nuts. I hope they put her away for the rest of her life."

"If you're willing to testify against her, Wally, you might be able to make a better deal for yourself with the police."

"Me? Like you just said, I didn't kill anybody. What do the cops have against me?"

"You covered up for the killer and tried to frame Cyndi."

"I didn't frame anybody."

"But you let an innocent person be arrested, knowing full well who the real killer was. It may have seemed like a good idea, but in hindsight it wasn't so clever. You may be a good musician, Wally, but you hit a wrong chord this time."

It seemed an eternity before Biddle arrived. He took in my disheveled appearance but was gentlemanly enough to not comment. We stepped away from the crowd.

"You have a way of intruding on my days off and now you've ruined my night at home in front of the TV."

"Should I apologize?"

He laughed. "Not unless you don't have the answer I'm expecting. Just wanted to lay a little guilt on you. Glad you had me called. This scene is more interesting than anything on television. Besides, the game was a blowout."

I gave him a quick rundown on what had transpired.

"Put out a BOLO on the truck," Biddle ordered, and instructed Wally to give the officers its description and plate number. "Driver's name is—" He turned to me. "What's her name?"

"Alicia Piedmont. Oh, and she's armed. She has his shotgun," I added.

"This is all a big mistake," Wally said.

"If it is, we'll sort it out down at headquarters." Biddle told the officers to place Brolin in the backseat of their patrol car and deliver him to the central precinct. "Coming?" he asked me.

"I wouldn't miss it for the world," I said. "I'll call Cyndi and Mr. Washburn on the way. I've never wanted to make a phone call so much in my life."

"What a drag," I heard Sally Prentice say to the other musicians. "Can you get another guitar player down here? This is messing up my whole appearance."

I climbed in the front of Biddle's unmarked sedan. As he was about to pull away, I said, "Please, wait just a minute."

He looked at me quizzically as I angled his rearview mirror to put on my Stetson. "Just a souvenir," I said. "How do I look?"

"You look like an old-time country-and-western star," he said.

"Old-time, huh?"

"Yeah," he said, ripping into a Goo Goo Cluster and handing another one to me. "But a good old-time."

Chapter Twenty-four

"Alicia had been having an affair with Marker," I said.

"He always did have a weakness for platinum blondes," Lynee said.

"She was furious when he put all his efforts into Sally Prentice. Alicia had expected that she'd be chosen to be his next country star. She'd gone to Marker & Whitson to confront him."

"Didn't she know that Cyndi was there?" Lynee asked.

"No, she didn't. Alicia used the door from the parking lot and the back stairs to go up to his office. When Marker told Alicia he wasn't interested in her anymore—he was already making plans to seduce his latest protégée—she went into a rage, grabbed the CMA award off his desk as he walked away, and swung it at his skull, knocking him out. As you know, he died later from his injuries."

Lynee shook her head. "I tried to tell my nephew that Alicia was a bad seed, a liar and a user, but he wouldn't listen, had a real crush on her."

"And just as you suspected, Mrs. Fletcher," Detective Biddle put in, "we found the key to that back door in her possessions. Apparently Marker gave all his girlfriends a key, but his wife didn't have one. That's why she always left her car out front at the fire hydrant and collected all those parking tickets."

"How did Wally get involved in all this?" Jamal asked.

"When Alicia realized what she'd done, she ran out," I said. "According to Wally, she called him in a panic. He told her to sit tight and he'd think of something."

"When Cyndi showed up at his door," Biddle added, "he called Alicia back and told her to relax. He had the perfect way to get her off the hook. Let Cyndi take the rap since he rightly guessed that we were already looking for her."

"If Cyndi hadn't run from the scene," I said, "she might never have been arrested. Once she did, however, she chose exactly the wrong man to run to. He had told me he encouraged her to go to the police, but Cyndi swears he scared her silly, telling her the police would never believe her, that she had better lie low until he could figure out a way to get her out of town."

"And all the while he was just trying to make her look more guilty," Lynee said. "And then he went and ratted her out, huh?"

"Yes," I said. "He was the one who told the police where she would be that morning."

"How did you know that, Jessica?"

"Our sheriff back home, Mort Metzger, had told me a man had tipped off the police as to her whereabouts. The police had a photo of Cyndi, but it was never published in the newspaper. I checked all the previous day's papers my first morning in Nashville. The only one who knew the police were looking for Cyndi, and knew where she would be that morning, was Wally."

"I wish she hadn't been afraid to call home."

"Oh, Janet," I said. "She was terrified for herself but worried more about your health. She knew if she called home, you'd know immediately that something was wrong. You could always tell by the sound of her voice. And if she told you the truth, that she was suspected of assault, later murder, and was being sought by the police, she feared it would trigger a heart attack or worse."

There were five of us sitting around the table. Detective Biddle had arrived first. Then Lynee Granger and Jamal Washburn came in. Finally, I'd joined them, bringing Cyndi's mother, Janet Blaskowitz. Thrilled that her daughter had been exonerated, she had accepted an offer from the committee Cabot Cove Mayor Jim Shevlin had headed up to raise money for Cyndi's defense. The committee insisted Janet use some of the contributions to fly down to Nashville for her daughter's singing debut at the Bluebird Café. The remainder of the funds would go to Cabot Cove Cares, the arts organization that had funded Cyndi's trip to Nashville.

"What happened to Alicia?" Janet asked. "I can't help feeling sorry for her even though she did a terrible thing."

"She didn't get far," Biddle replied. "My guys picked her up about a mile away, sitting in the truck, crying hysterically. She spent the night in the hospital psych unit before we took her to be booked. She's now at the same women's jail facility where Cyndi stayed. I'm guessing she'll plead temporary insanity."

"So are you going to charge Wally?" Lynee asked Biddle.

He raised his hand and counted on his fingers. "Let's see," he said, "we're holding him on aiding and abetting, accessory after the fact, perjury for lying to authorities— and the list goes on."

"A colleague of mine has been assigned to his case," Jamal added. "From what I hear, they're working on a plea bargain in exchange for his testimony against Alicia."

"Poor Wally," Lynee said. "His popularity with the girls was his undoing."

"Poor Wally, my foot," I said. "He was

the one who recognized how good Cyndi's song was and brought it to Sally Prentice. He wanted to get on her good side so she'd insist on having him play on her recording."

"You mean it wasn't Marker after all?" Janet asked.

"Oh, no. He shares plenty of the blame," I said. "At Wally's suggestion, Sally pushed Marker to give her the song, and demanded a cowriting credit. Marker was eager to please his swiftly rising star, so he conceded to everything she asked. They all got what they wanted. Sally got the song, Wally got the CD gig, and Marker got—"

"Murdered," Biddle put in.

"Yes," I said. "And he didn't deserve that—not that anyone ever does. But before he jilted Alicia, he managed to get Sally Prentice's signature on a Marker & Whitson contract, which I'm betting his partner is very happy about, even though Sally won't be singing 'Talkin' Through the Tears' on her album."

"She won't?"

"No. She came to the conclusion—with a little encouragement—that the song was bad luck for her. She gave it back to Cyndi."

There was some thumping on the sound system and we looked over to see a man with a long gray beard tied like a ponytail waving at the musicians. They sat in a ring of folding chairs at the center of the room, facing each other, a microphone in front of each one. Three songwriters holding guitars were performing this night, and three other musicians—a bass player, a young woman on a fiddle, and a fellow sitting on a cajón, a boxlike drum—were accompanying them. There was only one empty seat in the house, and it was at our table.

"We can't talk during the music," Lynee said. "House rules."

"I've had enough talking to last me a long time," Janet said. "Everyone has been asking me questions ever since I arrived. I'm ready just to listen."

Just before the house lights dimmed, the last one in our party slipped into his seat. "Sorry," Brian Krupp said, "got stuck over at Marilyn Marker's house doing an interview for an upcoming feature."

"Is she going to take over her husband's partnership in the firm?" I asked.

"If she can get it," he replied. "Her stepson is suing her for half of her share of the business. Anyone want to wager on who Whitson would prefer to work with? Never a dull day in Music City, USA."

A voice came over the sound system. "Ladies and gentlemen, we have a special treat tonight, a young songwriter in Nashville who's ready to make a *new* name for herself." There was a ripple of laughter. "She'd already passed one of our auditions, but was unfortunately delayed. She's ready now. And we're delighted to have her here. Please give a warm round of applause for Cindy Blaskowitz."

I looked at Janet, who couldn't take her eyes off her eldest daughter. "Blaskowitz?" I whispered.

Janet nodded, tears streaming down her smiling cheeks. "She decided she didn't want to change her name after all," she whispered back. "I'm so proud of her."

"As well you should be."

Cindy tapped the microphone in front of her and dipped her head. "I can't tell you how happy I am to be here," she said, grinning. "A little later, I'm going to sing a song I wrote that many of you have heard about, but I'd like to open up with something different. This song is not mine, but it was written for and about me by the song-writer David Stewart. It's a cautionary tale for every young country performer who comes to Music City. I hope you like it. It's called 'Nashville Noir.'"